GOLDEN TALES

of

ANATOLE FRANCE

PREFACE

No special plan has been followed in making this collection. The stories and tales demonstrate no theories of art or matter; they have been chosen simply to amuse. Indeed, a half-dozen similar collections might be made, each without trespassing in the domain of any other, and each with equal merit and interest. Let the reader of these tales remember, moreover, that in their perusal he has but sampled; if he smacks his lips and finds the dish to his taste, let him pass on to the author's complete works.

The genius of Anatole France was especially adapted to the short story. In its praise, he has said:

"What a superiority, in point of taste, does the short story exhibit in comparison with the novel. How much more delicate it is, more discreet and more certain in its appeal to people with active minds, people whose lives are fully occupied, and who know the value of their time. Is not brevity the primary courtesy that a writer owes to his readers? The short story suffices for every need; and, in it, a great deal may be conveyed in a few

words.   A well-turned tale is a feast for connois-
seurs, and a satisfaction to the critical.   It is, of
fiction, the elixir, the quintessence, the precious ointment."

CONTENTS

CONTENTS

THE GOLDEN TALES OF
ANATOLE FRANCE

THE PROCURATOR OF JUDÆA

ÆLIUS LAMIA, born in Italy of illustrious parents, had not yet discarded the *toga prætexta* when he set out for the schools of Athens to study philosophy. Subsequently he took up his residence at Rome, and in his house on the Esquiline, amid a circle of youthful wastrels, abandoned himself to licentious courses. But being accused of engaging in criminal relations with Lepida, the wife of Sulpicius Quirinus, a man of consular rank, and being found guilty, he was exiled by Tiberius Cæsar. At that time he was just entering his twenty-fourth year. During the eighteen years that his exile lasted he traversed Syria, Palestine, Cappadocia, and Armenia, and made prolonged visits to Antioch, Cæsarea, and Jerusalem. When, after the death of Tiberius, Caius was raised to the purple, Lamia obtained permission to return to Rome. He even regained a portion of his possessions. Adversity had taught him wisdom.

1

He avoided all intercourse with the wives and
daughters of Roman citizens, made no efforts towards obtaining office, held aloof from public
honours, and lived a secluded life in his house on
the Esquiline. Occupying himself with the task of
recording all the remarkable things he had seen
during his distant travels, he turned, as he said,
the vicissitudes of his years of expiation into a
diversion for his hours of rest. In the midst of
these calm employments, alternating with assiduous
study of the works of Epicurus, he recognized
with a mixture of surprise and vexation that age
was stealing upon him. In his sixty-second year,
being afflicted with an illness which proved in no
slight degree troublesome, he decided to have recourse to the waters at Baiæ. The coast at that
point, once frequented by the halcyon, was at this
date the resort of the wealthy Roman, greedy of
pleasure. For a week Lamia lived alone, without
a friend in the brilliant crowd. Then one day,
after dinner, an inclination to which he yielded
urged him to ascend the incline, which, covered
with vines that resembled bacchantes, looked out
upon the waves.

Having reached the summit he seated himself
by the side of a path beneath a terebinth, and let
his glances wander over the lovely landscape. To

his left, livid and bare, the Phlegræan plain stretched out towards the ruins of Cumæ. On his right, Cape Misenum plunged its abrupt spur beneath the Tyrrhenian sea. Beneath his feet luxurious Baiæ, following the graceful outline of the coast, displayed its gardens, its villas thronged with statues, its porticos, its marble terraces along the shores of the blue ocean where the dolphins sported. Before him, on the other side of the bay, on the Campanian coast, gilded by the already sinking sun, gleamed the temples which far away rose above the laurels of Posilippo, whilst on the extreme horizon Vesuvius looked forth smiling.

Lamia drew from a fold of his toga a scroll containing the *Treatise upon Nature,* extended himself upon the ground, and began to read. But the warning cries of a slave necessitated his rising to allow of the passage of a litter which was being carried along the narrow pathway through the vineyards. The litter being uncurtained, permitted Lamia to see stretched upon the cushions as it was borne nearer to him the figure of an elderly man of immense bulk, who, supporting his head on his hand, gazed out with a gloomy and disdainful expression. His nose, which was aquiline, and his chin, which was prominent, seemed desirous of meeting across his lips, and his jaws were powerful.

3

From the first moment Lamia was convinced that the face was familiar to him. He hesitated a moment before the name came to him. Then suddenly hastening towards the litter with a display of surprise and delight—

"Pontius Pilate!" he cried. "The gods be praised who have permitted me to see you once again!"

The old man gave a signal to the slaves to stop, and cast a keen glance upon the stranger who had addressed him.

"Pontius, my dear host," resumed the latter, "have twenty years so far whitened my hair and hollowed my cheeks that you no longer recognize your friend Ælius Lamia?"

At this name Pontius Pilate dismounted from the litter as actively as the weight of his years and the heaviness of his gait permitted him, and embraced Ælius Lamia again and again.

"Gods! what a treat it is to me to see you once more! But, alas, you call up memories of those long-vanished days when I was Procurator of Judæa in the province of Syria. Why, it must be thirty years ago that I first met you. It was at Cæsarea, whither you came to drag out your weary term of exile. I was fortunate enough to alleviate it a little, and out of friendship, Lamia, you followed me to that depressing place Jerusalem, where the Jews filled me with bitterness and disgust. You remained for more than ten years my guest and my companion, and in converse about Rome and things Roman we both of us managed to find consolation—you for your misfortunes, and I for my burdens of State."

Lamia embraced him afresh.

"You forget two things, Pontius; you are overlooking the facts that you used your influence on my behalf with Herod Antipas, and that your purse was freely open to me."

"Let us not talk of that," replied Pontius, "since after your return to Rome you sent me by one of your freedmen a sum of money which repaid me with usury."

"Pontius, I could never consider myself out of your debt by the mere payment of money. But tell me, have the gods fulfilled your desires? Are you in the enjoyment of all the happiness you deserve? Tell me about your family, your fortunes, your health."

"I have withdrawn to Sicily, where I possess estates, and where I cultivate wheat for the market. My eldest daughter, my best-beloved Pontia, who has been left a widow, lives with me, and directs my household. The gods be praised, I have preserved my mental vigour; my memory is not in the least degree enfeebled. But old age always brings in its train a long procession of griefs and infirmities. I am cruelly tormented with gout. And at this very moment you find me on my way to the Phlegræan plain in search of a remedy for my sufferings. From that burning soil, whence at night flames burst forth, proceed acrid exhalations of sulphur, which, so they say, ease the pains and restore suppleness to the joints. At least, the physicians assure me that it is so."

"May you find it so in your case, Pontius! But, despite the gout and its burning torments, you scarcely look as old as myself, although in reality you must be my senior by ten years. Unmistakably you have retained a greater degree of vigour than I ever possessed, and I am overjoyed to find you looking so hale. Why, dear friend, did you retire from the public service before the customary age? Why, on resigning your governorship in Judæa, did you withdraw to a voluntary exile on your Sicilian estates? Give me an account of your doings from the moment that I ceased to be a witness of them. You were preparing to suppress a Samaritan rising when I set out for Cappadocia, where I hoped to draw some profit from the breeding of horses and mules. I have not seen you since then. How did that expedition succeed? Pray tell me. Everything interests me that concerns you in any way."

Pontius Pilate sadly shook his head.

"My natural disposition," he said, "as well as a sense of duty, impelled me to fulfil my public responsibilities, not merely with diligence, but even with ardour. But I was pursued by unrelenting hatred. Intrigues and calumnies cut short my career in its prime, and the fruit it should have looked to bear has withered away. You ask me about the Samaritan insurrection. Let us sit down on this hillock. I shall be able to give you an answer in few words. Those occurrences are as vividly present to me as if they had happened yesterday.

"A man of the people, of persuasive speech— there are many such to be met with in Syria— induced the Samaritans to gather together in arms on Mount Gerizim (which in that country is looked upon as a holy place) under the promise that he would disclose to their sight the sacred vessels which in the ancient days of Evander and our father, Æneas, had been hidden away by an eponymous hero, or rather a tribal deity, named Moses. Upon this assurance the Samaritans rose in rebellion; but having been warned in time to forestall them, I dispatched detachments of infantry to occupy the mountain, and stationed cavalry to keep the approaches to it under observation.

"These measures of prudence were urgent. The rebels were already laying siege to the town of Tyrathaba, situated at the foot of Mount Gerizim. I easily dispersed them, and stifled the as yet scarcely organized revolt. Then, in order to give a forcible example with as few victims as possible, I handed over to execution the leaders of the rebellion. But you are aware, Lamia, in what strait dependence I was kept by the proconsul Vitellius, who governed Syria not in, but against the interests of Rome, and looked upon the provinces of the empire as territories which could be farmed out to tetrarchs. The head-men among the Samaritans, in their resentment against me, came and fell at his feet lamenting. To listen to them, nothing had been further from their thoughts than to disobey Cæsar. It was I who had provoked the rising, and it was purely in order to withstand my violence that they had gathered together round Tyrathaba. Vitellius listened to their complaints, and handing over the affairs of Judæa to his friend Marcellus, commanded me to go and justify my proceedings before the Emperor himself. With a heart overflowing with grief and resentment I took ship.

Just as I approached the shores of Italy, Tiberius, worn out with age and the cares of empire, died suddenly on the selfsame Cape Misenum, whose peak we see from this very spot magnified in the mists of evening. I demanded justice of Caius, his successor, whose perception was naturally acute, and who was acquainted with Syrian affairs. But marvel with me, Lamia, at the maliciousness of fortune, resolved on my discomfiture. Caius then had in his suite at Rome the Jew Agrippa, his companion, the friend of his childhood, whom he cherished as his own eyes. Now Agrippa favoured Vitellius, inasmuch as Vitellius was the enemy of Antipas, whom Agrippa pursued with his hatred. The Emperor adopted the prejudices of his beloved Asiatic, and refused even to listen to me. There was nothing for me to do but bow beneath the stroke of unmerited misfortune. With tears for my meat and gall for my portion, I withdrew to my estates in Sicily, where I should have died of grief if my sweet Pontia had not come to console her father. I have cultivated wheat, and succeeded in producing the fullest ears in the whole province. But now my life is ended; the future will judge between Vitellius and me."

"Pontius," replied Lamia, "I am persuaded that you acted towards the Samaritans according to the rectitude of your character, and solely in the interests of Rome. But were you not perchance on that occasion a trifle too much influenced by that impetuous courage which has always swayed you? You will remember that in Judæa it often happened that I who, younger than you, should naturally have been more impetuous than you, was obliged to urge you to clemency and suavity."

"Suavity towards the Jews!" cried Pontius Pilate. "Although you have lived amongst them, it seems clear that you ill understand those enemies of the human race. Haughty and at the same time base, combining an invincible obstinacy with a despicably mean spirit, they weary alike your love and your hatred. My character, Lamia, was formed upon the maxims of the divine Augustus. When I was appointed Procurator of Judæa, the world was already penetrated with the majestic ideal of the *pax romana*. No longer, as in the days of our internecine strife, were we witnesses to the sack of a province for the aggrandisement of a proconsul. I knew where my duty lay. I was careful that my actions should be governed by prudence and moderation. The gods are my witnesses that I was resolved upon mildness, and upon mildness only. Yet what did my benevolent intentions avail me? You were at my side, Lamia, when, at the outset of my career as ruler, the first rebellion came to a head. Is there any need for me to recall the details to you? The garrison had been transferred from Cæsarea to take up its winter quarters at Jerusalem. Upon the ensigns of the legionaries appeared the present-ment of Cæsar. The inhabitants of Jerusalem, who did not recognize the indwelling divinity of the Emperor, were scandalized at this, as though, when obedience is compulsory, it were not less abject to obey a god than a man. The priests of their nation appeared before my tribunal imploring me with supercilious humility to have the ensigns removed from within the holy city. Out of reverence for the divine nature of Cæsar and the majesty of the empire, I refused to comply. Then the rabble made common cause with the priests, and all around the pretorium portentous cries of supplication arose. I ordered the soldiers to stack their spears in front of the tower of Antonia, and to proceed, armed only with sticks like lictors, to disperse the insolent crowd. But, heedless of blows, the Jews continued their entreaties, and the more obstinate amongst them threw themselves on the ground and, exposing their throats to the rods, deliberately courted death. You were a witness of my humiliation on that occasion, Lamia. By the order of Vitellius I was forced to send the insignia back to Cæsarea. That disgrace I had certainly not merited. Before the immortal gods I swear that never once during my term of office did I flout justice and the laws. But I am grown old. My enemies and detractors are dead. I shall die unavenged. Who will now retrieve my character?"

He moaned and lapsed into silence. Lamia replied—

"That man is prudent who neither hopes nor fears anything from the uncertain events of the future. Does it matter in the least what estimate men may form of us hereafter? We ourselves are after all our own witnesses, and our own judges. You must rely, Pontius Pilate, on the testimony you yourself bear to your own rectitude. Be content with your own personal respect and that of your friends. For the rest, we know that mildness by itself will not suffice for the work of government. There is but little room in the actions of public men for that indulgence of human frailty which the philosophers recommend."

"We'll say no more at present," said Pontius. "The sulphureous fumes which rise from the Phlegræan plain are more powerful when the ground which exhales them is still warm beneath the sun's rays. I must hasten on. Adieu! But now that I have rediscovered a friend, I should wish to take advantage of my good fortune. Do me the favour, Ælius Lamia, to give me your company at supper at my house to-morrow. My house stands on the seashore, at the extreme end of the town in the direction of Misenum. You will easily recognize it by the porch which bears a painting representing Orpheus surrounded by tigers and lions, whom he is charming with the strains from his lyre.

"Till to-morrow, Lamia," he repeated, as he climbed once more into his litter. "To-morrow we will talk about Judæa."

The following day at the supper hour Lamia presented himself at the house of Pontius Pilate. Two couches only were in readiness for occupants. Creditably but simply equipped, the table held a silver service in which were set out beccaficos in honey, thrushes, oysters from the Lucrine lake, and lampreys from Sicily. As they proceeded with their repast, Pontius and Lamia interchanged inquiries with one another about their ailments, the symptoms of which they described at considerable length, mutually emulous of communicating the various remedies which had been recommended to them. Then, congratulating themselves on being thrown together once more at Baiæ, they vied with

one another in praise of the beauty of that enchanting coast and the mildness of the climate they en-
joyed. Lamia was enthusiastic about the charms
of the courtesans who frequented the seashore
laden with golden ornaments and trailing draperies
of barbaric broidery. But the aged Procurator
deplored the ostentation with which by means of
trumpery jewels and filmy garments foreigners and
even enemies of the empire beguiled the Romans
of their gold. After a time they turned to the
subject of the great engineering feats that had been
accomplished in the country; the prodigious bridge
constructed by Caius between Puteoli and Baiæ,
and the canals which Augustus excavated to convey
the waters of the ocean to Lake Avernus and the
Lucrine lake.

"I also," said Pontius, with a sigh, "I also wished
to set afoot public works of great utility. When,
for my sins, I was appointed Governor of Judæa, I
conceived the idea of furnishing Jerusalem with an
abundant supply of pure water by means of an aqueduct. The elevation of the levels, the proportion-
ate capacity of the various parts, the gradient for
the brazen reservoirs to which the distribution pipes
were to be fixed—I had gone into every detail, and
decided everything for myself with the assistance
of mechanical experts. I had drawn up regulations

for the superintendents so as to prevent individuals
from making unauthorized depredations. The
architects and the workmen had their instructions.
I gave orders for the commencement of operations.
But far from viewing with satisfaction the construction of that conduit, which was intended to carry to
their town upon its massive arches not only water
but health, the inhabitants of Jerusalem gave vent to
lamentable outcries. They gathered tumultuously
together, exclaiming against the sacrilege and im-
piousness, and, hurling themselves upon the workmen, scattered the foundation stones. Can you pic-
ture to yourself, Lamia, a filthier set of barbarians?
Nevertheless, Vitellius decided in their favour, and
I received orders to put a stop to the work."

"It is a knotty point," said Lamia, "how far one
is justified in devising things for the commonweal
against the will of the populace."

Pontius Pilate continued as though he had not
heard this interruption.

"Refuse an aqueduct! What madness! But
whatever is of Roman origin is distasteful to the
Jews. In their eyes we are an unclean race, and
our very presence appears a profanation to them.
You will remember that they would never venture
to enter the pretorium for fear of defiling themselves, and that I was consequently obliged to dis-

15

charge my magisterial functions in an open-air tribunal on that marble pavement your feet so often
trod.

"They fear us and they despise us. Yet is not
Rome the mother and warden of all those peoples
who nestle smiling upon her venerable bosom?
With her eagles in the van, peace and liberty have
been carried to the very confines of the universe.
Those whom we have subdued we look on as our
friends, and we leave those conquered races, nay,
we secure to them the permanence of their customs
and their laws. Did Syria, aforetime rent asunder
by its rabble of petty kings, ever even begin to taste
of peace and prosperity until it submitted to the
armies of Pompey? And when Rome might have
reaped a golden harvest as the price of her goodwill,
did she lay hands on the hoards that swell the treas-
uries of barbaric temples? Did she despoil the
shrine of Cybele at Pessinus, or the Morimene and
Cilician sanctuaries of Jupiter, or the temple of the
Jewish god at Jerusalem? Antioch, Palmyra, and
Apamea, secure despite their wealth, and no longer
in dread of the wandering Arab of the desert, have
erected temples to the genius of Rome and the
divine Cæsar. The Jews alone hate and withstand
us. They withhold their tribute till it is wrested

from them, and obstinately rebel against military service."

"The Jews," replied Lamia, "are profoundly attached to their ancient customs. They suspected you, unreasonably I admit, of a desire to abolish their laws and change their usages. Do not resent it, Pontius, if I say that you did not always act in such a way as to disperse their unfortunate illusion. It gratified you, despite your habitual self-restraint, to play upon their fears, and more than once have I seen you betray in their presence the contempt with which their beliefs and religious ceremonies inspired you. You irritated them particularly by giving instructions for the sacerdotal garments and ornaments of their high priest to be kept in ward by your legionaries in the Antonine tower. One must admit that though they have never risen like us to an appreciation of things divine, the Jews celebrate rites which their very antiquity renders venerable."

Pontius Pilate shrugged his shoulders.

"They have very little exact knowledge of the nature of the gods," he said. "They worship Jupiter, yet they abstain from naming him or erecting a statue of him. They do not even adore him under the semblance of a rude stone, as certain of the Asiatic peoples are wont to do. They know nothing of Apollo, of Neptune, of Mars, nor of Pluto, nor of any goddess. At the same time, I am convinced that in days gone by they worshipped Venus. For even to this day their women bring doves to the altar as victims; and you know as well as I that the dealers who trade beneath the arcades of their temple supply those birds in couples for sacrifice. I have even been told that on one occasion some madman proceeded to overturn the stalls bearing these offerings, and their owners with them. The priests raised an outcry about it, and looked on it as a case of sacrilege. I am of opinion that their custom of sacrificing turtle-doves was instituted in honour of Venus. Why are you laughing, Lamia?"

"I was laughing," said Lamia, "at an amusing idea which, I hardly know how, just occurred to me. I was thinking that perchance some day the Jupiter of the Jews might come to Rome and vent his fury upon you. Why should he not? Asia and Africa have already enriched us with a considerable number of gods. We have seen temples in honour of Isis and the dog-faced Anubis erected in Rome. In the public squares, and even on the race-courses, you may run across the Bona Dea of the Syrians mounted on an ass. And did you never hear how, in the reign of Tiberius, a young patrician passed himself off as the horned Jupiter of the Egyptians, Jupiter Ammon, and in this disguise procured the favours of an illustrious lady who was too virtuous to deny anything to a god? Beware, Pontius, lest the invisible Jupiter of the Jews disembark some day on the quay at Ostia!"

At the idea of a god coming out of Judæa, a fleeting smile played over the severe countenance of the Procurator. Then he replied gravely—

"How would the Jews manage to impose their sacred law on outside peoples when they are in a perpetual state of tumult amongst themselves as to the interpretation of that law? You have seen them yourselves, Lamia, in the public squares, split up into twenty rival parties, with staves in their hands, abusing each other and clutching one another by the beard. You have seen them on the steps of the temple, tearing their filthy garments as a symbol of lamentation, with some wretched creature in a frenzy of prophetic exaltation in their midst. They have never realized that it is possible to discuss peacefully and with an even mind those matters concerning the divine which yet are hidden from the profane and wrapped in uncertainty. For the nature of the immortal gods remains hidden from us, and we cannot arrive at a knowledge of it. Though I am of opinion, none the less, that it is a prudent thing to believe in the providence of the gods. But the Jews are devoid of philosophy, and cannot tolerate any diversity of opinions. On the contrary, they judge worthy of the extreme penalty all those who on divine subjects profess opinions opposed to their law. And as, since the genius of Rome has towered over them, capital sentences pronounced by their own tribunals can only be carried out with the sanction of the proconsul or the procurator, they harry the Roman magistrate at any hour to procure his signature to their baleful decrees, they besiege the pretorium with their cries of 'Death!' A hundred times, at least, have I known them, mustered, rich and poor together, all united under their priests, make a furious onslaught on my ivory chair, seizing me by the skirts of my robe, by the thongs of my sandals, and all to demand of me—nay, to exact from me—the death sentence on some unfortunate whose guilt I failed to perceive, and as to whom I could only pronounce that he was as mad as his accusers. A hundred times, do I say! Not a hundred, but every day and all day. Yet it was my duty to execute their law as if it were ours, since I was appointed by Rome not for the destruction, but for the upholding of their customs, and over them I had the power of the rod and the axe. At the outset of

my term of office I endeavoured to persuade them
to hear reason; I attempted to snatch their miserable victims from death. But this show of mildness only irritated them the more; they demanded
their prey, fighting around me like a horde of
vultures with wing and beak. Their priests reported to Cæsar that I was violating their law, and
their appeals, supported by Vitellius, drew down
upon me a severe reprimand. How many times
did I long, as the Greeks used to say, to dispatch
accusers and accused in one convoy to the crows!

"Do not imagine, Lamia, that I nourish the
rancour of the discomfited, the wrath of the super-
annuated, against a people which in my person has
prevailed against both Rome and tranquillity. But
I foresee the extremity to which sooner or later
they will reduce us. Since we cannot govern them,
we shall be driven to destroy them. Never doubt
it. Always in a state of insubordination, brewing
rebellion in their inflammatory minds, they will one
day burst forth upon us with a fury beside which
the wrath of the Numidians and the mutterings
of the Parthians are mere child's play. They are
secretly nourishing preposterous hopes, and madly
premeditating our ruin. How can it be otherwise,
when, on the strength of an oracle, they are living
in expectation of the coming of a prince of their

own blood whose kingdom shall extend over the whole earth? There are no half measures with such a people. They must be exterminated. Jerusalem must be laid waste to the very foundation. Perchance, old as I am, it may be granted me to behold the day when her walls shall fall and the flames shall envelop her houses, when her inhabitants shall pass under the edge of the sword, when salt shall be strown on the place where once the temple stood. And in that day I shall at length be justified."

Lamia exerted himself to lead the conversation back to a less acrimonious note.

"Pontius," he said, "it is not difficult for me to understand both your long-standing resentment and your sinister forebodings. Truly, what you have experienced of the character of the Jews is nothing to their advantage. But I lived in Jerusalem as an interested onlooker, and mingled freely with the people, and I succeeded in detecting certain obscure virtues in these rude folk which were altogether hidden from you. I have met Jews who were all mildness, whose simple manners and faithfulness of heart recalled to me what our poets have related concerning the Spartan lawgiver. And you yourself, Pontius, have seen perish beneath the cudgels of your legionaries simple-minded men who have died for a cause they believed to be just without revealing their names. Such men do not deserve our contempt. I am saying this because it is desirable in all things to preserve moderation and an even mind. But I own that I never experienced any lively sympathy for the Jews. The Jewesses, on the contrary, I found extremely pleasing. I was young then, and the Syrian women stirred all my senses to response. Their ruddy lips, their liquid eyes that shone in the shade, their sleepy gaze pierced me to the very marrow. Painted and stained, smelling of nard and myrrh, steeped in odours, their physical attractions are both rare and delightful."

Pontius listened impatiently to these praises.

"I was not the kind of man to fall into the snares of the Jewish women," he said; " and since you have opened the subject yourself, Lamia, I was never able to approve of your laxity. If I did not express with sufficient emphasis formerly how culpable I held you for having intrigued at Rome with the wife of a man of consular rank, it was because you were then enduring heavy penance for your misdoings. Marriage from the patrician point of view is a sacred tie; it is one of the institutions which are the support of Rome. As to foreign women and slaves, such relations as one

may enter into with them would be of little account were it not that they habituate the body to
a humiliating effeminacy. Let me tell you that
you have been too liberal in your offerings to the
Venus of the Market-place; and what, above all, I
blame in you is that you have not married in
compliance with the law and given children to the
Republic, as every good citizen is bound to do."

But the man who had suffered exile under Tiberius was no longer listening to the venerable magistrate. Having tossed off his cup of Falernian, he
was smiling at some image visible to his eye alone.

After a moment's silence he resumed in a very
deep voice, which rose in pitch by little and little—

"With what languorous grace they dance, those
Syrian women! I knew a Jewess at Jerusalem who
used to dance in a poky little room, on a thread-
bare carpet, by the light of one smoky little lamp,
waving her arms as she clanged her cymbals. Her
loins arched, her head thrown back, and, as it were,
dragged down by the weight of her heavy red hair,
her eyes swimming with voluptuousness, eager, lan-
guishing, compliant, she would have made Cleo-
patra herself grow pale with envy. I was in love
with her barbaric dances, her voice—a little raucous
and yet so sweet—her atmosphere of incense, the
semi-somnolescent state in which she seemed to live.

I followed her everywhere. I mixed with the vile rabble of soldiers, conjurers, and extortioners with which she was surrounded. One day, however, she disappeared, and I saw her no more. Long did I seek her in disreputable alleys and taverns. It was more difficult to learn to do without her than to lose the taste for Greek wine. Some months after I lost sight of her, I learned by chance that she had attached herself to a small company of men and women who were followers of a young Galilean thaumaturgist. His name was Jesus; he came from Nazareth, and he was crucified for some crime, I don't quite know what. Pontius, do you remember anything about the man?"

Pontius Pilate contracted his brows, and his hand rose to his forehead in the attitude of one who probes the deeps of memory. Then after a silence of some seconds—

"Jesus?" he murmured, "Jesus—of Nazareth? I cannot call him to mind."

PUTOIS

I

HEN we were children, our tiny garden, which you could go from end to end of in twenty strides, seemed to us a vast universe, made up of joys and terrors," said Monsieur Bergeret.

"Do you remember Putois, Lucien?" asked Zoé, smiling as was her wont, with lips compressed and her nose over her needlework.

"Do I remember Putois! . . . Why, of all the figures which pass before my childhood's eyes, that of Putois remains the clearest in my memory. Not a single feature of his face or his character have I forgotten. He had a long head. . . ."

"A low forehead," added Mademoiselle Zoé.

Then antiphonally, in a monotonous voice, with mock gravity, the brother and sister recited the following points of a kind of police description:

"A low fore-head."

"Wall-eyed."

"Furtive looking."

"A crow's foot on his temple."

"High cheek-bones, red and shiny."

"His ears were ragged."

"His face was blank and expressionless."

"It was only by his hands, which were constantly moving, that you divined his thoughts."

"Thin, rather bent, weak in appearance."

"In reality of unusual strength."

"He could easily bend a five-franc piece between his thumb and forefinger."

"His thumb was huge."

"He spoke with a drawl."

"His tone was unctuous."

Suddenly Monsieur Bergeret cried eagerly:

"Zoé! We have forgotten his yellow hair and his scant beard. We must begin again."

Pauline had been listening with astonishment to this strange recital. She asked her father and her aunt how they had come to learn this prose passage by heart, and why they recited it like a Litany.

Monsieur Bergeret replied gravely:

"Pauline, what you have just heard is the sacred text, I may say the liturgy of the Bergeret family. It is right that it should be transmitted to you in order that it may not perish with your aunt and me. Your grandfather, my child, your grandfather, Eloi Bergeret, who was not one to be amused with trifles, set a high value on this passage, principally on account of its origin. He entitled it 'The Anatomy of Putois.' And he was accustomed to say that in certain respects he set the anatomy of Putois above the anatomy of Quaresmeprenant. 'If the description written by Xenomanes,' he said, 'is more learned and richer in rare and precious terms, the description of Putois greatly excels it in the lucidity of its ideas and the clearness of its style.' Such was his opinion, for in those days Doctor Ledouble, of Tours, had not yet expounded chapters thirty, thirty-one and thirty-two of the fourth book of Rabelais."

"I can't understand you," said Pauline.

"It is because you don't know Putois, my daughter. You must learn that, in the childhood of your father and your Aunt Zoé, there was no more familiar figure than Putois. In the home of your grandfather Bergeret, Putois was a household word. We all, in turn, believed that we had seen him."

"But who was Putois?" asked Pauline.

Instead of replying her father began to laugh, and Mademoiselle Bergeret also laughed, though her lips were closed.

Pauline looked first at one and then at the other. It seemed to her odd that her aunt should laugh so heartily, and odder still that she should laugh at the same thing as her brother; for strange to say the minds of the brother and sister moved in different grooves.

"Tell me who Putois was, papa. Since you want me to know, tell me."

"Putois, my child, was a gardener. The son of honest farmers of Artois, he had set up as a nursery-man at Saint-Omer. But he was unable to please his customers and failed in business. He gave up his nursery and went out to work by the day. His employers were not always satisfied."

At these words, Mademoiselle Bergeret, still laughing, remarked:

"You remember, Lucien, when father couldn't find his ink-pot, his pens, his sealing-wax or his scissors on his desk, how he used to say: 'I think Putois must have been here.'"

"Ah!" said Monsieur Bergeret, "Putois had not a good reputation."

"Is that all?" asked Pauline.

"No, my child, it is not all. There was something odd about Putois; we knew him, he was familiar to us and yet . . ."

. . . . "He did not exist," said Zoé.

Monsieur Bergeret looked reproachfully at her.

"What a thing to say, Zoé! Why thus break the

charm? Putois did not exist! Dare you say so, Zoé? Can you maintain it? Before affirming that Putois did not exist, that Putois never was, you should consider the condition of being and the modes of existence. Putois existed, sister. But it is true that his was a peculiar existence."

"I understand less and less," said Pauline, growing discouraged.

"The truth will dawn upon you directly, child. Know that Putois was born in the fullness of age. I was still a child; your aunt was a little girl. We lived in a small house, in a suburb of Saint-Omer. Our parents led a quiet retired life, until they were discovered by an old lady of Saint-Omer, Madame Cornouiller, who lived in her manor of Monplaisir, some twelve miles from the town, and who turned out to be my mother's great aunt. She took advantage of the privilege of friendship, to insist on our father and mother coming to dine with her at Monplaisir every Sunday. There they were bored to death. But the old lady said it was right for relatives to dine together on Sundays, and that only ill-bred persons neglected the observance of this ancient custom. Our father was miserable. His sufferings were pitiful to behold. But Madame Cornouiller did not see them. She saw nothing.

My mother bore it better. She suffered as much as my father, and perhaps more, but she contrived to smile."

"Women are made to suffer," said Zoé.

"Every living creature in the world is born to suffer, Zoé. It was in vain that our parents refused these terrible invitations; Madame Cornouiller's carriage came to fetch them every Sunday afternoon. They were bound to go to Monplaisir; it was an obligation which they could not possibly avoid. It was an established order which only open rebellion could disturb. At length my father revolted, and swore he would not accept another of Madame Cornouiller's invitations. To my mother he left the task of finding decent pretexts and varying reasons for their repeated refusals; it was a task for which she was ill fitted; for she was incapable of dissimulation."

"Say, rather, Lucien, that she was not willing to dissimulate. Had she wished she could have fibbed like anyone else."

"It is true that when she had good reasons she preferred giving them to inventing bad ones. You remember, sister, that one day she said at table: 'Fortunately Zoé has whooping-cough: so we shall not have to go to Monplaisir for a long time.'"

"Yes, that did happen," said Zoé.

"You recovered, Zoé. And one day Madame Cornouiller came and said to our mother: 'My dear, I am counting on you and your husband to dine at Monplaisir on Sunday.' Our mother had been expressly enjoined by her husband to give Madame Cornouiller some plausible pretext for refusing. In her extremity the only excuse she could think of was absolutely devoid of probability: 'I am extremely sorry, madame, but it will be impossible. On Sunday I expect the gardener.'

"At these words Madame Cornouiller looked through the glazed door of the drawing-room at the wilderness of a little garden, where the spindle-trees and the lilacs looked as if they never had and never would make the acquaintance of a pruning-hook. 'You are expecting the gardener! What for? To work in your garden!'

"Then, our mother, having involuntarily cast eyes on the patch of rough grass and half-wild plants, which she had just called a garden, realized with alarm that her excuse must appear a mere invention. 'Why couldn't this man come on Monday or Tuesday to work in your . . . garden? Either of these days would be better. It is wrong to work on Sunday. Is he occupied during the week?'

"I have often noticed that the most impudent and the most absurd reasons meet with the least

resistance; they disconcert the opponent. Madame
Cornouiller insisted less than might have been expected of a person so disinclined to give in.
Rising from her chair she asked: 'What is your
gardener's name, dear?'

" 'Putois,' replied our mother promptly.

"Putois had a name. Henceforth he existed.
Madame Cornouiller went off mumbling: 'Putois!
I seem to know that name. Putois? Putois!
Why, yes, I know him well enough. But I can't
recall him. Where does he live? He goes out to
work by the day. When people want him, they
send for him to some house where he is working.
Ah! Just as I thought; he is a loafer, a vagabond
. . . a good-for-nothing. You should beware of
him, my dear.'

"Henceforth Putois had a character."

ONSIEUR GOUBIN and Monsieur Jean Marteau came in. Monsieur Bergeret told them the subject of the conversation:

"We were talking of the man whom my mother one day caused to exist, and created gardener at Saint-Omer. She gave him a name. Henceforth he acted."

"I beg your pardon, sir?" said Monsieur Goubin, wiping his eye-glasses. "Do you mind saying that over again?"

"Willingly," replied Monsieur Bergeret. "There was no gardener. The gardener did not exist. My mother said: 'I expect the gardener!' Straightway the gardener existed—and acted."

"But, Professor," inquired Monsieur Goubin, "how can he have acted if he did not exist?"

"In a manner, he did exist," replied Monsieur Bergeret.

"You mean he existed in imagination," scornfully retorted Monsieur Goubin.

"And is not imaginary existence, existence?" exclaimed the Professor. "Are not mythical person-

ages capable of influencing men? Think of mythology, Monsieur Goubin, and you will perceive that
it is not the real characters, but rather the imaginary ones that exercise the profoundest and the
most durable influence over our minds. In all
times and in all lands, beings who were no more
real than Putois, have inspired nations with love
and hatred, with terror and hope, they have coun-
selled crimes, they have received offerings, they
have moulded manners and laws. Monsieur Goubin, think on the mythology of the ages. Putois
is a mythological personage, obscure, I admit, and
of the humblest order. The rude satyr, who used
to sit at a table with our northern peasants, was
deemed worthy to figure in one of Jordaëns' pictures, and in a fable of La Fontaine. The hairy
son of Sycorax was introduced into the sublime
world of Shakespeare. Putois, less fortunate, will
be for ever scorned by poets and artists. He is
lacking in grandeur and mystery; he has no distinction, no character. He is the offspring of too rational a mind; he was conceived by persons who
knew how to read and write, who lacked the enchanting imagination which gives birth to fables.
Gentlemen, I think what I have said is enough to
reveal to you the true nature of Putois."

"I understand it," said Monsieur Goubin.

35

Then Monsieur Bergeret continued:

"Putois existed. I maintain it. He was. Consider, gentlemen, and you will conclude that the condition of being in no way implies matter; it signifies only the connexion between attribute and subject, it expresses merely a relation."

"Doubtless," said Jean Marteau, "but to be without attributes is to be practically nothing. Some one said long ago: 'I am that I am.' Pardon my bad memory; but one can't recollect everything. Whoever it was who spoke thus committed a great imprudence. By those thoughtless words he implied that he was devoid of attributes and without relation, wherefore he asserted his own non-existence and rashly suppressed himself. I wager that he has never been heard of since."

"Then your wager is lost," replied Monsieur Bergeret. "He corrected the bad effect of those egotistical words by applying to himself a whole string of adjectives. He has been greatly talked of, but generally without much sense."

"I don't understand," said Monsieur Goubin.

"That does not matter," replied Jean Marteau.

And he requested Monsieur Bergeret to tell them about Putois.

"It is very kind of you to ask me," said the Professor. "Putois was born in the second half of the nineteenth century, at Saint-Omer. It would have been better for him had he been born some centuries earlier, in the Forest of Arden or in the Wood of Broceliande. He would then have been an evil spirit of extraordinary cleverness."

"A cup of tea, Monsieur Goubin," said Pauline.

"Was Putois an evil spirit then?" inquired Jean Marteau.

"He was evil," replied Monsieur Bergeret; "in a certain way, and yet not absolutely evil. He was like those devils who are said to be very wicked, but in whom, when one comes to know them, one discovers good qualities. I am disposed to think that justice has not been done to Putois. Madame Cornouiller was prejudiced against him; she immediately suspected him of being a loafer, a drunkard, a thief. Then, reflecting that since he was employed by my mother, who was not rich, he could not ask for high pay, she wondered whether it might not be to her advantage to engage him in the place of her own gardener, who had a better reputation, but also, alas! more requirements. It would soon be the season for trimming the yew-trees. She thought that if Madame Eloi Bergeret, who was poor, paid Putois little, she who was rich might give him still less, since it is the custom for the rich to pay less than the poor. And already in her mind's eye she beheld her yew-trees cut into walls, spheres and pyramids, all for but a trifling outlay. 'I should look after Putois,' she said to herself, 'and see that he did not loaf and thieve. I risk nothing and save a good deal. These casual labourers sometimes do better than skilled workmen.' She resolved to make the experiment, she said to my mother: 'Send Putois to me, my dear. I will give him work at Monplaisir.' My mother promised. She would willingly have done it. But really it was impossible. Madame Cornouiller expected Putois at Monplaisir and expected him in vain. She was a persistent person, and, once having made a resolve, she was determined to carry it out. When she saw my mother, she complained of having heard nothing of Putois. 'Did you not tell him, my dear, that I was expecting him?' 'Yes, but he is so strange, so erratic . . .' 'Oh! I know that sort of person. I know your Putois through and through. But no workman can be so mad as to refuse to come to work at Monplaisir. My house is well known, I should think. Putois will come for my instructions, and quickly, my dear. Only tell me where he lives; and I will go and find him myself.' My mother replied that she did not know where Putois lived, he was not known to have a home, he was without an address. 'I have not seen

him again, Madame. He seems to have gone into
hiding.' She could not have come nearer the truth.
And yet Madame Cornouiller listened to her with
mistrust. She suspected her of beguiling Putois
and keeping him out of sight for fear of losing him
or rendering him more exacting. And she men-
tally pronounced her overselfish. Many a judgment generally accepted and ratified by history has
no better foundation."

"That is quite true," said Pauline.

"What is true?" asked Zoé, who was half asleep.

"That the judgments of history are often false.
I remember, papa, that you said one day: 'It was
very naïve of Madame Roland to appeal to an impartial posterity, and not to see that if her con-
temporaries were malevolent, those who came after
them would be equally so.' "

"Pauline," inquired Mademoiselle Zoé, sternly,
"what has that to do with the story of Putois?"

"A great deal, aunt."

"I don't see it."

Monsieur Bergeret, who did not object to di-
gressions, replied to his daughter:

"If every injustice were ultimately repaired in
this world, it would never have been necessary to
invent another for the purpose. How can posterity judge the dead justly? Into the shades whither

they pass can they be pursued, can they there be questioned? As soon as it is possible to regard them justly they are forgotten. But is it possible ever to be just? What is justice? At any rate, in the end, Madame Cornouiller was obliged to admit that my mother was not deceiving her, and that Putois was not to be found.

"Nevertheless, she did not give up looking for him. Of all her relations, friends, neighbours, servants and tradesmen she inquired whether they knew Putois. Only two or three replied that they had never heard of him. The majority thought they had seen him. 'I have heard the name,' said the cook, 'but I can't put a face to it.' 'Putois! Why! I know him very well,' said the road surveyor, scratching his ear. 'But I couldn't exactly point him out to you.' The most precise information came from Monsieur Blaise, the registrar, who declared that he had employed Putois to chop wood in his yard, from the 19th until the 23rd of October, in the year of the comet.

"One morning, Madame Cornouiller rushed panting into my father's study: 'I have just seen Putois,' she exclaimed. 'Ah! Yes. I've just seen him. Do I think so? But I am sure. He was creeping along by Monsieur Tenchant's wall. He turned into the Rue des Abbesses; he was walking quickly. Then I lost him. Was it really he? There's no doubt of it. A man about fifty, thin, bent, looking like a loafer, wearing a dirty blouse.' 'Such is indeed Putois' description,' said my father. 'Ah! I told you so! Besides, I called him. I cried: Putois! and he turned round. That is what detectives do when they want to make sure of the identity of a criminal they are in search of. Didn't I tell you it was he! . . . I managed to get on his track, your Putois. Well! he is very evil looking. And it was extremely imprudent of you and your wife to employ him. I can read character; and though I only saw his back, I would swear that he is a thief, and perhaps a murderer. His ears are ragged; and that is an infallible sign.' 'Ah! you noticed that his ears were ragged?' 'Nothing escapes me. My dear Monsieur Bergeret, if you don't want to be murdered with your wife and children, don't let Putois come into your house again. Take my advice and have all your locks changed.'

"Now a few days later it happened that Madame Cornouiller had three melons stolen from her kitchen garden. As the thief was not discovered, she suspected Putois. The *gendarmes* were summoned to Monplaisir, and their statements confirmed Madame Cornouiller's suspicions. Just then gangs of thieves were prowling around the gardens of the countryside. But this time the theft seemed to have been committed by a single person, and with extraordinary skill. He had not damaged anything, and had left no footprint on the moist ground. The delinquent could be none other than Putois. Such was the opinion of the police sergeant who had long known all about Putois, and was making every effort to put his hand on the fellow.

"In the *Journal de Saint-Omer* appeared an article on the three melons of Madame Cornouiller. It contained a description of Putois, according to information obtained in the town. 'His forehead is low,' said the newspaper, 'he is wall-eyed; his look is shifty, he has a crow's foot on the temple, high cheek-bones red and shiny. His ears are ragged. Thin, slightly bent, weak in appearance, in reality he is extraordinarily strong: he can easily bend a five-franc piece between his thumb and forefinger.

" 'There were good reasons,' said the newspaper, 'for attributing to him a long series of robberies perpetrated with marvellous skill.'

"Putois was the talk of the town. One day it was said that he had been arrested and committed to prison. But it was soon discovered that the man who had been taken for Putois was a pedlar named Rigobert. As nothing could be proved against him, he was discharged after a fortnight's precautionary detention. And still Putois could not be found. Madame Cornouiller fell a victim to another robbery still more audacious than the first. Three silver teaspoons were stolen from her sideboard.

"She recognized the hand of Putois, had a chain put on her bedroom door and lay awake at night."

III

ABOUT ten o'clock, when Pauline had gone to bed, Mademoiselle Bergeret said to her brother:

"Don't forget to tell how Putois seduced Madame Cornouiller's cook."

"I was just thinking of it, sister," replied her brother. "To omit that incident would be to omit the best part of the story. But we must come to it in its proper place. The police made a careful search for Putois but they did not find him. When it was known that he could not be found, every one made it a point of honour to discover him; and the malicious succeeded. As there were not a few malicious folk at Saint-Omer and in the neighbourhood, Putois was observed at one and the same time in street, field and wood. Thus, another trait was added to his character. To him was attributed that gift of ubiquity which is possessed by so many popular heroes. A being capable of travelling long distances in a moment, and of appearing suddenly in the place where he is least expected, is naturally alarming. Putois was the terror of Saint-Omer.

Madame Cornouiller, convinced that Putois had robbed her of three melons and three teaspoons, barricaded herself at Monplaisir and lived in perpetual fear. Bars, bolts and locks were powerless to reassure her. Putois was for her a terribly subtle creature, who could pass through closed doors. A domestic event redoubled her alarm. Her cook was seduced; and a time came when she could conceal her fault no longer. But she obstinately refused to indicate her betrayer."

"Her name was Gudule," said Mademoiselle Zoé.

"Her name was Gudule; and she was thought to be protected against the perils of love by a long and forked beard. A beard, which suddenly appeared on the chin of that saintly royal maiden venerated at Prague, protected her virginity. A beard, which was no longer young, sufficed not to protect the virtue of Gudule. Madame Cornouiller urged Gudule to utter the name of the man who had betrayed her and then abandoned her to distress. Gudule burst into tears, but refused to speak. Threats and entreaties were alike useless. Madame Cornouiller made a long and minute inquiry. She diplomatically questioned her neighbours—both men and women—the tradesmen, the gardener, the road surveyor, the *gendarmes;* nothing put her on the track of the culprit. Again she endeavoured to extract a full confession from Gudule. 'In your own interest, Gudule, tell me who it is.' Gudule remained silent. Suddenly Madame Cornouiller had a flash of enlightenment: 'It is Putois!' The cook wept and said nothing. 'It is Putois! Why did I not guess it before? It is Putois! You unhappy girl! Oh you poor, unhappy girl!'

"Henceforth Madame Cornouiller was persuaded that Putois was the father of her cook's child. Every one at Saint-Omer, from the President of the Tribunal to the lamplighter's mongrel dog, knew Gudule and her basket. The news that Putois had seduced Gudule filled the town with laughter, astonishment and admiration. Putois was hailed as an irresistible lady-killer and the lover of the eleven thousand virgins. On these slight grounds there was ascribed to him the paternity of five or six other children born that year, who, considering the happiness that awaited them and the joy they brought to their mothers, would have done just as well not to put in an appearance. Among others were included the servant of Monsieur Maréchal, who kept the general shop with the sign of 'Le

Rendezvous des Pêcheurs,' a baker's errand girl, and the little cripple of the Pont-Biquet, who had all fallen victims to Putois' charms. 'The monster!' cried the gossips.

"Thus Putois, invisible satyr, threatened with woes irretrievable all the maidens of a town, wherein, according to the oldest inhabitants, virgins had from time immemorial lived free from danger.

"Though celebrated thus throughout the city and its neighbourhood, he continued in a subtle manner to be associated especially with our home. He passed by our door, and it was believed that from time to time he climbed over our garden wall. He was never seen face to face. But we were constantly recognizing his shadow, his voice, his footprints. More than once, in the twilight, we thought we saw his back at the bend of the road. My sister and I were changing our opinions of him. He remained wicked and malevolent, but he was becoming child-like and simple. He was growing less real, and, if I may say so, more poetical. He was about to be included in the naïve cycle of children's fairy tales. He was turning into Croquemitaine, into Père Fouettard, into the dustman who shuts little children's eyes at night. He was not that sprite who by night entangles the colt's tail in the stable. Not so rustic or so charming, yet he was just as frankly mischievous; he used to draw ink moustaches on my sister's dolls. In our beds we used to hear him before we went to sleep: he was caterwauling on the roofs with the cats, he was barking with the dogs; he was groaning in the mill-hopper; he was mimicking the songs of belated drunkards in the street.

"What rendered Putois present and familiar to us, what interested us in him was that his memory was associated with all the objects that surrounded us. Zoé's dolls, my exercise-books, the pages of which he had so often blotted and crumpled, the garden wall over which we had seen his red eyes gleam in the shadow, the blue flower-pot one winter's night cracked by him if it were not by the frost; trees, streets, benches, everything reminded us of Putois, our Putois, the children's Putois, a being local and mythical. In grace and in poetry he fell far short of the most awkward wild man of the woods, of the uncouthest Sicilian or Thessalian faun. But he was a demi-god all the same.

"To our father Putois' character appeared very differently, it was symbolical and had a philosophical signification. Our father had a vast pity for humanity. He did not think men very reasonable.

Their errors, when they were not cruel, entertained
and amused him. The belief in Putois interested
him as a compendium and abridgment of all the
beliefs of humanity. Our father was ironical and
sarcastic; he spoke of Putois as if he were an actual
being. He was sometimes so persistent, and described each detail with such precision, that our
mother was quite astonished. 'Anyone would say
that you are serious, my love,' she would say
frankly, 'and yet you know perfectly . . .' He replied gravely, 'The whole of Saint-Omer believes
in the existence of Putois. Could I be a good citizen and deny it? One must think well before sup-
pressing an article of universal belief.'

"Only very clear-headed persons are troubled by
such scruples. At heart my father was a follower
of Gassendi. He compromised between his individual views and those of the public: with the Saint-
Omerites he believed in the existence of Putois, but
he did not admit his direct intervention in the theft
of the melons and the seduction of the cook. In
short, like a good citizen he professed his faith in
the existence of Putois, and he dispensed with Putois
when explaining the events which happened in the
town. Wherefore, in this case as in all others, he
proved himself a good man and a thoughtful.

"As for our mother, she felt herself in a way re-

sponsible for the birth of Putois, and she was right.
For in reality Putois was born of our mother's tara-
diddle, as Caliban was born of a poet's invention.
The two crimes, of course, differed greatly in magnitude, and my mother's guilt was not so great as
Shakespeare's. Nevertheless, she was alarmed and
dismayed at seeing so tiny a falsehood grow indefi-
nitely, and so trifling a deception meet with a success
so prodigious that it stopped nowhere, spread
throughout the whole town, and threatened to
spread throughout the whole world. One day she
grew pale, believing that she was about to see her
fib rise in person before her. On that day, her
servant, who was new to the house and neighbourhood, came and told her that a man was asking for
her. He wanted, he said, to speak to Madame.
'What kind of a man is he?' 'A man in a blouse.
He looked like a country labourer.' 'Did he give
his name?' 'Yes, Madame.' 'Well, what is it?'
'Putois.' 'Did he tell you that that was his name?'
'Putois, yes Madame.' 'And he is here?' 'Yes,
Madame. He is waiting in the kitchen.' 'You
have seen him?' 'Yes, Madame.' 'What does he
want?' 'He did not say. He will only tell
Madame.' 'Go and ask him.'

"When the servant returned to the kitchen,
Putois was no longer there. This meeting between

Putois and the new servant was never explained. But I think that from that day my mother began to believe that Putois might possibly exist, and that perhaps she had not invented."

A GOOD LESSON WELL LEARNT

N the days of King Louis XI there lived at Paris, in a matted chamber, a citizen dame called Violante, who was comely and well-liking in all her person. She had so bright a face that Master Jacques Tribouillard, doctor in law and a renowned cosmographer, who was often a visitor at her house, was used to tell her:

"Seeing you, madame, I deem credible and even hold it proven, what Cucurbitus Piger lays down in one of his scholia on Strabo, to wit, that the famous city and university of Paris was of old known by the name of Lutetia or Leucecia, or some such-like word coming from *Leuké,* that is to say, 'the white,' forasmuch as the ladies of the same had bosoms white as snow,—yet not so clear and bright and white as is your own, madame."

To which Violante would say in answer:

" 'Tis enough for me if my bosom is not fit to fright folks, like some I wot of. And, if I show it, why, 'tis to follow the fashion. I have not the hardihood to do otherwise than the rest of the world."

A GOOD LESSON WELL LEARNT

Now Madame Violante had been wedded, in the flower of her youth, to an Advocate of the Parlement, a man of a harsh temper and sorely set on the arraignment and punishing of unfortunate prisoners. For the rest, he was of sickly habit and a weakling, of such a sort he seemed more fit to give pain to folks outside his doors than pleasure to his wife within. The old fellow thought more of his blue bags than of his better half, though these were far otherwise shapen, being bulgy and fat and formless. But the lawyer spent his nights over them.

Madame Violante was too reasonable a woman to love a husband that was so unlovable. Master Jacques Tribouillard upheld she was a good wife, as steadfastly and surely confirmed and stablished in conjugal virtue as Lucretia the Roman. And for proof he alleged that he had altogether failed to turn her aside from the path of honour. The judicious observed a prudent silence on the point, holding that what is hid will only be made manifest at the last Judgment Day. They noted how the lady was over fond of gewgaws and laces and wore in company and at church gowns of velvet and silk and cloth of gold, purfled with miniver; but they were too fair-minded folk to decide whether, damning as she did Christian men who saw her so comely

and so finely dressed to the torments of vain longing, she was not damning her own soul too with one
of them. In a word, they were well ready to stake
Madame Violante's virtue on the toss of a coin,
cross or pile,—which is greatly to the honour of
that fair lady.

The truth is her Confessor, Brother Jean Turelure, was for ever upbraiding her.

"Think you, madame," he would ask her, "that
the blessed St. Catherine won heaven by leading
such a life as yours, baring her bosom and sending
to Genoa for lace ruffles?"

But he was a great preacher, very severe on
human weaknesses, who could condone naught and
thought he had done everything when he had inspired terror. He threatened her with hell fire
for having washed her face with ass's milk.

As a fact, no one could say if she had given her
old husband a meet and proper head-dress, and
Messire Philippe de Coetquis used to warn the
honest dame in a merry vein:

"See to it, I say! He is bald, he will catch his
death of cold!"

Messire Philippe de Coetquis was a knight of
gallant bearing, as handsome as the knave of hearts
in the noble game of cards. He had first encoun-

tered Madame Violante one evening at a ball, and after dancing with her far into the night, had carried her home on his crupper, while the Advocate splashed his way through the mud and mire of the kennels by the dancing light of the torches his four tipsy lackeys bore. In the course of these merry doings, a-foot and on horseback, Messire Philippe de Coetquis had formed a shrewd notion that Madame Violante had a limber waist and a full, firm bosom of her own, and there and then had been smit by her charms. He was a frank and guileless wight and made bold to tell her outright what he would have of her,—to wit, to hold her naked in his two arms.

To which she would make answer:

"Messire Philippe, you know not what you say. I am a virtuous wife,"—

Or another time:

"Messire Philippe, come back again tomorrow,—"

And when he came next day she would ask innocently:

"Nay, where is the hurry?"

These never-ending postponements caused the Chevalier no little distress and chagrin. He was ready to believe, with Master Tribouillard, that

Madame Violante was indeed a Lucretia, so true is it that all men are alike in fatuous self-conceit! And we are bound to say she had not so much as suffered him to kiss her mouth,—only a pretty diversion after all and a bit of wanton playfulness.

Things were in this case when Brother Jean Turelure was called to Venice by the General of his Order, to preach to sundry Turks lately converted to the true Faith.

Before setting forth, the good Brother went to take leave of his fair Penitent, and upbraided her with more than usual sternness for living a dissolute life. He exhorted her urgently to repent and pressed her to wear a hair-shirt next her skin,—an incomparable remedy against naughty cravings and a sovran medicine for natures over prone to the sins of the flesh.

She besought him: "Good Brother, never ask too much of me."

But he would not hearken, and threatened her with the pains of hell if she did not amend her ways. Then he told her he would gladly execute any commissions she might be pleased to entrust him with. He was in hopes she would beg him to bring her back some consecrated medal, a rosary, or, better still, a little of the soil of the Holy Sepulchre which the Turks carry from Jerusalem together with dried roses, and which the Italian monks sell.

But Madame Violante preferred a quite other request:

"Good Brother, dear Brother, as you are going to Venice, where such cunning workmen in this sort are to be found, I pray you bring me back a Venetian mirror, the clearest and truest can be gotten."

Brother Jean Turelure promised to content her wish.

While her Confessor was abroad, Madame Violante led the same life as before. And when Messire Philippe pressed her: "Were it not well to take our pleasure together?" she would answer: "Nay! 'tis too hot. Look at the weathercock if the wind will not change anon." And the good folk who watched her ways were in despair of her ever giving a proper pair of horns to her crabbed old husband. " 'Tis a sin and a shame!" they declared.

On his return from Italy Brother Jean Turelure presented himself before Madame Violante and told her he had brought what she desired.

"Look, madame," he said, and drew from under his gown a death's-head.

"Here, madame, is your mirror. This death's-head was given me for that of the prettiest woman in all Venice. She was what you are, and you will be much like her anon."

57

Madame Violante, mastering her surprise and horror, answered the good Father in a well-assured voice that she understood the lesson he would teach her and she would not fail to profit thereby.

"I shall aye have present in my mind, good Brother, the mirror you have brought me from Venice, wherein I see my likeness not as I am at present, but as doubtless I soon shall be. I promise you to govern my behaviour by this salutary thought."

Brother Jean Turelure was far from expecting such pious words. He expressed some satisfaction.

"So, madame," he murmured, "you see yourself the need of altering your ways. You promise me henceforth to govern your behaviour by the thought this fleshless skull hath brought home to you. Will you not make the same promise to God as you have to me?"

She asked if indeed she must, and he assured her it behoved her so to do.

"Well, I will give this promise then," she declared.

"Madame, this is very well. There is no going back on your word now."

"I shall not go back on it, never fear."

Having won this binding promise, Brother Jean

58

Turelure left the place, radiant with satisfaction. And as he went from the house, he cried out loud in the street:

"Here is a good work done! By Our Lord God's good help, I have turned and set in the way toward the gate of Paradise a lady, who, albeit not sinning precisely in the way of fornication spoken of by the Prophet, yet was wont to employ for men's temptation the clay whereof the Creator had kneaded her that she might serve and adore him withal. She will forsake these naughty habits to adopt a better life. I have thoroughly changed her. Praise be to God!"

Hardly had the good Brother gone down the stairs when Messire Philippe de Coetquis ran up them and scratched at Madame Violante's door. She welcomed him with a beaming smile, and let him into a closet, furnished with carpets and cushions galore, wherein he had never been admitted before. From this he augured well. He offered her sweetmeats he had in a box.

"Here be sugar-plums to suck, madame; they are sweet and sugared, but not so sweet as your lips."

To which the lady retorted he was a vain, silly fop to make boast of a fruit he had never tasted.

He answered her meetly, kissing her forthwith on the mouth.

She manifested scarce any annoyance and said only she was an honest woman and a true wife. He congratulated her and advised her not to lock up this jewel of hers in such close keeping that no man could enjoy it. "For, of a surety," he swore, "you will be robbed of it, and that right soon."

"Try then," said she, cuffing him daintily over the ears with her pretty pink palms.

But he was master by this time to take whatsoever he wished of her. She kept protesting with little cries:

"I won't have it. Fie! fie on you, messire! You must not do it. Oh! sweetheart . . . oh! my love . . . my life! You are killing me!"

Anon, when she had done sighing and dying, she said sweetly:

"Messire Philippe, never flatter yourself you have mastered me by force or guile. You have had of me what you craved, but 'twas of mine own free will, and I only resisted so much as was needful that I might yield me as I liked best. Sweetheart, I am yours. If, for all your handsome face, which I loved from the first, and despite the tenderness of your wooing, I did not before grant you what you have just won with my consent, 'twas because I had no true understanding of things. I had no thought of the flight of time and the shortness of life and love; plunged in a soft languor of indolence, I reaped no harvest of my youth and beauty. However, the good Brother Jean Turelure hath given me a profitable lesson. He hath taught me the preciousness of the hours. But now he showed me a death's-head, saying: 'Suchlike you will be soon.' This taught me we must be quick to enjoy the pleasures of love and make the most of the little space of time reserved to us for that end."

These words and the caresses wherewith Madame Violante seconded them persuaded Messire Philippe to turn the time to good account, to set to work afresh to his own honour and profit and the pleasure and glory of his mistress, and to multiply the sure proofs of prowess which it behoves every good and loyal servant to give on suchlike an occasion.

After which, she was ready to cry quits. Taking him by the hand, she guided him back to the door, kissed him daintily on the eyes, and asked:

"Sweetheart Philippe, is it not well done to follow the precepts of the good Brother Jean Turelure?"

THE SEVEN WIVES OF BLUEBEARD

CHAPTER I

HE strangest, the most varied, the most erroneous opinions have been expressed with regard to the famous individual commonly known as Blue-beard. None, perhaps, was less tenable than that which made of this gentleman a personification of the Sun. For this is what a certain school of comparative mythology set itself to do, some forty years ago. It informed the world that the seven wives of Bluebeard were the Dawns, and that his two brothers-in-law were the morning and the evening Twilight, identifying them with the Dioscuri, who delivered Helena when she was rapt away by Theseus. We must remind those readers who may feel tempted to believe this that in 1817 a learned librarian of Agen, Jean-Baptiste Pérés, demonstrated, in a highly plausible manner, that Napoleon had never existed, and that the story of this supposed great captain was nothing but a

solar myth. Despite the most ingenious diversions of the wits, we cannot possibly doubt that Bluebeard and Napoleon did both actually exist.

An hypothesis no better founded is that which consists in identifying Bluebeard with the Marshal de Rais, who was strangled by the arm of the Law above the bridges of Nantes on 26th of October, 1440. Without inquiring, with M. Salomon Reinach, whether the Marshal committed the crimes for which he was condemned, or whether his wealth, coveted by a greedy prince, did not in some degree contribute to his undoing, there is nothing in his life that resembles what we find in Bluebeard's; this alone is enough to prevent our confusing them or merging the two individuals into one.

Charles Perrault, who, about 1600, had the merit of composing the first biography of this *seigneur,* justly remarkable for having married seven wives, made him an accomplished villain, and the most perfect model of cruelty that ever trod the earth. But it is permissible to doubt, if not his sincerity, at least the correctness of his information. He may, perhaps, have been prejudiced against his hero. He would not have been the first example of a poet or historian who liked to darken the colours of his pictures. If we have what seems a flattering portrait of Titus, it would seem, on the other hand, that Tacitus has painted Tiberius much blacker than the reality. Macbeth, whom legend and Shakespeare accuse of crimes, was in reality a just and a wise king. He never treacherously murdered the old king, Duncan. Duncan, while yet young, was defeated in a great battle, and was found dead on the morrow at a spot called the Armourer's Shop. He had slain several of the kinsfolk of Gruchno, the wife of Macbeth. The latter made Scotland prosperous; he encouraged trade, and was regarded as the defender of the middle classes, the true King of the townsmen. The nobles of the clans never forgave him for defeating Duncan, nor for protecting the artisans. They destroyed him, and dishonoured his memory. Once he was dead the good King Macbeth was known only by the statements of his enemies. The genius of Shakespeare imposed these lies upon the human consciousness. I had long suspected that Bluebeard was the victim of a similar fatality. All the circumstances of his life, as I found them related, were far from satisfying my mind, and from gratifying that craving for logic and lucidity by which I am incessantly consumed. On reflection, I

perceived that they involved insurmountable difficulties. There was so great a desire to make me
believe in the man's cruelty that it could not fail to
make me doubt it.

These presentiments did not mislead me. My
intuitions, which have their origin in a certain
knowledge of human nature, were soon to be
changed into certainty, based upon irrefutable
proofs.

In the house of a stone-cutter in St. Jean-des-
Bois, I found several papers relating to Bluebeard;
amongst others his defence, and an anonymous complaint against his murderers, which was not proceeded with, for what reasons I know not. These
papers confirmed me in the belief that he was good
and unfortunate, and that his memory has been
overwhelmed by unworthy slanders. From that
time forth, I regarded it as my duty to write his
true history, without permitting myself any illusion
as to the success of such an undertaking. I am well
aware that this attempt at rehabilitation is destined
to fall into silence and oblivion. How can the cold,
naked Truth fight against the glittering enchant-
ments of Falsehood?

CHAPTER II

SOMEWHERE about 1650 there lived on his estate, between Compiègne and Pierrefonds, a wealthy noble, by name Bernard de Montragoux, whose ancestors had held the most important posts in the kingdom. But he dwelt far from the Court, in that peaceful obscurity which then veiled all save that on which the king bestowed his glance. His castle of Guillettes abounded in valuable furniture, gold and silver ware, tapestry and embroideries, which he kept in coffers; not that he hid his treasures for fear of damaging them by use; he was, on the contrary, generous and magnificent. But in those days, in the country, the nobles willingly led a very simple life, feeding their people at their own table, and dancing on Sundays with the girls of the village.

On certain occasions, however, they gave splendid entertainments, which contrasted with the dullness of everyday life. So it was necessary that they should hold a good deal of handsome furniture and beautiful tapestries in reserve. This was the case with Monsieur de Montragoux.

66

His castle, built in the Gothic period, had all its rudeness. From without it looked wild and gloomy enough, with the stumps of its great towers, which had been thrown down at the time of the monarchy's troubles, in the reign of the late King Louis. Within it offered a much pleasanter prospect. The rooms were decorated in the Italian taste, as was the great gallery on the ground floor, loaded with embossed decorations in high relief, pictures and gilding.

At one end of this gallery there was a closet usually known as "the little cabinet." This is the only name by which Charles Perrault refers to it. It is as well to note that it was also called the "Cabinet of the Unfortunate Princesses," because a Florentine painter had portrayed on the walls the tragic stories of Dirce, daughter of the Sun, bound by the sons of Antiope to the horns of a bull, Niobe weeping on Mount Sipylus for her children, pierced by the divine arrows, and Procris inviting to her bosom the javelin of Cephalus. These figures had a look of life about them, and the porphyry tiles with which the floor was covered seemed dyed in the blood of these unhappy women. One of the doors of the Cabinet gave upon the moat, which had no water in it.

The stables formed a sumptuous building, situated at some distance from the castle. They contained stalls for sixty horses, and coach-houses for twelve gilded coaches. But what made Guillettes so bewitching a residence were the woods and canals surrounding it, in which one could devote oneself to the pleasures of angling and the chase.

Many of the dwellers in that country-side knew Monsieur de Montragoux only by the name of Bluebeard, for this was the only name that the common people gave him. And in truth his beard was blue, but it was blue only because it was black, and it was because it was so black that it was blue. Monsieur de Montragoux must not be imagined as having the monstrous aspect of the threefold Typhon whom one sees in Athens, laughing in his triple indigo-blue beard. We shall get much nearer the reality by comparing the *seigneur* of Guillettes to those actors or priests whose freshly shaven cheeks have a bluish gloss.

Monsieur de Montragoux did not wear a pointed beard like his grandfather at the Court of King Henry II; nor did he wear it like a fan, as did his great-grandfather who was killed at the battle of Marignan. Like Monsieur de Turenne, he had only a slight moustache and a chin-tuft; his cheeks had

a bluish look; but whatever may have been said of
him, this good gentleman was by no means disfig-
ured thereby, nor did he inspire any fear on that
account. He only looked the more virile, and if
it made him look a little fierce, it had not the effect
of making the women dislike him. Bernard de
Montragoux was a very fine man, tall, broad across
the shoulders, moderately stout, and well favoured;
albeit of a rustic habit, smacking of the woods
rather than of drawing-rooms and assemblies.
Still, it is true that he did not please the ladies as
much as he should have pleased them, built as he
was, and wealthy. Shyness was the reason; shyness, not his beard. Women exercised an invincible
attraction for him, and at the same time inspired
him with an insuperable fear. He feared them as
much as he loved them. This was the origin and
initial cause of all his misfortunes. Seeing a lady
for the first time, he would have died rather than
speak to her, and however much attracted he may
have been, he stood before her in gloomy silence.
His feelings revealed themselves only through his
eyes, which he rolled in a terrible manner. This
timidity exposed him to every kind of misfortune,
and, above all, it prevented his forming a becoming connection with modest and reserved women;

and betrayed him, defenceless, to the attempts of
the most impudent and audacious. This was his
life's misfortune.

Left an orphan from his early youth, and having rejected, owing to this sort of bashfulness and
fear, which he was unable to overcome, the very
advantageous and honourable alliances which had
presented themselves, he married a Mademoiselle
Colette Passage, who had recently settled down in
that part of the country, after amassing a little
money by making a bear dance through the towns
and villages of the kingdom. He loved her with all
his soul. And to do her justice, there was something pleasing about her, though she was what she
was: a fine woman with an ample bosom and a complexion that was still sufficiently fresh, although a
little sunburnt by the open air. Great were her
joy and surprise on first becoming a lady of quality.
Her heart, which was not bad, was touched by the
kindness of a husband in such a high position, and
with such a stout, powerful body, who was to her
the most obedient of servants and devoted of lovers. But after a few months she grew weary because she could no longer go to and fro on the face
of the earth. In the midst of wealth, overwhelmed
with love and care, she could find no greater pleas-

ure than that of going to see the companion of her wandering life, in the cellar where he languished with a chain round his neck and a ring through his nose, and kissing him on the eyes and weeping.

Seeing her full of care, Monsieur de Montragoux himself became careworn, and this only added to his companion's melancholy. The consideration and forethought which he lavished on her turned the poor woman's head. One morning, when he awoke, Monsieur de Montragoux found Colette no longer at his side. In vain he searched for her throughout the castle.

The door of the Cabinet of the Unfortunate Princesses was open. It was through this door that she had gone to reach the open country with her bear. The sorrow of Bluebeard was painful to behold. In spite of the innumerable messengers sent forth in search of her, no news was ever received of Colette Passage.

Monsieur de Montragoux was still mourning her when he happened to dance, at the fair of Guillettes, with Jeanne de La Cloche, daughter of the Police Lieutenant of Compiègne, who inspired him with love. He asked her in marriage, and obtained her forthwith. She loved wine, and drank it to excess. So much did this taste increase that after

71

a few months she looked like a leather bottle with a round red face atop of it. The worst of it was that this leather bottle would run mad, incessantly rolling about the reception-rooms and the stair-cases, crying, swearing, and hiccoughing; vomiting wine and insults at everything that got in her way. Monsieur de Montragoux was dazed with disgust and horror. But he quite suddenly recovered his courage, and set himself, with as much firmness as patience, to cure his wife of so disgusting a vice. Prayers, remonstrances, supplications, and threats: he employed every possible means. All was useless. He forbade her wine from his cellar: she got it from outside, and was more abominably drunk than ever.

To deprive her of her taste for a beverage that she loved too well, he put valerian in the bottles. She thought he was trying to poison her, sprang upon him, and drove three inches of kitchen knife into his belly. He expected to die of it, but he did not abandon his habitual kindness.

"She is more to be pitied than blamed," he said.

One day, when he had forgotten to close the door of the Cabinet of the Unfortunate Princesses, Jeanne de La Cloche entered by it, quite out of her mind, as usual, and seeing the figures on the walls

in postures of affliction, ready to give up the ghost,
she mistook them for living women, and fled terror-
stricken into the country, screaming murder. Hearing Bluebeard calling her and running after her, she
threw herself, mad with terror, into a pond, and
was there drowned. It is difficult to believe, yet
certain, that her husband, so compassionate was his
soul, was much afflicted by her death.

Six weeks after the accident he quietly married
Gigonne, the daughter of his steward, Traignel.
She wore wooden shoes, and smelt of onions. She
was a fine-looking girl enough, except that she
squinted with one eye, and limped with one foot.
As soon as she was married, this goose-girl, bitten
by foolish ambition, dreamed of nothing but further
greatness and splendour. She was not satisfied
that her brocade dresses were rich enough, her pearl
necklaces beautiful enough, her rubies big enough,
her coaches sufficiently gilded, her lakes, woods, and
lands sufficiently vast. Bluebeard, who had never
had any leaning toward ambition, trembled at the
haughty humour of his spouse. Unaware, in his
straightforward simplicity, whether the mistake lay
in thinking magnificently like his wife, or modestly
as he himself did, he accused himself of a medioc-
rity of mind which was thwarting the noble desires

73

of his consort, and, full of uncertainty, he would sometimes exhort her to taste with moderation the good things of this world, while at others he roused himself to pursue fortune along the verge of precipitous heights. He was prudent, but conjugal affection bore him beyond the reach of prudence. Gigonne thought of nothing but cutting a figure in the world, being received at Court, and becoming the King's mistress. Unable to gain her point, she pined away with vexation, contracting a jaundice, of which she died. Bluebeard, full of lamentation, built her a magnificent tomb.

This worthy *seigneur,* overwhelmed by constant domestic adversity, would not perhaps have chosen another wife: but he was himself chosen for a husband by Mademoiselle Blanche de Gibeaumex, the daughter of a cavalry officer, who had but one ear; he used to relate that he had lost the other in the King's service. She was full of intelligence, which she employed in deceiving her husband. She betrayed him with every man of quality in the neighbourhood. She was so dexterous that she deceived him in his own castle, almost under his very eyes, without his perceiving it. Poor Bluebeard assuredly suspected something, but he could not say what. Unfortunately for her, while she gave her whole mind to tricking her husband, she was not sufficiently careful in deceiving her lovers; by which I mean that she betrayed them, one for another. One day she was surprised in the Cabinet of the Unfortunate Princesses, in the company of a gentleman whom she loved, by a gentleman whom she had loved, and the latter, in a transport of jealousy, ran her through with his sword. A few hours later the unfortunate lady was there found dead by one of the castle servants, and the fear inspired by the room increased.

Poor Bluebeard, learning at one blow of his ample dishonour, and the tragic death of his wife, did not console himself for the latter misfortune by any consideration of the former. He had loved Blanche de Gibeaumex with a strange ardour, more dearly than he had loved Jeanne de La Cloche, Gigonne Traignel, or even Colette Passage. On learning that she had consistently betrayed him, and that now she would never betray him again, he experienced a grief and mental perturbation which, far from being appeased, daily increased in violence. So intolerable were his sufferings that he contracted a malady which caused his life to be despaired of.

The physicians, having employed various medi-

cines without effect, advised him that the only
remedy proper to his complaint was to take a
young wife. He then thought of his young cousin,
Angèle de La Garandine, whom he believed would
be willingly bestowed upon him, as she had no property. What encouraged him to take her to wife
was the fact that she was reputed to be simple and
ignorant of the world. Having been deceived by
a woman of intelligence, he felt more comfortable
with a fool. He married Mademoiselle de La
Garandine, and quickly perceived the falsity of his
calculations. Angèle was kind, Angèle was good,
and Angèle loved him; she had not, in herself, any
leanings toward evil, but the least astute person
could quickly lead her astray at any moment. It
was enough to tell her: "Do this for fear of
bogies; come in here or the were-wolf will eat
you;" or "Shut your eyes, and take this drop of
medicine," and the innocent girl would straightway
do so, at the will of the rascals who wanted of her
that which it was very natural to want of her, for
she was pretty. Monsieur de Montragoux, injured
and betrayed by this innocent girl, as much as and
more than he had been by Blanche de Gibeaumex,
had the additional pain of knowing it, for Angèle
was too candid to conceal anything from him. She

used to tell him: "Sir, some one told me this; some one did that to me; some one took so and so away from me; I saw that; I felt so and so." And by her ingenuousness she caused her lord to suffer torments beyond imagination. He endured them like a Stoic. Still he finally had to tell the simple creature that she was a goose, and to box her ears. This, for him, was the beginning of a reputation for cruelty, which was not fated to be diminished. A mendicant monk, who was passing Guillettes while Monsieur de Montragoux was out shooting woodcock, found Madame Angèle sewing a doll's petticoat. This worthy friar, discovering that she was as foolish as she was beautiful, took her away on his donkey, having persuaded her that the Angel Gabriel was waiting in a wood, to give her a pair of pearl garters. It is believed that she must have been eaten by a wolf, for she was never seen again.

After such a disastrous experience, how was it that Bluebeard could make up his mind to contract yet another union? It would be impossible to understand it, were we not well aware of the power which a fine pair of eyes exerts over a generous heart.

The honest gentleman met, at a neighbouring

château which he was in the habit of frequenting, a young orphan of quality, by name Alix de Pontalcin, who, having been robbed of all her property by a greedy trustee, thought only of entering a convent. Officious friends intervened to alter her determination and persuade her to accept the hand of Monsieur de Montragoux. Her beauty was perfect. Bluebeard, who was promising himself the enjoyment of an infinite happiness in her arms, was once more deluded in his hopes, and this time experienced a disappointment, which, owing to his disposition, was bound to make an even greater impression upon him than all the afflictions which he had suffered in his previous marriages. Alix de Pontalcin obstinately refused to give actuality to the union to which she had nevertheless consented.

In vain did Monsieur de Montragoux press her to become his wife; she resisted prayers, tears, and objurgations, she refused her husband's lightest caresses, and rushed off to shut herself into the Cabinet of the Unfortunate Princesses, where she remained, alone and intractable, for whole nights at a time.

The cause of a resistance so contrary to laws both human and divine was never known; it was attributed to Monsieur de Montragoux's blue beard, but our previous remarks on the subject of his beard render such a supposition far from probable. In any case, it is a difficult subject to discuss. The unhappy husband underwent the cruellest sufferings. In order to forget them, he hunted with desperation, exhausting horses, hounds, and huntsmen. But when he returned home, foundered and over-tired, the mere sight of Mademoiselle de Pontalcin was enough to revive his energies and his torments. Finally, unable to endure the situation any longer, he applied to Rome for the annulment of a marriage which was nothing better than a trap; and in consideration of a handsome present to the Holy Father he obtained it in accordance with canon law. If Monsieur de Montragoux discarded Mademoiselle de Pontalcin with all the marks of respect due to a woman, and without breaking his cane across her back, it was because he had a valiant soul, a great heart, and was master of himself as well as of Guillettes. But he swore that, for the future, no female should enter his apartments. Happy had he been if he had held to his oath to the end!

CHAPTER III

OME years had elapsed since Monsieur de Montragoux had rid himself of his sixth wife, and only a confused recollection remained in the countryside of the domestic calamities which had fallen upon this worthy *seigneur's* house. Nobody knew what had become of his wives, and hairraising tales were told in the village at night; some believed them, others did not. About this time, a widow, past the prime of life, Dame Sidonie de Lespoisse, came to settle with her children in the manor of La Motte-Giron, about two leagues, as the crow flies, from the castle of Guillettes. Whence she came, or who her husband had been, not a soul knew. Some believed, because they had heard it said, that he had held certain posts in Savoy or Spain; others said that he had died in the Indies; many had the idea that the widow was possessed of immense estates, while others doubted it strongly. However, she lived in a notable style, and invited all the nobility of the country-side to La Motte-Giron. She had two daughters, of whom

the elder, Anne, on the verge of becoming an old
maid, was a very astute person: Jeanne, the younger,
ripe for marriage, concealed a precocious knowledge of the world under an appearance of simplicity. The Dame de Lespoisse had also two sons, of
twenty and twenty-two years of age; very fine well-
made young fellows, of whom one was a Dragoon,
and the other a Musketeer. I may add, having
seen his commission, that he was a Black Musketeer.
When on foot, this was not apparent, for the Black
Musketeers were distinguished from the Grey not
by the colour of their uniform, but by the hides of
their horses. All alike wore blue surcoats laced
with gold. As for the Dragoons, they were to be
recognized by a kind of fur bonnet, of which the
tail fell gallantly over the ear. The Dragoons
had the reputation of being scamps, a scapegrace
crowd, witness the song:

> "Mama, here the dragoons come:
> Let us haste away."

But you might have searched in vain through His
Majesty's two regiments of Dragoons for a bigger
rake, a more accomplished sponger, or a viler rogue
than Cosme de Lespoisse. Compared with him,
his brother was an honest lad. Drunkard and

gambler, Pierre de Lespoisse pleased the ladies, and won at cards; these were the only ways of gaining a living known to him.

Their mother, Dame de Lespoisse, was making a splash at Motte-Giron only in order to catch gulls. As a matter of fact, she had not a penny, and owed for everything, even to her false teeth. Her clothes and furniture, her coach, her horses, and her servants had all been lent by Parisian money-lenders, who threatened to withdraw them all if she did not presently marry one of her daughters to some rich nobleman, and the respectable Sidonie was expecting to find herself at any moment naked in an empty house. In a hurry to find a son-in-law, she had at once cast her eye upon Monsieur de Montragoux, whom she summed up as being simple-minded, easy to deceive, extremely mild, and quick to fall in love under his rude and bashful exterior. Her two daughters entered into her plans, and every time they met him, riddled poor Bluebeard with glances which pierced him to the depths of his heart. He soon fell a victim to the potent charms of the two Demoiselles de Lespoisse. Forgetting his oath, he thought of nothing but marrying one of them, finding them equally beautiful. After some delay, caused less by hesitation than timidity, he went to Motte-Giron in great state, and made his petition to the Dame de Lespoisse, leaving to her the choice of which daughter she would give him. Madame Sidonie obligingly replied that she held him in high esteem, and that she authorised him to pay his court to whichever of the ladies he should prefer.

"Learn to please, monsieur," she said. "I shall be the first to applaud your success."

In order to make their better acquaintance, Bluebeard invited Anne and Jeanne de Lespoisse, with their mother, brothers, and a multitude of ladies and gentlemen to pass a fortnight at the castle of Guillettes. There was a succession of walking, hunting, and fishing parties, dances and festivities, dinners and entertainments of every sort. A young *seigneur*, the Chevalier de Merlus, whom the ladies Lespoisse had brought with them, organised the beats. Bluebeard had the best packs of hounds and the largest turnout in the country-side. The ladies rivalled the ardour of the gentlemen in hunting the deer. They did not always hunt the animal down, but the hunters and their ladies wandered away in couples, found one another, and again wandered off into the woods. For choice, the Chevalier de la Merlus would lose himself with Jeanne de Les-

83

poisse, and both would return to the castle at night, full of their adventures, and pleased with their day's sport.

After a few days' observation, the good *seigneur* of Montragoux felt a decided preference for Jeanne, the younger sister, rather than the elder, as she was fresher, which is not saying that she was less experienced. He allowed his preference to appear; there was no reason why he should conceal it, for it was a befitting preference; moreover, he was a plain dealer. He paid court to the young lady as best he could, speaking little, for want of practice; but he gazed at her, rolling his rolling eyes, and emitting from the depths of his bowels sighs which might have overthrown an oak tree. Sometimes he would burst out laughing, whereupon the crockery trembled, and the windows rattled. Alone of all the party, he failed to remark the assiduous attentions of the Chevalier de la Merlus to Madame de Lespoisse's younger daughter, or if he did remark them he saw no harm in them. His experience of women was not sufficient to make him suspicious, and he trusted when he loved. My grandmother used to say that in life experience is worthless, and that one remains the same as when one begins. I believe she was right, and the true

84

story that I am now unfolding is not of a nature to
prove her wrong.

Bluebeard displayed an unusual magnificence in
these festivities. When night arrived the lawns
before the castle were lit by a thousand torches,
and tables served by men-servants and maids dressed
as fauns and dryads groaned under all the tastiest
things which the country-side and the forest produced. Musicians provided a continual succession
of beautiful symphonies. Towards the end of the
meal the schoolmaster and schoolmistress, followed
by the boys and girls of the village, appeared before
the guests, and read a complimentary address to
the *seigneur* of Montragoux and his friends. An
astrologer in a pointed cap approached the ladies,
and foretold their future love-affairs from the lines
of their hands. Bluebeard ordered drink to be
given for all his vassals, and he himself distributed
bread and meat to the poor families.

At ten o'clock, for fear of the evening dew, the
company retired to the apartments, lit by a multitude of candles, and there tables were prepared for
every sort of game: lansquenet, billiards, reversi,
bagatelle, pigeon-holes, turnstile, porch, beast, hoca,
brelan, draughts, backgammon, dice, basset, and
calbas. Bluebeard was uniformly unfortunate in

these various games, at which he lost large sums every night. He could console himself for his continuous run of bad luck by watching the three Lespoisse ladies win a great deal of money. Jeanne, the younger, who often backed the game of the Chevalier de la Merlus, heaped up mountains of gold. Madame de Lespoisse's two sons also did very well at reversi and basset; their luck was invariably best at the more hazardous games. The play went on until late into the night. No one slept during these marvellous festivities, and as the earliest biographer of Bluebeard has said: "They spent the whole night in playing tricks on one another." These hours were the most delightful of the whole twenty-four; for then, under cover of jesting, and taking advantage of the darkness, those who felt drawn toward one another would hide together in the depths of some alcove. The Chevalier de la Merlus would disguise himself at one time as a devil, at another as a ghost or a werewolf in order to frighten the sleepers, but he always ended by slipping into the room of Mademoiselle Jeanne de Lespoisse. The good *seigneur* of Montragoux was not over-looked in these games. The two sons of Madame de Lespoisse put irritant powder in his bed, and burnt in his room substances which emitted a disgusting smell. Or they would arrange a jug of water over his door so that the worthy *seigneur* could not open the door without the whole of the water being upset upon his head. In short, they played on him all sorts of practical jokes, to the diversion of the whole company, and Bluebeard bore them with his natural good humour.

He made his request, to which Madame de Lespoisse acceded, although, as she said, it wrung her heart to think of giving her girls in marriage.

The marriage was celebrated at Motte-Giron with extraordinary magnificence. The Demoiselle Jeanne, amazingly beautiful, was dressed entirely in *point de France,* her head covered with a thousand ringlets. Her sister Anne wore a dress of green velvet embroidered with gold. Their mother's dress was of golden tissue, trimmed with black chenille, with a *parure* of pearls and diamonds. Monsieur de Montragoux wore all his great diamonds on a suit of black velvet; he made a very fine appearance; his expression of timidity and innocence contrasting strongly with his blue chin and his massive build. The bride's brothers were of course handsomely arrayed but the Chevalier de la Merlus, in a suit of rose velvet trimmed with pearls, shone with unparalleled splendour.

Immediately after the ceremony, the Jews who had hired out to the bride's family and her lover all these fine clothes and rich jewels resumed possession of them and posted back to Paris with them.

OR a month Monsieur de Montragoux was the happiest of men. He adored his wife, and regarded her as an angel. of purity. She was something quite different, but far shrewder men than poor Bluebeard might have been deceived as he was, for she was a person of great cunning and astuteness, and allowed herself submissively to be ruled by her mother, who was the cleverest jade in the whole kingdom of France. She established herself at Guillettes with her eldest daughter Anne, her two sons, Pierre and Cosme, and the Chevalier de la Merlus, who kept as close to Madame de Montragoux as if he had been her shadow. Her good husband was a little annoyed at this; he would have liked to keep his wife always to himself, but he did not take exception to the affection which she felt for this young gentleman, as she had told him that he was her foster-brother.

Charles Perrault relates that a month after having contracted this union, Bluebeard was compelled to make a journey of six weeks' duration on some important business. He does not seem to be aware of the reasons for this journey, and it has been suspected that it was an artifice, which the jealous husband resorted to, according to custom, in order to surprise his wife. The truth is quite otherwise. Monsieur de Montragoux went to Le Perche to receive the heritage of his cousin of Outarde, who had been killed gloriously by a cannon-ball at the battle of the Dunes, while casting dice upon a drum.

Before leaving, Monsieur de Montragoux begged his wife to indulge in every possible distraction during his absence.

"Invite all your friends, madame," he said, "go riding with them, amuse yourselves, and have a pleasant time."

He handed over to her all the keys of the house, thus indicating that in his absence she was the sole and sovereign mistress of all the *seigneurie* of Guillettes.

"This," he said, "is the key of the two great wardrobes; this of the gold and silver not in daily use; this of the strong-boxes which contain my gold and silver; this of the caskets where my jewels are kept; and this is a pass-key into all the rooms. As for this little key, it is that of the Cabinet, at the end of the Gallery, on the ground floor; open everything, and go where you will."

Charles Perrault claims that Monsieur de Montragoux added:

"But as for the little Cabinet, I forbid you to enter that; and I forbid you so expressly that if you do enter it, I cannot say to what lengths my anger will not go."

The historian of Bluebeard in placing these words on record, has fallen into the error of adopting, without verification, the version concocted after the event by the ladies Lespoisse. Monsieur de Montragoux expressed himself very differently. When he handed to his wife the key of the little Cabinet, which was none other than the Cabinet of the Unfortunate Princesses, to which we have already frequently alluded, he expressed the desire that his beloved Jeanne should not enter that part of the house which he regarded as fatal to his domestic happiness. It was through this room, indeed, that his first wife, and the best of all of them, had fled, when she ran away with her bear; here Blanche de Gibeaumex had repeatedly betrayed him with various gentlemen; and lastly, the porphyry pavement was stained by the blood of a beloved criminal. Was not this enough to make Monsieur de Montragoux

connect the idea of this room with cruel memories
and fateful forebodings?

The words which he addressed to Jeanne de Lespoisse convey the desires and impressions which
were troubling his mind. They were actually as
follows:

"For you, madame, nothing of mine is hidden,
and I should feel that I was doing you an injury
did I fail to hand over to you all the keys of a dwelling which belongs to you. You may therefore enter this little cabinet, as you may enter all the other
rooms of the house; but if you will take my advice
you will do nothing of the kind, to oblige me, and
in consideration of the painful ideas which, for me,
are connected with this room, and the forebodings
of evil which these ideas, despite myself, call up into
my mind. I should be inconsolable were any mis-
chance to befall you, or were I to bring misfortune
upon you. You will, madame, forgive these fears,
which are happily unfounded, as being only the outcome of my anxious affection and my watchful love."

With these words the good *seigneur* embraced
his wife and posted off to Le Perche.

"The friends and neighbours," says Charles Perrault, "did not wait to be asked to visit the young
bride; so full were they of impatience to see all the

wealth of her house. They proceeded at once to inspect all the rooms, cabinets, and wardrobes, each of which was richer and more beautiful than the last; and there was no end to their envy and their praises of their friend's good fortune."

All the historians who have dealt with this subject have added that Madame de Montragoux took no pleasure in the sight of all these riches, by reason of her impatience to open the little Cabinet. This is perfectly correct, and as Perrault has said: "So urgent was her curiosity that, without considering that it was unmannerly to leave her guests, she went down to it by a little secret staircase, and in such a hurry that two or three times she thought she would break her neck." The fact is beyond question. But what no one has told us is that the reason why she was so anxious to reach this apartment was that the Chevalier de la Merlus was awaiting her there.

Since she had come to make her home in the castle of Guillettes she had met this young gentleman in the Cabinet every day, and oftener twice a day than once, without wearying of an intercourse so unseemly in a young married woman. It is impossible to hesitate as to the nature of the ties connecting Jeanne with the Chevalier: they were anything but respectable, anything but chaste. Alas, had Madame de Montragoux merely betrayed her husband's honour, she would no doubt have incurred the blame of posterity; but the most austere of moralists might have found excuses for her. He might allege, in favour of so young a woman, the laxity of the morals of the period; the examples of the city and the Court; the too certain effects of a bad training, and the advice of an immoral mother, for Madame Sidonie de Lespoisse countenanced her daughter's intrigues. The wise might have forgiven her a fault too amiable to merit their severity; her errors would have seemed too common to be crimes, and the world would simply have considered that she was behaving like other people. But Jeanne de Lespoisse, not content with betraying her husband's honour, did not hesitate to attempt his life.

It was in the little Cabinet, otherwise known as the Cabinet of the Unfortunate Princesses, that Jeanne de Lespoisse, Dame de Montragoux, in concert with the Chevalier de la Merlus, plotted the death of a kind and faithful husband. She declared later that, on entering the room, she saw hanging there the bodies of six murdered women, whose congealed blood covered the tiles, and that recognising in these unhappy women the first six wives of

Bluebeard, she foresaw the fate which awaited herself. She must, in this case, have mistaken the paintings on the walls for mutilated corpses, and her hallucinations must be compared with those of Lady Macbeth. But it is extremely probable that Jeanne imagined this horrible sight in order to relate it afterwards, justifying her husband's murderers by slandering their victim.

The death of Monsieur de Montragoux was determined upon. Certain letters which lie before me compel the belief that Madame Sidonie Lespoisse had her part in the plot. As for her elder daughter, she may be described as the soul of the conspiracy. Anne de Lespoisse was the wickedest of the whole family. She was a stranger to sensual weakness, remaining chaste in the midst of the profligacy of the house; it was not a case of refusing pleasures which she thought unworthy of her; the truth was that she took pleasure only in cruelty. She engaged her two brothers, Cosme and Pierre, in the enterprise by promising them the command of a regiment.

CHAPTER V.

T now rests with us to trace, with the aid of authentic documents, and reliable evidence, the most atrocious, treacherous, and cowardly domestic crime of which the record has come down to us. The murder whose circumstances we are about to relate can only be compared to that committed on the night of the 9th March, 1449, on the person of Guillaume de Flavy, by his wife Blanche d'Overbreuc, a young and slender woman, the bastard d'Orbandas, and the barber Jean Bocquillon. They stifled Guillaume with a pillow, battered him pitilessly with a club, and bled him at the throat like a calf. Blanche d'Overbreuc proved that her husband had determined to have her drowned, while Jeanne de Lespoisse betrayed a loving husband to a gang of unspeakable scoundrels. We will record the facts with all possible restraint.

Bluebeard returned rather earlier than expected. This it was gave rise to the quite mistaken idea that, a prey to the blackest jealousy, he was wishful to surprise his wife. Full of joy and confidence, if he thought of giving her a surprise it was an agreeable one. His kindness and tenderness, and his joyous, peaceful air would have softened the most savage hearts. The Chevalier de la Merlus, and the whole execrable brood of Lespoisse saw therein nothing but an additional facility for taking his life, and possessing themselves of his wealth, still further increased by his new inheritance.

His young wife met him with a smiling face, allowing herself to be embraced and led to the conjugal chamber, where she did everything to please the good man. The following morning she returned him the bunch of keys which had been confided to her care. But there was missing that of the Cabinet of the Unfortunate Princesses, commonly called that little Cabinet. Bluebeard gently demanded its delivery, and after putting him off for a time on various pretexts Jeanne returned it to him.

There now arises a question which cannot be solved without leaving the limited domain of history to enter the indeterminate regions of philosophy.

Charles Perrault specifically states that the key of the little Cabinet was a fairy key, that is to say, it was magical, enchanted, endowed with properties contrary to the laws of nature, at all events, as we conceive them. We have no proof to the contrary.

This is a fitting moment to recall the precept of my illustrious master, Monsieur du Clos des Lunes, a member of the Institute: "When the supernatural makes its appearance, it must not be rejected by the historian." I shall therefore content myself with recalling as regards this key, the unanimous opinion of all the old biographers of Bluebeard; they all affirm that it was a fairy key. This is a point of great importance. Moreover, this key is not the only object created by human industry which has proved to be endowed with marvellous properties. Tradition abounds with examples of enchanted swords. Arthur's was a magic sword. And so was that of Joan of Arc, on the undeniable authority of Jean Chartier; and the proof afforded by that illustrious chronicler is that when the blade was broken the two pieces refused to be welded together again despite all the efforts of the most competent armourers. Victor Hugo speaks in one of his poems of those "magic stairways still obscured below." Many authors even admit that there are men-magicians who can turn themselves into wolves. We shall not undertake to combat such a firm and constant belief, and we shall not pretend to decide whether the key of the little Cabinet was or was not enchanted, for our reserve does not imply that we are in any uncertainty, and therein resides its merit. But where we find ourselves in our proper domain, or to be more precise within our own jurisdiction, where we once more become judges of facts, and writers of circumstances, is where we read that the key was flecked with blood. The authority of the texts does not so far impress us as to compel us to believe this. It was not flecked with blood. Blood had flowed in the little cabinet, but at a time already remote. Whether the key had been washed or whether it had dried, it was impossible that it should be so stained, and what, in her agitation, the criminal wife mistook for a blood-stain on the iron, was the reflection of the sky still empurpled by the roses of dawn.

Monsieur de Montragoux, on seeing the key, perceived none the less that his wife had entered the little cabinet. He noticed that it now appeared cleaner and brighter than when he had given it to her, and was of opinion that this polish could only come from use.

This produced a painful impression upon him, and he said to his wife, with a mournful smile:

"My darling, you have been into the little cabinet. May there result no grievous outcome for either of us! From that room emanates a malign influence from which I would have protected you. If you, in your turn should become subjected to it, I should never get over it. Forgive me; when we love we are superstitious."

On these words, although Bluebeard cannot have frightened her, for his words and demeanour expressed only love and melancholy, the young lady of Montragoux began shrieking at the top of her voice:

"Help! Help! he's killing me!"

This was the signal agreed upon. On hearing it, the Chevalier de la Merlus and the two sons of Madame de Lespoisse were to have thrown themselves upon Bluebeard and run him through with their swords.

But the Chevalier, whom Jeanne had hidden in a cupboard in the room, appeared alone. Monsieur de Montragoux, seeing him leap forth sword in hand, placed himself on guard. Jeanne fled terror-stricken, and met her sister Anne in the gallery. She was not, as has been related, on a tower; for all the towers had been thrown down by order of Cardinal Richelieu. Anne was striving to put heart into her two brothers, who, pale and quaking, dared not risk so great a stake.

Jeanne hastily implored them:

"Quick, quick, brothers, save my lover!"

Pierre and Cosme then rushed at Bluebeard. They found him, having disarmed the Chevalier de la Merlus, holding him down with his knee; they treacherously ran their swords through his body from behind, and continued to strike at him long after he had breathed his last.

Bluebeard had no heirs. His wife remained mistress of his property. She used a part of it to provide a dowry for her sister Anne, another part to buy captains' commissions for her two brothers and the rest to marry the Chevalier de la Merlus, who became a very respectable man as soon as he was wealthy.

OUR LADY'S JUGGLER

N the days of King Louis there was a poor juggler in France, a native of Compiègne, Barnaby by name, who went about from town to town performing feats of skill and strength.

On fair days he would unfold an old worn-out carpet in the public square, and when by means of a jovial address, which he had learned of a very ancient juggler, and which he never varied in the least, he had drawn together the children and loafers, he assumed extraordinary attitudes, and balanced a tin plate on the tip of his nose. At first the crowd would feign indifference.

But when, supporting himself on his hands face downwards, he threw into the air six copper balls, which glittered in the sunshine, and caught them again with his feet; or when throwing himself backwards until his heels and the nape of the neck met, giving his body the form of a perfect wheel, he would juggle in this posture with a dozen knives, a murmur of admiration would escape the spectators, and pieces of money rain down upon the carpet.

Nevertheless, like the majority of those who live

by their wits, Barnaby of Compiègne had a great struggle to make a living.

Earning his bread in the sweat of his brow, he bore rather more than his share of the penalties consequent upon the misdoings of our father Adam.

Again, he was unable to work as constantly as he would have been willing to do. The warmth of the sun and the broad daylight were as necessary to enable him to display his brilliant parts as to the trees if flower and fruit should be expected of them. In winter time he was nothing more than a tree stripped of its leaves, and as it were dead. The frozen ground was hard to the juggler, and, like the grasshopper of which Marie de France tells us, the inclement season caused him to suffer both cold and hunger. But as he was simple-natured he bore his ills patiently.

He had never meditated on the origin of wealth, nor upon the inequality of human conditions. He believed firmly that if this life should prove hard, the life to come could not fail to redress the balance, and this hope upheld him. He did not re-semble those thievish and miscreant Merry Andrews who sell their souls to the devil. He never blas-phemed God's name; he lived uprightly, and al-though he had no wife of his own, he did not covet his neighbour's, since woman is ever the enemy of the strong man, as it appears by the history of Samson recorded in the Scriptures.

In truth, his was not a nature much disposed to carnal delights, and it was a greater deprivation to him to forsake the tankard than the Hebe who bore it. For whilst not wanting in sobriety, he was fond of a drink when the weather waxed hot. He was a worthy man who feared God, and was very devoted to the Blessed Virgin.

Never did he fail on entering a church to fall upon his knees before the image of the Mother of God, and offer up this prayer to her:

"Blessed Lady, keep watch over my life until it shall please God that I die, and when I am dead, ensure to me the possession of the joys of paradise."

OW on a certain evening after a dreary wet day, as Barnaby pursued his road, sad and bent, carrying under his arm his balls and knives wrapped up in his old carpet, on the watch for some barn where, though he might not sup, he might sleep, he perceived on the road, going in the same direction as himself, a monk, whom he saluted courteously. And as they walked at the same rate they fell into conversation with one another.

"Fellow traveller," said the monk, "how comes it about that you are clothed all in green? Is it perhaps in order to take the part of a jester in some mystery play?"

"Not at all, good father," replied Barnaby. "Such as you see me, I am called Barnaby, and for my calling I am a juggler. There would be no pleasanter calling in the world if it would always provide one with daily bread."

"Friend Barnaby," returned the monk, "be careful what you say. There is no calling more pleasant than the monastic life. Those who lead it are occupied with the praises of God, the Blessed Virgin, and the saints; and, indeed, the religious life is one ceaseless hymn to the Lord."

Barnaby replied—

"Good father, I own that I spoke like an ignorant man. Your calling cannot be in any respect compared to mine, and although there may be some merit in dancing with a penny balanced on a stick on the tip of one's nose, it is not a merit which comes within hail of your own. Gladly would I, like you, good father, sing my office day by day, and especially, the office of the most Holy Virgin, to whom I have vowed a singular devotion. In order to embrace the monastic life I would willingly abandon the art by which from Soissons to Beauvais I am well known in upwards of six hundred towns and villages."

The monk was touched by the juggler's simplicity, and as he was not lacking in discernment, he at once recognized in Barnaby one of those men of whom it is said in the Scriptures: Peace on earth to men of good will. And for this reason he replied—

"Friend Barnaby, come with me, and I will have you admitted into the monastery of which I am Prior. He who guided St. Mary of Egypt in the desert set me upon your path to lead you into the way of salvation."

It was in this manner, then, that Barnaby became a monk. In the monastery into which he was received the religious vied with one another in the worship of the Blessed Virgin, and in her honour each employed all the knowledge and all the skill which God had given him.

The prior on his part wrote books dealing according to the rules of scholarship with the virtues of the Mother of God.

Brother Maurice, with a deft hand copied out these treatises upon sheets of vellum.

Brother Alexander adorned the leaves with delicate miniature paintings. Here were displayed the Queen of Heaven seated upon Solomon's throne, and while four lions were on guard at her feet, around the nimbus which encircled her head hovered seven doves, which are the seven gifts of the Holy Spirit, the gifts, namely, of Fear, Piety, Knowledge, Strength, Counsel, Understanding, and Wisdom. For her companions she had six virgins with hair of gold, namely, Humility, Prudence, Seclusion, Submission, Virginity, and Obedience.

At her feet were two little naked figures, perfectly white, in an attitude of supplication. These were souls imploring her all-powerful intercession for their soul's health, and we may be sure not imploring in vain.

Upon another page facing this, Brother Alexander represented Eve, so that the Fall and the Redemption could be perceived at one and the same time—Eve the Wife abased, and Mary the Virgin exalted.

Furthermore, to the marvel of the beholder, this book contained presentments of the Well of Living Waters, the Fountain, the Lily, the Moon, the Sun, and the Garden enclosed of which the Song of Songs tells us, the Gate of Heaven and the City of God, and all these things were symbols of the Blessed Virgin.

Brother Marbode was likewise one of the most loving children of Mary.

He spent all his days carving images in stone, so that his beard, his eyebrows, and his hair were white with dust, and his eyes continually swollen and weeping; but his strength and cheerfulness were not diminished, although he was now well gone in years, and it was clear that the Queen of Paradise still cherished her servant in his old age. Marbode represented her seated upon a throne, her brow encircled with an orb-shaped nimbus set with pearls. And he took care that the folds of her dress should cover the feet of her, concerning whom the prophet declared: My be-loved is as a garden enclosed.

Sometimes, too, he depicted her in the sem-blance of a child full of grace, and appearing to say, "Thou art my God, even from my mother's womb."

In the priory, moreover, were poets who com-posed hymns in Latin, both in prose and verse, in honour of the Blessed Virgin Mary, and amongst the company was even a brother from Picardy who sang the miracles of Our Lady in rhymed verse and in the vulgar tongue.

III

EING a witness of this emulation in praise and the glorious harvest of their labours, Barnaby mourned his own ignorance and simplicity.

"Alas!" he sighed, as he took his solitary walk in the little shelterless garden of the monastery, " wretched wight that I am, to be unable, like my brothers, worthily to praise the Holy Mother of God, to whom I have vowed my whole heart's affection. Alas! alas! I am but a rough man and unskilled in the arts, and I can render you in service, blessed Lady, neither edifying sermons, nor treatises set out in order according to rule, nor ingenious paintings, nor statues truthfully sculptured, nor verses whose march is measured to the beat of feet. No gift have I, alas!"

After this fashion he groaned and gave himself up to sorrow. But one evening, when the monks were spending their hour of liberty in conversation, he heard one of them tell the tale of a religious man who could repeat nothing other than the Ave Maria. This poor man was despised for his ignorance; but after his death there issued forth from his mouth five roses in honour of the five letters of the name Mary (Marie), and thus his sanctity was made manifest.

Whilst he listened to this narrative Barnaby marvelled yet once again at the loving kindness of the Virgin; but the lesson of that blessed death did not avail to console him, for his heart overflowed with zeal, and he longed to advance the glory of his Lady, who is in heaven.

How to compass this he sought but could find no way, and day by day he became the more cast down, when one morning he awakened filled full with joy, hastened to the chapel, and remained there alone for more than an hour. After dinner he returned to the chapel once more.

And, starting from that moment, he repaired daily to the chapel at such hours as it was deserted, and spent within it a good part of the time which the other monks devoted to the liberal and mechanical arts. His sadness vanished, nor did he any longer groan.

A demeanour so strange awakened the curiosity of the monks.

These began to ask one another for what purpose Brother Barnaby could be indulging so persistently in retreat.

The prior, whose duty it is to let nothing escape him in the behaviour of his children in religion, resolved to keep a watch over Barnaby during his withdrawals to the chapel. One day, then, when he was shut up there after his custom, the prior, accompanied by two of the older monks, went to discover through the chinks in the door what was going on within the chapel.

They saw Barnaby before the altar of the Blessed Virgin, head downwards, with his feet in the air, and he was juggling with six balls of copper and a dozen knives. In honour of the Holy Mother of God he was performing those feats, which aforetime had won him most renown. Not recognizing that the simple fellow was thus placing at the service of the Blessed Virgin his knowledge and skill, the two old monks exclaimed against the sacrilege.

The prior was aware how stainless was Barnaby's soul, but he concluded that he had been seized with madness. They were all three preparing to lead him swiftly from the chapel, when they saw the Blessed Virgin descend the steps of the altar and advance to wipe away with a fold of her azure robe the sweat which was dropping from her juggler's forehead.

Then the prior, falling upon his face upon the pavement, uttered these words—

"Blessed are the simple-hearted, for they shall see God."

"Amen!" responded the old brethren, and kissed the ground.

BALTHASAR

"Magos reges fere habuit Oriens." [1]

TERTULLIAN.

N those days Balthasar, whom the Greeks called Saracin, reigned in Ethiopia. He was black, but comely of countenance. He had a simple soul and a generous heart.

The third year of his reign, which was the twenty-second of his age, he left his dominions on a visit to Balkis, Queen of Sheba. The mage Sembobitis and the eunuch Menkera accompanied him. He had in his train seventy-five camels bearing cinnamon, myrrh, gold dust, and elephants' tusks.

As they rode, Sembobitis instructed him in the influences of the planets,[1] as well as in the virtues of precious stones, and Menkera sang to him canticles from the sacred mysteries. He paid but little heed to them, but amused himself instead watching the jackals with their ears pricked up, sitting erect on the edge of the desert.

At last, after a march of twelve days, Balthasar became conscious of the fragrance of roses, and

---

[1] The East commonly held kings versed in magic.

very soon they saw the gardens that surround the city of Sheba. On their way they passed young girls dancing under pomegranate trees in full bloom.

"The dance," said Sembobitis the mage, "is a prayer."

"One could sell these women for a great price," said Menkera the eunuch.

As they entered the city they were amazed at the extent of the sheds and warehouses and workshops that lay before them, and also at the immense quantities of merchandise with which these were piled.

For a long time they walked through streets thronged with chariots, street porters, donkeys and donkey-drivers, until all at once the marble walls, the purple awnings and the gold cupolas of the palace of Balkis, lay spread out before them.

The Queen of Sheba received them in a courtyard cooled by jets of perfumed water which fell with a tinkling cadence like a shower of pearls.

Smiling, she stood before them in a jewelled robe.

At sight of her Balthasar was greatly troubled.

She seemed to him lovelier than a dream and more beautiful than desire.

"My lord," and Sembobitis spoke under his breath, "remember to conclude a good commercial treaty with the queen."

"Have a care, my lord," Menkera added. "It is

said she employs magic with which to gain the love of men.".

Then, having prostrated themselves, the mage and the eunuch retired.

Balthasar, left alone with Balkis, tried to speak; he opened his mouth but he could not utter a word. He said to himself, "The queen will be angered at my silence."

But the queen still smiled and looked not at all angry. She was the first to speak with a voice sweeter than the sweetest music.

"Be welcome, and sit down at my side." And with a slender finger like a ray of white light she pointed to the purple cushions on the ground. Balthasar sat down, gave a great sigh, and grasping a cushion in each hand he cried hastily:

"Madam, I would these two cushions were two giants, your enemies; I would wring their necks."

And as he spoke he clutched the cushions with such violence in his hands that the delicate stuff cracked and out flew a cloud of snow-white down. One of the tiny feathers swayed a moment in the air and then alighted on the bosom of the queen.

"My lord Balthasar," Balkis said, blushing; "why do you wish to kill giants?"

"Because I love you," said Balthasar.

"Tell me," Balkis asked, "is the water good in the wells of your capital?"

"Yes," Balthasar replied in some surprise.

"I am also curious to know," Balkis continued, "how a dry conserve of fruit is made in Ethiopia?"

The king did not know what to answer.

"Now please tell me, please," she urged.

Whereupon with a mighty effort of memory he tried to describe how Ethiopian cooks preserve quinces in honey. But she did not listen. And suddenly, she interrupted him.

"My lord, it is said that you love your neighbour, Queen Candace. Is she more beautiful than I am? Do not deceive me."

"More beautiful than you, madam," Balthasar cried as he fell at the feet of Balkis," how could that possibly be!"

"Well, then, her eyes? her mouth, her colour? her throat?" the queen continued.

With his arms outstretched towards her, Balthasar cried:

"Give me but the little feather that has fallen on your neck and in return you shall have half my kingdom as well as the wise Sembobitis and Menkera the eunuch."

But she rose and fled with a ripple of clear laughter.

When the mage and the eunuch returned they found their master plunged deep in thought which was not his custom.

"My lord!" asked Sembobitis, "have you concluded a good commercial treaty?"

That day Balthasar supped with the Queen of Sheba and drank the wine of the palm-tree.

"It is true, then," said Balkis as they supped together, "that Queen Candace is not so beautiful as I?"

"Queen Candace is black," replied Balthasar.

Balkis looked expressively at Balthasar.

"One may be black and yet not ill-looking," she said.

"Balkis!" cried the king.

He said no more, but seized her in his arms, and the head of the queen sank back under the pressure of his lips. But he saw that she was weeping. Thereupon he spoke to her in the low, caressing tones that nurses use to their nurslings. He called her his little blossom and his little star.

"Why do you weep?" he asked. "And what must one do to dry your tears? If you have a desire tell me and it shall be fulfilled."

She ceased weeping, but she was sunk deep in thought. He implored her a long time to tell him her desire. And at last she spoke.

"I wish to know fear."

And as Balthasar did not seem to understand, she explained to him that for a long time past she had greatly longed to face some unknown danger, but she could not, for the men and gods of Sheba watched over her.

"And yet," she added with a sigh, "during the night I long to feel the delicious chill of terror penetrate my flesh. To have my hair stand up on my head with horror. O! it would be such joy to be afraid!"

She twined her arms about the neck of the dusky king, and said with the voice of a pleading child:

"Night has come. Let us go through the town in disguise. Are you willing?"

He agreed. She ran to the window at once and looked through the lattice into the square below.

"A beggar is lying against the palace wall. Give him your garments and ask him in exchange for his camel-hair turban and the coarse cloth about his loins. Be quick and I will dress myself."

And she ran out of the banqueting-hall joyfully clapping her hands one against the other.

Balthasar took off his linen tunic embroidered with gold and girded himself with the skirt of the beggar. It gave him the look of a real slave. The queen soon reappeared dressed in the blue seamless garment of the women who work in the fields.

"Come!" she said.

And she dragged Balthasar along the narrow corridors towards a little door which opened on the fields.

II

HE night was dark, and in the darkness of the night Balkis looked very small.

She led Balthasar to one of the taverns where wastrels and street porters foregathered along with prostitutes. The two sat down at a table and saw through the foul air by the light of a fetid lamp, unclean human brutes attack each other with fists and knives for a woman or a cup of fermented liquor, while others with clenched fists snored under the tables. The tavern-keeper, lying on a pile of sacking, watched the drunken brawlers with a prudent eye. Balkis, having seen some salt fish hanging from the rafters of the ceiling, said to her companion:

"I much wish to eat one of these fish with pounded onions."

Balthasar gave the order. When she had eaten he discovered that he had forgotten to bring money. It gave him no concern, for he thought that he could slip out with her without paying the reckoning. But the tavern-keeper barred their way, calling them a vile slave and a worthless she-ass. Balthasar struck him to the ground with a blow of his fist. Whereupon some of the drinkers drew their knives and flung themselves on the two strangers. But the black man, seizing an enormous pestle used to pound Egyptian onions, knocked down two of his assailants and forced the others back. And all the while he was conscious of the warmth of Balkis' body as she cowered close against him; it was this which made him invincible.

The tavern-keeper's friends, not daring to approach again, flung at him from the end of the pot-house jars of oil, pewter vessels, burning lamps, and even the huge bronze cauldron in which a whole sheep was stewing. This cauldron fell with a horrible crash on Balthasar's head and split his skull. For a moment he stood as if dazed, and then summoning all his strength he flung the cauldron back with such force that its weight was increased tenfold. The shock of the hurtling metal was mingled with indescribable roars and death rattles. Profiting by the terror of the survivors, and fearing that Balkis might be injured, he seized her in his arms and fled with her through the silence and darkness of the lonely byways. The stillness of night enveloped the earth, and the fugitives heard the clamour of the women and the carousers, who pursued them at haphazard, die away in the darkness.

Soon they heard nothing more than the sound of dripping blood as it fell from the brow of Balthasar on the breast of Balkis.

"I love you," the queen murmured.

And by the light of the moon as it emerged from behind a cloud the king saw the white and liquid radiance of her half-closed eyes. They descended the dry bed of a stream, and suddenly Balthasar's foot slipped on the moss and they fell together locked in each other's embrace. They seemed to sink forever into a delicious void, and the world of the living ceased to exist for them. They were still plunged in the enchanting forgetfulness of time, space and separate existence, when at daybreak the gazelles came to drink out of the hollows among the stones.

At that moment a passing band of brigands discovered the two lovers lying on the moss.

"They are poor," they said, "but we shall sell them for a great price, for they are so young and beautiful."

Upon which they surrounded them, and having bound them they tied them to the tail of an ass and proceeded on their way.

The black man so bound threatened the brigands with death. But Balkis, who shivered in the cool, fresh air of the morning, only smiled, as if at something unseen.

They tramped through frightful solitudes until the heat of mid-day made itself felt. The sun was already high when the brigands unbound their prisoners, and, letting them sit in the shade of a rock, threw them some mouldy bread which Balthasar disdained to touch but which Balkis ate greedily.

She laughed. And when the brigand chief asked why she laughed, she replied:

"I laugh at the thought that I shall have you all hanged."

"Indeed!" cried the chief, "a curious assertion in the mouth of a scullery wench like you, my love! Doubtless you will hang us all by aid of that blackamoor gallant of yours?"

At this insult Balthasar flew into a fearful rage, and he flung himself on the brigand and clutched his neck with such violence that he nearly strangled him.

But the other drew his knife and plunged it into his body to the very hilt. The poor king rolled to earth, and as he turned on Balkis a dying glance his sight faded.

III

T this moment was heard an uproar of men, horses and weapons, and Balkis recognised her trusty Abner who had come at the head of her guards to rescue his queen, of whose mysterious disappearance he had heard during the night.

Three times he prostrated himself at the feet of Balkis, and ordered the litter to advance which had been prepared to receive her. In the meantime the guards bound the hands of the brigands. The queen turned towards the chief and said gently: "You cannot accuse me of having made you an idle promise, my friend, when I said you would be hanged."

The mage Sembobitis and Menkera the eunuch, who stood beside Abner, gave utterance to terrible cries when they saw their king lying motionless on the ground with a knife in his stomach. They raised him with great care. Sembobitis, who was highly versed in the science of medicine, saw that he still breathed. He applied a temporary bandage

125

while Menkera wiped the foam from the king's lips. Then they bound him to a horse and led him gently to the palace of the queen.

For fifteen days Balthasar lay in the agonies of delirium. He raved without ceasing of the steaming cauldron and the moss in the ravine, and he incessantly cried aloud for Balkis. At last, on the sixteenth day, he opened his eyes and saw at his bedside Sembobitis and Menkera, but he did not see the queen.

"Where is she? What is she doing?"

"My lord," replied Menkera, "she is closeted with the King of Comagena."

"They are doubtless agreeing to an exchange of merchandise," added the mage Sembobitis.

"But be not so disturbed, my lord, or you will redouble your fever."

"I must see her," cried Balthasar. And he flew towards the apartments of the queen, and neither the sage nor the eunuch could restrain him. On nearing the bedchamber he beheld the King of Comagena come forth covered with gold and glittering like the sun. Balkis, smiling and with eyes closed, lay on a purple couch.

"My Balkis, my Balkis!" cried Balthasar.

She did not even turn her head but seemed to prolong a dream.

Balthasar approached and took her hand which she rudely snatched away.

"What do you want?" she said.

"Do you ask?" the black king answered, and burst into tears.

She turned on him her hard, calm eyes.

Then he realised that she had forgotten everything, and he reminded her of the night of the stream.

"In truth, my lord," said she, "I do not know to what you refer. The wine of the palm does not agree with you. You must have dreamed."

"What," cried the unhappy king, wringing his hands, "your kisses, and the knife which has left its mark on me, are these dreams?"

She rose; the jewels on her robe made a sound as of hail and flashed forth lightnings.

"My lord," she said, "it is the hour my council assembles. I have not the leisure to interpret the dreams of your suffering brain. Take some repose. Farewell."

Balthasar felt himself sinking, but with a supreme effort not to betray his weakness to this wicked woman, he ran to his room where he fell in a swoon and his wound re-opened.

IV.

OR three weeks he remained uncon-scious and as one dead, but having on the twenty-second day recovered his senses, he seized the hand of Sembobitis, who, with Menkera, watched over him, and cried, weeping:

"O, my friends, how happy you are, one to be old and the other the same as old. But no! there is no happiness on earth, everything is bad, for love is an evil and Balkis is wicked."

"Wisdom confers happiness," replied Sembobitis.

"I will try it," said Balthasar. "But let us de-part at once for Ethiopia." And as he had lost all he loved he resolved to consecrate himself to wisdom and to become a mage. If this decision gave him no especial pleasure it at least restored to him something of tranquillity. Every evening, seated on the terrace of his palace in company with the sage Sembobitis and Menkera the eunuch, he gazed at the palm-trees standing motionless against the horizon, or watched the crocodiles by the light of the moon float down the Nile like trunks of trees.

"One never wearies of admiring the beauties of Nature," said Sembobitis.

"Doubtless," said Balthasar, "but there are other things in Nature more beautiful even than palm-trees and crocodiles."

This he said thinking of Balkis. But Sembobitis, who was old, said:

"There is of course the phenomenon of the rising of the Nile which I have explained. Man is created to understand."

"He is created to love," replied Balthasar sighing. "There are things which cannot be explained."

"And what may those be?" asked Sembobitis.

"A woman's treason," the king replied.

Balthasar, however, having decided to become a mage, had a tower built from the summit of which might be discerned many kingdoms and the infinite spaces of Heaven. The tower was constructed of brick and rose high above all other towers. It took no less than two years to build, and Balthasar expended in its construction the entire treasure of the king, his father. Every night he climbed to the top of this tower and there he studied the heavens under the guidance of the sage Sembobitis.

"The constellations of the heavens disclose our destiny," said Sembobitis.

And he replied:

"It must be admitted nevertheless that these signs are obscure. But while I study them I forget Balkis, and that is a great boon."

And among truths most useful to know, the mage taught that the stars are fixed like nails in the arch of the sky, and that there are five planets, namely: Bel, Merodach, and Nebo, which are male, while Sin and Mylitta are female.

"Silver," he further explained, "corresponds to Sin, which is the moon, iron to Merodach, and tin to Bel."

And the worthy Balthasar answered: "Such is the kind of knowledge I wish to acquire. While I study astronomy I think neither of Balkis nor anything else on earth. The sciences are beneficent; they keep men from thinking. Teach me the knowledge, Sembobitis, which destroys all feeling in men and I will raise you to great honour among my people."

This was the reason that Sembobitis taught the king wisdom.

He taught him the power of incantation, according to the principles of Astrampsychos, Gobryas and Pazatas. And the more Balthasar studied the twelve houses of the sun, the less he thought of Balkis, and Menkera, observing this, was filled with a great joy.

"Acknowledge, my lord, that Queen Balkis under her golden robes has little cloven feet like a goat's."

"Who ever told you such nonsense?" asked the King.

"My lord, it is the common report both in Sheba and Ethiopia," replied the eunuch. "It is universally said that Queen Balkis has a shaggy leg and a foot made of two black horns."

Balthasar shrugged his shoulders. He knew that the legs and feet of Balkis were like the legs and feet of all other women and perfect in their beauty. And yet the mere idea spoiled the remembrance of her whom he had so greatly loved. He felt a grievance against Balkis that her beauty was not without blemish in the imagination of those who knew nothing about it. At the thought that he had possessed a woman who, though in reality perfectly formed, passed as a monstrosity, he was seized with such a sense of repugnance that he had no further desire to see Balkis again. Balthasar had a simple soul, but love is a very complex emotion.

From that day on the king made great progress both in magic and astrology. He studied the conjunction of the stars with extreme care, and he drew horoscopes with an accuracy equal to that of Sembobitis himself.

"Sembobitis," he asked, "are you willing to answer with your head the truth of my horoscopes?"

And the sage Sembobitis replied:

"My lord, science is infallible, but the learned often err."

Balthasar was endowed with fine natural sense.

He said:

"Only that which is true is divine, and what is divine is hidden from us. In vain we search for truth. And yet I have discovered a new star in the sky. It is a beautiful star, and it seems alive; and when it sparkles it looks like a celestial eye that blinks gently. I seem to hear it call to me. Happy, happy, happy is he who is born under this star. See, Sembobitis, how this charming and splendid star looks at us."

But Sembobitis did not see the star because he would not see it. Wise and old, he did not like novelties.

And alone in the silence of night Balthasar repeated: "Happy, happy, happy he who is born under this star."

V

HE rumour spread over all Ethiopia and the neighbouring kingdoms that King Balthasar had ceased to love Balkis.

When the tidings reached the country of Sheba, Balkis was as indignant as if she had been betrayed. She ran to the King of Comagena who was employing his time in forgetting his country in the city of Sheba.

"My friend," she cried, "do you know what I have just heard? Balthasar loves me no longer!"

"What does it matter," said the King of Comagena, "since we love one another?"

"But do you not feel how this blackamoor has insulted me?"

"No," said the King of Comagena, "I do not."

Whereupon she drove him ignominiously out of her presence, and ordered her grand vizier to prepare for a journey into Ethiopia.

"We shall set out this very night. And I shall cut off your head if all is not ready by sundown."

But when she was alone she began to sob.

133

"I love him! He loves me no longer, and I love him," she sighed in the sincerity of her heart.

And one night, when on his tower watching the miraculous star, Balthasar, casting his eyes towards earth, saw a long black line sinuously curving over the distant sands of the desert like an army of ants. Little by little what seemed to be ants grew larger and sufficiently distinct for the king to be able to recognise horses, camels and elephants.

The caravan having approached the city, Balthasar distinguished the glittering scimitars and the black horses of the guards of the Queen of Sheba. He even recognised the queen herself, and he was profoundly disturbed, for he felt that he would again love her. The star shone in the zenith with a marvellous brilliancy. Below, extended on a litter of purple and gold, Balkis looked small and brilliant like the star.

Balthasar was conscious of being drawn towards her by some terrible power. Still he turned his head away with a desperate effort, and lifting his eyes he again saw the star. Thereupon the star spoke and said: "Glory to God in the Heavens and peace on earth to men of good will!

"Take a measure of myrrh, gentle King Balthasar, and follow me. I will guide thee to the feet of a little child who is about to be born in a stable between an ass and an ox.

"And this little child is the King of Kings. He will comfort all those who need comforting.

"He calls thee to Him, O Balthasar, thou whose soul is as dark as thy face, but whose heart is as guileless as the heart of a child.

"He has chosen thee because thou hast suffered, and He will give thee riches, happiness and love.

"He will say to thee: 'Be poor joyfully, for that is true riches.' He will also say to thee: 'True happiness is in the renunciation of happiness. Love Me and love none other but Me, because I alone am love.'"

At these words a divine peace fell like a flood of light over the dark face of the king.

Balthasar listened with rapture to the star. He felt himself becoming a new man.

Prostrate beside him, Sembobitis and Menkera worshipped, their faces touching the stone.

Queen Balkis watched Balthasar. She realised that never again would there be love for her in that heart filled with a love divine. She turned white with rage and gave orders for the caravan to return at once to the land of Sheba.

As soon as the star had ceased to speak, Balthasar and his companions descended from the tower. Then, having prepared a measure of myrrh, they formed a caravan and departed in the direction towards which they were guided by the star. They journeyed a long time through unknown countries, the star always journeying in front of them.

One day, finding themselves in a place where three roads met, they saw two kings advance accompanied by a numerous retinue; one was young and fair of face. He greeted Balthasar and said:

"My name is Gaspar. I am a king, and I bear gold as a gift to the child that is about to be born in Bethlehem of Judea."

The second king advanced in turn. He was an old man, and his white beard covered his breast.

"My name is Melchior," he said, "and I am a king, and I bring frankincense to the holy child who is to teach Truth to mankind."

"I am bound whither you are," said Balthasar. "I have conquered my lust, and for that reason the star has spoken to me."

"I," said Melchior, "have conquered my pride, and that is why I have been called."

"I," said Gaspar, "have conquered my cruelty, and for that reason I go with you."

And the three mages proceeded on their journey together. The star which they had seen in the East preceded them until, arriving above the place where the child lay, it stood still. And seeing the star standing still they rejoiced with a great joy.

And, entering the house they found the child with Mary his mother, and prostrating themselves, they worshipped him. And opening their treasures they offered him gold, frankincense and myrrh, as it is written in the Gospel.

OLIVIER'S BRAG

HE Emperor Charlemagne and his twelve peers, having taken the palmer's staff at Saint-Denis, made a pilgrimage to Jerusalem. They prostrated themselves before the tomb of Our Lord, and sat in the thirteen chairs of the great hall wherein Jesus Christ and his Apostles met together to celebrate the blessed sacrifice of the Mass. Then they fared to Constantinople, being fain to see King Hugo, who was renowned for his magnificence.

The King welcomed them in his Palace, where, beneath a golden dome, birds of ruby, wrought with a wondrous art, sat and sang in bushes of emerald.

He seated the Emperor of France and the twelve Counts about a table loaded with stags, boars, cranes, wild geese, and peacocks, served in pepper. And he offered his guests, in oxhorns, the wines of Greece and Asia to drink. Charlemagne and his companions quaffed all these wines in honour of the King and his daughter, the Princess Helen. After supper Hugo led them to the chamber where they were to sleep. Now this chamber was circular, and a column, springing in the midst thereof, carried the vaulted roof. Nothing could be finer to look upon. Against the walls, which were hung with gold and purple, twelve beds were ranged, while another greater than the rest stood beside the pillar.

Charlemagne lay in this, and the Counts stretched themselves round about him on the others. The wine they had drunk ran hot in their veins, and their brains were afire. They could not sleep, and fell to making brags instead, and laying of wagers, as is the way of the knights of France, each striving to outdo the other in warranting himself to do some doughty deed for to manifest his prowess. The Emperor opened the game. He said:

"Let me fetch me, a-horseback and fully armed, the best knight King Hugo hath. I will lift my sword and bring it down upon him in such wise it shall cleave helm and hauberk, saddle and steed, and the blade shall delve a foot deep underground."

Guillaume d'Orange spake up after the Emperor and made the second brag.

"I will take," said he, "a ball of iron sixty men can scarce lift, and hurl it so mightily against the Palace wall that it shall beat down sixty fathoms' length thereof."

Ogier, the Dane, spake next.

"Ye see yon proud pillar which bears up the vault. To-morrow will I tear it down and break it like a straw."

After which Renaud de Montauban cried with an oath:

" 'Od's life! Count Ogier, whiles you overset the pillar, I will clap the dome on my shoulders and hale it down to the seashore."

Gérard de Rousillon it was made the fifth brag.

He boasted he would uproot single-handed, in one hour, all the trees in the Royal pleasaunce.

Aïmer took up his parable when Gérard was done.

"I have a magic hat," said he, "made of a sea-calf's skin, which renders me invisible. I will set it on my head, and to-morrow, whenas King Hugo is seated at meat, I will eat up his fish and drink down his wine, I will tweak his nose and buffet his ears. Not knowing whom or what to blame, he will clap all his serving-men in gaol and scourge them sore,— and we shall laugh."

"For me," declared Huon de Bordeaux, whose turn it was, "for me, I am so nimble I will trip up to the King and cut off his beard and eyebrows without his knowing aught about the matter. 'Tis a piece of sport I will show you to-morrow. And I shall have no need of a sea-calf hat either!"

Doolin de Mayence made his brag too. He promised to eat up in one hour all the figs and all the lemons in the King's orchards.

Next the Duc Naisme said in this wise:

"By my faith! *I* will go into the banquet hall, I will catch up flagons and cups of gold and fling them so high they will never light down again save to tumble into the moon."

Bernard de Brabant then lifted his great voice:

"I will do better yet," he roared. "Ye know the river that flows by Constantinople is broad and deep, for it is come nigh its mouth by then, after traversing Egypt, Babylon, and the Earthly Paradise. Well, I will turn it from its bed and make it flood the Great Square of the City."

Gérard de Viane said:

"Put a dozen knights in line of array. And I will tumble all the twelve on their noses, only by the wind of my sword."

It was the Count Roland laid the twelfth wager, in the fashion following:

"I will take my horn, I will go forth of the city and I will blow such a blast all the gates of the town will drop from their hinges."

Olivier alone had said no word yet. He was young and courteous, and the Emperor loved him dearly.

"Olivier, my son," he asked, "will you not make your brag like the rest of us?"

"Right willingly, sire," Olivier replied. "Do you know the name of Hercules of Greece?"

"Yea, I have heard some discourse of him," said Charlemagne. "He was an idol of the misbelievers, like the false god Mahound."

"Not so, sire," said Olivier. "Hercules of Greece was a knight among the Pagans and King of a Pagan kingdom. He was a gallant champion and stoutly framed in all his limbs. Visiting the Court of a certain Emperor who had fifty daughters, virgins, he wedded them all on one and the same night, and that so well and thoroughly that next morning they all avowed themselves well-contented women and with naught left to learn. He had not slighted ever a one of them. Well, sire, an you will, I will lay my wager to do after the fashion of Hercules of Greece."

"Nay, beware, Olivier, my son," cried the Emperor, "beware what you do; the thing would be a sin. I felt sure this King Hercules was a Saracen!"

"Sire," returned Olivier, "know this—I warrant me to show in the same space of time the selfsame prowess with one virgin that Hercules of Greece did with fifty. And the maid shall be none other but the Princess Helen, King Hugo's daughter."

"Good and well," agreed Charlemagne; "that will be to deal honestly and as a good Christian should. But you were in the wrong, my son, to drag the fifty virgins of King Hercules into your business, wherein, the Devil fly away with me else, I can see but one to be concerned."

"Sire," answered Olivier mildly, "there is but one of a truth. But she shall win such satisfaction of me that, an I number the tokens of my love, you will to-morrow see fifty crosses scored on the wall, and that is *my* brag."

The Count Olivier was yet speaking when lo! the column which bare the vault opened. The pillar was hollow and contrived in such sort that a man could lie hid therein at his ease to see and hear everything. Charlemagne and the twelve Counts had never a notion of this; so they were sore surprised to behold the King of Constantinople step forth. He was white with anger and his eyes flashed fire.

He said in a terrible voice:

"So this is how ye show your gratitude for the hospitality I offer you. Ye are ill-mannered guests. For a whole hour have ye been insulting me with your bragging wagers. Well, know this,—you, Sir Emperor, and ye, his knights; if to-morrow ye do not all of you make good your boasts, I will have your heads cut off."

Having said his say, he stepped back within the pillar, which shut to again closely behind him. For a while the twelve paladins were dumb with wonder and consternation. The Emperor was the first to break the silence.

"Comrades," he said, " 'tis true we have bragged too freely. Mayhap we have spoken things better unsaid. We have drunk overmuch wine, and have shown unwisdom. The chiefest fault is mine; I am your Emperor, and I gave you the bad example. I will devise with you to-morrow of the means whereby we may save us from this perilous pass; meantime, it behoves us to get to sleep. I wish you a good night. God have you in his keeping!"

A moment later the Emperor and the twelve peers were snoring under their coverlets of silk and cloth of gold.

They awoke on the morrow, their minds still distraught and deeming the thing was but a nightmare. But anon soldiers came to lead them to the Palace, that they might make good their brags before the King's face.

"Come," cried the Emperor, "come; and let us pray God and His Holy Mother. By Our Lady's help shall we easily make good our brags."

He marched in front with a more than human majesty of port. Arriving anon at the King's Palace, Charlemagne, Naisme, Aïmer, Huon, Doolin, Guillaume, Ogier, Bernard, Renaud, the two Gérards, and Roland fell on their knees and, joining their hands in prayer, made this supplication to the Holy Virgin:

"Lady, which art in Paradise, look on us now in our extremity; for love of the Realm of the Lilies, which is thine own, protect the Emperor of France and his twelve peers, and give them the puissance to make good their brags."

Thereafter they rose up comforted and fulfilled of bright courage and gallant confidence, for they knew that Our Lady would answer their prayer.

King Hugo, seated on a golden throne, accosted them, saying:

"The hour is come to make good your brags. But an if ye fail so to do, I will have your heads cut off. Begone therefore, straightway, escorted by my men-at-arms, each one of you to the place meet for the doing of the fine things ye have insolently boasted ye will accomplish."

At this order they separated and went divers ways, each followed by a little troop of armed men. Whiles some returned to the hall where they had

passed the night, others betook them to the gardens
and orchards. Bernard de Brabant made for the
river, Roland hied him to the ramparts, and all
marched valiantly. Only Olivier and Charlemagne
tarried in the Palace, waiting, the one for the knight
that he had sworn to cleave in twain, the other for
the maiden he was to wed.

But in very brief while a fearful sound arose,
awful as the last trump that shall proclaim to mankind the end of the world. It reached the Great
Hall of the Palace, set the birds of ruby trembling
on their emerald perches and shook King Hugo on
his throne of gold.

'Twas a noise of walls crumbling into ruin and
floods roaring, and high above the din blared out an
ear-splitting trumpet blast. Meanwhile messengers
had come hurrying in from all quarters of the city,
and thrown themselves trembling at the King's feet,
bearing strange and terrible tidings.

"Sire," said one, "sixty fathoms' length of the
city walls is fallen in at one crash."

"Sire," cried another, "the pillar which bare up
your vaulted hall is broken down, and the dome
thereof we have seen walking like a tortoise toward
the sea."

"Sire," faltered a third, "the river, with its ships
and its fishes, is pouring through the streets, and

146

will soon be beating against your Palace walls."

King Hugo, white with terror, muttered:

"By my faith! these men are wizards."

"Well, Sir King," Charlemagne addressed him with a smile on his lips, "the Knight I wait for is long of coming."

The King sent for him, and he came. He was a knight of stately stature and well armed. The good Emperor clave him in twain, as he had said.

Now while these things were a-doing, Olivier thought to himself:

"The intervention of Our Most Blessed Lady is plain to see in these marvels; and I am rejoiced to behold the manifest tokens she vouchsafes of her love for the Realm of France. Not in vain have the Emperor and his companions implored the succour of the Holy Virgin, Mother of God. Alas! *I* shall pay for all the rest, and have my head cut off. For I cannot well ask the Virgin Mary to help me make good *my* brag. 'Tis an enterprise of a sort wherein 'twould be indiscreet to crave the interference of Her who is the *Lily of Purity,* the *Tower of Ivory,* the *Guarded Door* and the *Fenced Orchard-Close.* And, lacking aid from on high, I am sore afraid I may not do so much as I have said."

Thus ran Olivier's thoughts, when King Hugo roughly accosted him with the words:

" 'Tis now your turn, Count, to fulfill your promise."

"Sire," replied Olivier, "I am waiting with great impatience for the Princess your daughter. For you must needs do me the priceless grace of giving me her hand."

"That is but fair," said King Hugo. "I will therefore bid her come to you and a chaplain with her for to celebrate the marriage."

At church, during the ceremony, Olivier reflected:

"The maid is sweet and comely as ever a man could desire, and too fair am I to clip her in my arms to regret the brag I have made."

That evening, after supper, the Princess Helen and the Count Olivier were escorted by twelve ladies and twelve knights to a chamber, wherein the twain were left alone together.

There they passed the night, and on the morrow guards came and led them both before King Hugo. He was on his throne, surrounded by his knights. Near by stood Charlemagne and the peers.

"Well, Count Olivier," demanded the King, "is your brag made good?"

Olivier held his peace, and already was King Hugo rejoiced at heart to think his new son-in-law's head must fall. For of all the brags and boasts, it was Olivier's had angered him worst.

"Answer," he stormed. "Do you dare to tell me your brag is accomplished?"

Thereupon the Princess Helen, blushing and smiling, spake with eyes downcast and in a faint voice, yet clear withal, and said,—"Yea!"

Right glad were Charlemagne and the peers to hear the Princess say this word.

"Well, well," said Hugo, "these Frenchmen have God and the Devil o' their side. It was fated I should cut off none of these knights' heads. . . . Come hither, son-in-law,"—and he stretched forth his hand to Olivier, who kissed it.

The Emperor Charlemagne embraced the Princess and said to her:

"Helen, I hold you for my daughter and my son's wife. You will go along with us to France, and you will live at our Court."

Then, as his lips lay on the Princess's cheek, he rounded softly in her ear:

"You spake as a loving-hearted woman should. But tell me this in closest confidence,—Did you speak the truth?"

She answered:

"Sire, Olivier is a gallant man and a courteous. He was so full of pretty ways and dainty devices

for to distract my mind, *I* never thought of counting.   Nor yet did *he* keep score.   Needs therefore
must I hold him quit of his promise."

King Hugo made great rejoicings for his daughter's nuptials.   Thereafter Charlemagne and his
twelve peers returned back to France, taking with
them the Princess Helen.

THE OCEAN CHRIST

HAT year many of the fishers of Saint-Valéry had been drowned at sea. Their bodies were found on the beach cast up by the waves with the wreckage of their boats; and for nine days, up the steep road leading to the church were to be seen coffins borne by hand and followed by widows, who were weeping beneath their great black-hooded cloaks, like women in the Bible.

Thus were the skipper Jean Lenoël and his son Désiré laid in the great nave, beneath the vaulted roof from which they had once hung a ship in full rigging as an offering to Our Lady. They were righteous men and God-fearing. Monsieur Guillaume Truphème, priest of Saint-Valéry, having pronounced the Absolution, said in a tearful voice:

"Never were laid in consecrated ground there to await the judgment of God better men and better Christians than Jean Lenoël and his son Désiré."

And while barques and their skippers perished near the coast, in the high seas great vessels foundered. Not a day passed that the ocean did not

bring in some flotsam of wreck. Now one morning some children who were steering a boat saw a
figure lying on the sea. It was a figure of Jesus
Christ, life-size, carved in wood, painted in natural
colouring, and looking as if it were very old. The
Good Lord was floating upon the sea with arms
outstretched. The children towed the figure ashore
and brought it up into Saint-Valéry. The head
was encircled with the crown of thorns. The feet
and hands were pierced. But the nails were missing as well as the cross. The arms were still outstretched ready for sacrifice and blessing, just as
He appeared to Joseph of Arimathea and the holy
women when they were burying him.

The children gave it to Monsieur le Curé
Truphème, who said to them:

"This image of the Saviour is of ancient work-
manship. He who made it must have died long
ago. Although to-day in the shops of Amiens and
Paris excellent statues are sold for a hundred francs
and more, we must admit that the earlier sculptors
were not without merit. But what delights me
most is the thought that if Jesus Christ be thus
come with open arms to Saint-Valéry, it is in order
to bless the parish, which has been so cruelly tried,
and in order to announce that he has compassion
on the poor folk who go a-fishing at the risk of

their lives. He is the God who walked upon the sea and blessed the nets of Cephas."

And Monsieur le Curé Truphème, having had the Christ placed in the church on the cloth of the high altar, went off to order from the carpenter Lemerre a beautiful cross in heart of oak.

When it was made, the Saviour was nailed to it with brand new nails, and it was erected in the nave above the churchwarden's pew.

Then it was noticed that His eyes were filled with mercy and seemed to glisten with tears of heavenly pity.

One of the churchwardens, who was present at the putting up of the crucifix, fancied he saw tears streaming down the divine face. The next morning when Monsieur le Curé with a choir-boy entered the church to say his mass, he was astonished to find the cross above the churchwarden's pew empty and the Christ lying upon the altar.

As soon as he had celebrated the divine sacrifice he had the carpenter called and asked him why he had taken the Christ down from his cross. But the carpenter replied that he had not touched it. Then, after having questioned the beadle and the sidesmen, Monsieur Truphème made certain that no one had entered the church since the crucifix had been placed over the churchwarden's pew.

Thereupon he felt that these things were miraculous, and he meditated upon them discreetly. The following Sunday in his exhortation he spoke of them to his parishioners, and he called upon them to contribute by their gifts to the erection of a new cross more beautiful than the first and more worthy to bear the Redeemer of the world.

The poor fishers of Saint-Valéry gave as much money as they could and the widows brought their wedding-rings. Wherefore Monsieur Truphème was able to go at once to Abbeville and to order a cross of ebony highly polished and surmounted by a scroll with the inscription I.N.R.I. in letters of gold. Two months later it was erected in the place of the former and the Christ was nailed to it between the lance and the sponge.

But Jesus left this cross as He had left the other; and as soon as night fell He went and stretched Himself upon the altar.

Monsieur le Curé, when he found Him there in the morning, fell on his knees and prayed for a long while. The fame of this miracle spread throughout the neighbourhood, and the ladies of Amiens made a collection for the Christ of Saint-Valéry. Monsieur Truphème received money and jewels from Paris, and the wife of the Minister of Marine, Madame Hyde de Neuville, sent him a heart of diamonds. Of all these treasures, in the space of two years, a goldsmith of La Rue St. Sulpice, fashioned a cross of gold and precious stones which was set up with great pomp in the church of Saint-Valéry on the second Sunday after Easter in the year 18—. But He who had not refused the cross of sorrow, fled from this cross of gold and again stretched Himself upon the white linen of the altar.

For fear of offending Him He was left there this time; and He had lain upon the altar for more than two years, when Pierre, son of Pierre Caillou, came to tell Monsieur le Curé Truphème that he had found the true cross of Our Lord on the beach.

Pierre was an innocent; and, because he had not sense enough to earn a livelihood, people gave him bread out of charity; he was liked because he never did any harm. But he wandered in his talk and no one listened to him.

Nevertheless Monsieur Truphème, who had never ceased meditating on the Ocean Christ, was struck by what the poor imbecile had just said. With the beadle and two sidesmen he went to the spot, where the child said he had seen a cross, and there he found two planks studded with nails, which had long been washed by the sea and which did indeed form a cross.

They were the remains of some old shipwreck. On one of these boards could still be read two letters painted in black, a J and an L; and there was no doubt that this was a fragment of Jean Lenoël's barque, he who with his son Désiré had been lost at sea five years before.

At the sight of this, the beadle and the sidesmen began to laugh at the innocent who had taken the broken planks of a boat for the cross of Jesus Christ. But Monsieur le Curé Truphème checked their merriment. He had meditated much and prayed long since the Ocean Christ had arrived among the fisherfolk, and the mystery of infinite charity began to dawn upon him. He knelt down upon the sand, repeated the prayer for the faithful departed, and then told the beadle and the sidesmen to carry the flotsam on their shoulders and to place it in the church. When this had been done he raised the Christ from the altar, placed it on the planks of the boat and himself nailed it to them, with the nails that the ocean had corroded.

By the priest's command, the very next day this cross took the place of the cross of gold and precious stones over the churchwarden's pew. The

Ocean Christ has never left it.   He has chosen to remain nailed to the planks on which men died invoking His name and that of His Mother.   There, with parted lips, august and afflicted He seems to say:

"My cross is made of all men's woes, for I am in truth the God of the poor and the heavy-laden."

THE MANUSCRIPT OF A VILLAGE
DOCTOR

OCTOR H——, who recently died
at Servigny (Aisne), where he had
practised medicine for more than
forty years, left behind him a journal never intended for the public
eye. I should not feel justified in publishing the
manuscript *in extenso,* nor even in printing frag-
ments of any considerable length, although, like
Monsieur Taine, there is a large number of persons
nowadays of the opinion that it is above all things
desirable to print and circulate what was never
planned for publication. Whatever these worthy
folk may say, the fact that a writer is an amateur
does not afford any guarantee that what he has to
say will be interesting. The memoirs of Doctor
H—— would be wearisome from their mere mo-
notonously moral note. And yet the man who wrote
them, in his lowly environment, possessed an intellect quite out of the ordinary. This village doctor
was philosopher as well as physician. Perhaps the
closing pages of his journal might be perused with-

out any exceptional distaste. I venture to transcribe them here:—

Extract from the Journal of the late Doctor H——,
Physician at Servigny (Aisne).

"It is an axiom of philosophy that nothing in this world is either altogether bad or altogether good. Pity, the tenderest, the most natural, the most useful of the virtues, is not at all times in place either with the soldier or the priest; both with priest and soldier there are occasions when it must be held in restraint—when confronted by the enemy, for instance. Officers do not make a practice of recommending it on the eve of battle, and in some old book I have read that Monsieur Nicole held it in distrust as the motive principle of concupiscence. There is nothing of the priest about me, and still less of the soldier. I am a doctor, and amongst the most insignificant of that profession, a country doctor. I have practised my art for long years and in obscurity, and I would assert that if pity alone can be a worthy stimulus to the adoption of our profession, we must lay it aside finally when we encounter those miseries which it has inspired us with the desire to alleviate. A doctor whom pity accompanies to the bedside of his patients will find his observation not sufficiently acute, his hands not sufficiently steady. We go wherever comparison for the human race calls, but we must leave pity behind us. Moreover, doctors for the most part find it an easy task to attain the callousness which is so necessary to them. That is a mental condition which cannot long elude them, and there are moral reasons for this. Pity speedily becomes blunted when brought into contact with suffering; there is less disposition to deplore those misfortunes for which alleviation can be procured; finally, to the physician an illness offers a succession of interesting phenomena.

"From the time when I began the practice of medicine I flung myself into it with ardour. In the bodily ills disclosed to me I saw only opportunities for the practical application of my art. When a complaint developed without complications, I was able to see beauty in its conformity to the normal type. Those phenomena of disease, which offered apparent anomalies, awakened curiosity in my mind; so that I was enamoured of disease. What am I saying? From the point of view I espoused disease and health were possessed of indisputable personality. As an enthusiastic observer of the human mechanism, I found as much to admire in its more baleful affections as in its most healthy compliance with law. Willingly

should I have exclaimed with Pinel: 'What a
magnificent cancer!' That was a fine attitude of
mind, and I was on my way to become a philos-
opher-physician. I only needed to have a genius
for my art in order to enjoy completely, and enter
into possession of, the full beauty of the theory of
disease classification. It is the privilege of genius
to unveil the splendour of things. Where the
ordinary man would see only a disgusting wound,
the naturalist worthy of the name stands enraptured
before a battlefield on which the mysterious forces
of life struggle for supremacy, in an encounter
more inexorable, more terrifying than any that the
strenuous abandon of Salvator Rosa ever depicted.
I only caught glimpses of that spectacle of which
the Magendies and Claude Bernards were familiar
witnesses, and it was a distinction for me to do so;
but though resigned to the career of a humble
practitioner, I fortified myself, as a professional
duty, in the habit of confronting grievous situations
unemotionally. I gave my patients my energies
and my intellect. I did not give them pity. God
forbid that I should place any gift, howsoever
precious, above His gift of pity! Pity is the
widow's mite; it is the incomparable offering of the
poor man, who with generosity outstripping that of
all the wealthy in this world of ours, gives with the

gift of his tears a piece torn from his heart. For that very reason it is that pity must be dissociated from the carrying out of a professional duty, how noble soe'er that profession may be.

"To enter upon more particular considerations, I would say that the folk in whose midst I am living evoke in their misfortunes a sentiment which is not pity. There is something of truth in the theory that a man cannot inspire in another an emotion which he is incapable of experiencing himself. Now the peasantry in our part of the country are not tender-hearted. Harsh to others as to themselves, they drag out an existence morose in its gravity. That gravity, too, is contagious, and in their company sadness and dejection affect one's mind. What is fine about their moral outlook is that they preserve unscathed the nobler features of humanity. As they are not accustomed to think with any frequency or profundity, their thoughts assume naturally in certain circumstances a solemn tone. I have heard some of them give utterance at the point of death to brief, forcible speeches worthy of the patriarchs of the Old Testament. They can call forth one's admiration, but do not awaken one's sympathies. With them everything is quite simple, even their illnesses. Their sufferings are not accentuated by their imagination. They are not like those oversensitive creatures who construct from their ills a monster more harassing than the ills themselves. They meet death so much as a matter of course that it is impossible to be greatly disturbed. To sum up, I might say that they are all so much alike that no shred of individuality vanishes as each one passes away.

"For the reasons which I have just set down it follows that I practise my profession of village doctor very peacefully. I never regret having chosen it. I sometimes think I am a little above it; but if it is vexatious to a man to feel himself above his position, the annoyance would certainly be greater if he felt unequal to it. I am not rich, and never shall be so long as I live. But of what use would money be to one who leads a solitary village life? My little grey mare, Jenny, is as yet only fifteen years old, and she still trots as easily as in the days of her first youth, especially when we are going in the direction of the stable. I do not, like my illustrious fellow-physicians in Paris, possess a gallery of pictures for the entertainment of my visitors, but I can show pear trees which the towns-men have nothing like. My orchard is famous for twenty leagues round, and the owners of the neigh-bouring châteaux come to beg cuttings from me.

"Now on a certain Monday—it will be a year ago

this very day—as I was busy in my garden inspecting my espaliers, a farm servant came to beg me to call as soon as possible at Les Alies.

"I asked him whether Jean Blin, the farmer at Les Alies, had sustained a fall the previous day as he came home in the evening. For in my part of the country a sprain is a common Sunday occurrence, and it is not at all rare for a man to break two or three ribs that day on leaving the public-house. Jean Blin is not exactly a bad sort, but he likes drinking in company, and more than once he has known what it is like to wait for Monday's dawn at the bottom of a miry ditch.

"The farm servant replied that there was nothing the matter with Jean Blin, but that Éloi, Jean's little son, was seized with fever.

"Without another thought for my espaliers, I went in search of my hat and stick, and set out on foot for Les Alies, which is only twenty minutes' walk from my house. As I walked, my thoughts were on ahead with Jean Blin's little boy in the grip of a fever. His father was a peasant much like every other peasant, with this peculiar difference, that the Intelligence which created him forgot to provide him with a brain. This great hulking Jean Blin has a head as thick as his fist. Divine wisdom has only furnished that particular skull with what was strictly indispensable, there's no getting over that. His wife, the best looking woman in the place, is a noisy, bustling housewife, stolidly virtuous. Well, well! To this worthy couple a child had been given, who was easily the most delicate, the most spiritual little being that ever adorned this old world of ours. Heredity is responsible for some of the surprises in nature, and it has been well said that nobody knows what he is about when he fathers a child. Heredity, according to our honoured Nysten, is the biological phenomenon which is responsible for the fact that, in addition to the normal type of the species, ancestors transmit to their descendants certain peculiarities of organization and of aptitude. I admit it. But what peculiarities are transmitted and what are not, that is what is not very clear, even after a perusal of the learned works of Doctor Lucas and Monsieur Ribot. My neighbour, the notary, lent me last year a volume by Monsieur Émile Zola, and I observe that that author takes credit for particular discernment in this respect. 'Here,' he says, in substance, 'is an ancestor afflicted with neurosis; his descendants will show neuropathic tendencies, that is to say, when they do not do so; amongst them will be found some foolish and some intelligent individuals; one of them may even be a genius.' He has

165

gone to the trouble of drawing up a genealogical chart to make his idea more easily apprehended. Well and good! The discovery is not particularly novel, and its expounder would unquestionably be ill-advised to vaunt himself upon it; it is none the less true, however, that it embraces practically all we know on the subject of heredity. And this is how it came about that Éloi, Jean Blin's little son, was an embodied intellect. He had a creative imagination. Many a time, when he was no higher than my walking-stick, I have come across him playing truant with the village urchins. Whilst they were reaching after nests, I have watched the little fellow constructing model mills and miniature syphons with pipes of straw. Inventive and unsociable he turned to nature. His schoolmaster despaired of ever making anything of so inattentive a child; and, to tell the truth, at eight years old Éloi was still ignorant of his letters. But at that age he learned to read and write with astonishing rapidity, and in six months became the best scholar in the village.

"He was the most affectionate and the most clinging child. I gave him a few lessons in mathematics, and was astounded at the fertility that his mind displayed at this early age. In fact—I own it without any fear of being ridiculed, for in an old man cut off from civilization some exaggeration is pardonable—I rejoiced to have detected in this little peasant the premonitions of one of those enlightened spirits which at long intervals shine forth in the midst of our purblind race, and, impelled alike by the need of lavishing their affection and the desire for knowledge, are bound to effect something useful or beautiful wherever fate may assign them a place.

"My mind was occupied with musings of this kind as far as Les Alies. Entering the low-ceiled roof, I found little Éloi ensconced in the big bed with cotton hangings, to which no doubt his parents had removed him on account of the gravity of his condition. He was lethargic, his head, though small and delicate, nevertheless made as great a dent in the pillow as if it had been of enormous weight. I stole near. His forehead was on fire; there was a disquieting redness about the conjunctive membrane; the temperature of the body was altogether too high. His mother and grandmother kept close to him, anxiously. Jean Blin, whose uneasiness prevented him from working, not knowing what to do, and being afraid to go away, stood with his hands in his pockets looking inquiringly first at one and then at another. The child turned his drawn face towards me, and scrutinizing me with an affectionate but heartbreaking glance, said in reply to my questions that his forehead and his eyes were both very painful, that he could hear noises which he knew were imaginary, and that he knew perfectly well who I was, his dear old friend.

" 'First he has shivering fits, and then he is feverishly hot,' said his mother.

"Jean Blin, after ruminating for several minutes, remarked—

" 'My belief is that what ails him is his inside.'

"Then he relapsed into silence.

"It had been only too easy for me to diagnose the symptoms of acute meningitis. I prescribed revulsive applications to the feet, and leeches behind the ears. I drew near to my little friend a second time, and tried to say something cheerful to him, more cheerful, alas! than facts warranted. But I was suddenly aware of an entirely new personal experience. Although I was completely self possessed I seemed to see the sick child through a veil, and at such a distance that he appeared quite, quite small. This upsetting of my ideas of space was speedily followed by an analogous upheaval of my ideas of time. Although my visit had not lasted above five minutes, I received the impression that I had been in that low-ceiled room, in front of that bed with its white cotton hangings, for a long time, for a very long time, and that months and even years had rolled by whilst I was held motionless.

"By a mental effort which is perfectly natural to me, I there and then put these singular impressions under analysis, and the cause of them became quite clear to me. It was simple enough. Éloi was dear to me. At the sight of him so unexpectedly and so seriously ill I could not 'get my bearings.' It is the popular phrase and it is appropriate. Moments of anguish appear to us unnaturally long. That is why I received the impression that the five or six minutes I had passed beside Éloi had something interminable about them. As to the fancy that the child was at a great distance from me, that came from the idea that I was about to lose him. This idea, impressed on me against my will, had from the first moment assumed a character of absolute certainty.

"The following day Éloi was in a less alarming condition. The improvement continued for several days. I had sent into the town to procure ice, and this had had a good effect. But on the fifth day I recognized that he was in violent delirium. He talked a good deal, and amongst the disconnected words I heard him pouring out I could distinguish these—

" 'The balloon! the balloon! I have hold of the

169

helm of the balloon. It rises. The sky is inky. Mamma, mamma! why won't you come with me? I am steering my balloon to a place where it will be so beautiful! Come, it is stifling here.'

"That day Jean Blin followed me up the road. He slouched along with that air of embarrassment a man has who wants to say something and is yet afraid to say it. At last, after walking some twenty paces with me in silence, he stopped, and laying his hand on my arm said—

" 'See here, Doctor, it's my belief that what ails the little chap is his inside.'

"I continued my way sorrowfully, and for the first time in my life my eagerness to see once more my pears and apricots did not avail to mend my pace. For the first time in forty years of practice I found the plight of one of my patients heart-rending, and in my innermost self I bewailed the child I was powerless to save.

"Distracting pangs soon came to magnify my grief. I feared that my treatment had contributed to the development of the disease. I caught myself forgetting in the morning what I had prescribed the night before, uncertain in my diagnosis, nervous, and worried. I called in one of my fellow-practitioners, a clever young fellow, who had a practice in the next village. When he arrived, the poor little fellow, whose sight was already gone, was plunged in a profound coma.

"The following day he died.

"A year having elapsed after this misfortune, it happened that I was called in consultation to the county town. The fact is singular. The causes which led up to it are extraordinary; but as they have no connection with what I am relating, I do not record them here. After the consultation, Dr. C——, physician to the prefecture, did me the honour to invite me to lunch with him and two other members of the profession. After lunch, where I found refreshment in conversation at once erudite and diversified, coffee was served to us in the doctor's sanctum. As I approached the mantel-piece to put down my empty cup, I saw hanging upon the mirror-frame a portrait which aroused in me so profound an emotion that it was with difficulty I refrained from crying out. It was a miniature, the portrait of a child. This child resembled in so striking a fashion the one I had been unable to cure—the child of whom I had been constantly thinking for a year past—that for a moment I could not avoid the thought that it was he himself. That supposition, however, was of course absurd. The black wooden frame, with the circlet of gold surrounding the miniature, proclaimed the taste of the end of the eighteenth century, and the child was depicted in a vest of pink and white striped material such as the little Louis XVII might have worn; but the face was out-and-out the face of my little Éloi. The same forehead, imperious and powerful —the forehead of a man beneath the curls of a cherub; the same fire in the eyes, the same suffering grace on the lips! Indeed, to the very same features was joined the identical expression!

"I had probably been examining this portrait for quite a long while when Dr. C——, clapping me on the shoulder, said—

" 'Ah, my friend, you have before you a family relic which I am proud to possess. My maternal grandfather was the friend of the illustrious man whom you see painted there in the days of his early boyhood, and it was from my grandfather that that miniature came into my possession.'

"I asked him to be good enough to tell me the name of his grandfather's illustrious friend. Upon this he unhooked the miniature and held it out to me:

" 'See,' he said, 'on the exergue . . . *Lyon,* 1787. Doesn't that recall anything to you? No? Well, that child of twelve was the great Ampère.'

"Then, in a flash, I had an exact perception, an unequivocal estimate of what death had swept away one year previously in the farmhouse of Les Alies."

THE DAUGHTER OF LILITH

 HAD left Paris late in the evening, and I spent a long, silent and snowy night in the corner of the railway carriage. I waited six mortal hours at X——, and the next afternoon I found nothing better than a farm-wagon to take me to Artigues. The plain whose furrows rose and fell by turns on either side of the road, and which I had seen long ago lying radiant in the sunshine, was now covered with a heavy veil of snow over which straggled the twisted black stems of the vines. My driver gently urged on his old horse, and we proceeded through an infinite silence broken only at intervals by the plaintive cry of a bird, sad even unto death. I murmured this prayer in my heart: "My God, God of Mercy, save me from despair and after so many transgressions, let me not commit the one sin Thou dost not forgive." Then I saw the sun, red and rayless, blood-hued, descending on the horizon, as it were, the sacred Host, and remembering the divine Sacrifice of Calvary, I felt hope enter into my soul. For some time longer the wheels crunched the snow. At last the driver

pointed with the end of his whip to the spire of
Artigues as it rose like a shadow against the dull
red haze.

"I say," said the man, "are you going to stop at
the presbytery? You know the curé?"

"I have known him ever since I was a child. He
was my master when I was a student."

"Is he learned in books?"

"My friend, M. Safrac, is as learned as he is
good."

"So they say. But they also say other things."

"What do they say, my friend?"

"They say what they please, and I let them talk."

"What more do they say?"

"Well, there are those who say he is a sorcerer,
and that he can tell fortunes."

"What nonsense!"

"For my part I keep a still tongue! But if M.
Safrac is not a sorcerer and fortune-teller, why does
he spend his time reading books?"

The waggon stopped in front of the presbytery.

I left the idiot, and followed the curé's servant,
who conducted me to her master in a room where
the table was already laid. I found M. Safrac
greatly changed in the three years since I had last
seen him. His tall figure was bent. He was ex-
cessively emaciated. Two piercing eyes glowed in

his thin face. His nose, which seemed to have grown longer, descended over his shrunken lips. I fell into his arms.

"My father, my father," I cried, sobbing, "I have come to you because I have sinned. My father, my dear old master, whose profound and mysterious knowledge overawed my mind, and who yet reassured it with a revelation of material tenderness, save your child from the brink of a precipice. O my only friend, save me; enlighten me, you my only beacon!"

He embraced me, and smiled on me with that exquisite kindness of which he had given so many proofs during my childhood, and then he stepped back, as if to see me better.

"Well, adieu!" he said, greeting me according to the custom of his country, for M. Safrac was born on the banks of the Garonne, in the home of those famous wines which seemed the symbol of his own generous and fragrant soul.

After having taught philosophy with great distinction in Bordeaux, Poitiers and Paris, he asked as his only reward the gift of a poor cure in the country where he had been born and where he wished to die. He had now been priest at Artigues for six years, and in this obscure village he practised the most humble piety and the most enlightened sciences.

"Well, adieu! my child," he repeated. "You wrote me a letter to announce your coming which has moved me deeply. It is true, then, that you have not forgotten your old master?"

I tried to throw myself at his feet.

"Save me! save me!" I stammered.

But he stopped me with a gesture at once imperious and gentle.

"You shall tell me to-morrow, Ary, what you have to tell. First, warm yourself. Then we will have supper, for you must be very hungry and very thirsty."

The servant placed on the table the soup-tureen out of which rose a fragrant column of steam. She was an old woman, her hair hidden under a black kerchief, and in her wrinkled face were strongly mingled the beauty of race and the ugliness of decay. I was in profound distress, and yet the peace of this saintly dwelling, the gaiety of the wood fire, the white table-cloth, the wine and the steaming dishes entered, little by little, into my soul. Whilst I ate I nearly forgot that I had come to the fireside of this priest to exchange the sereness of remorse for the fertilising dew of repentance. Monsieur Safrac reminded me of the hours, already long since past, which we had spent together in the college when he had taught philosophy.

176

"You, Ary," he said to me, "were my best pupil. Your quick intelligence was always in advance of the thought of the teacher. For that reason I at once became attached to you. I like a Christian to be daring. Faith should not be timid when unbelief shows an indominable audacity. The Church nowadays has lambs only; and it needs lions. Who will give us back those learned fathers and doctors whose erudition embraced all sciences? Truth is like the sun; it requires the eye of an eagle to contemplate it."

"Ah, M. Safrac, you brought to bear on all questions that daring vision which nothing dazzles. I remember that your opinions sometimes even startled those of your colleagues whom the holiness of your life filled with admiration. You did not fear new ideas. Thus, for instance, you were inclined to admit the plurality of inhabited worlds."

His eyes kindled.

"What will the cowards say when they read my book? I have meditated, and I have worked under this beautiful sky, in this land which God has created with a special love. You know that I have some knowledge of Hebrew, Arabic, Persian, and certain of the Indian dialects. You also know that I have brought here a library rich in ancient manuscripts. I have plunged profoundly into the knowl-

177

edge of the tongues and traditions of the primitive East. This great work, by the help of God, will not have been in vain. I have nearly finished my book on 'Origins,' which re-establishes and upholds that Biblical exegesis of which an impious science already foresaw the imminent overthrow. God in His mercy has at last permitted science and faith to be reconciled. To effect this reconciliation I have started with the following premises:

"The Bible, inspired by the Holy Ghost, tells only the truth, but it does not tell all the truth. And how could it, seeing that its only object is to inform us of what is needful for our eternal salvation? Apart from this great purpose it has no other. Its design is as simple as it is infinite. It includes the fall and the redemption; it is the sacred history of man; it is complete and restricted. Nothing has been admitted to satisfy profane curiosity. A godless science must not be permitted to triumph any longer over the silence of God. It is time to say, 'No, the Bible has not lied, because it has not revealed all.' That is the truth which I proclaim. By the help of geology, prehistoric archæology, the Oriental cosmogonies, Hittite and Sumerian monuments, Chaldean and Babylonian traditions preserved in the Talmud, I assert the existence of the pre-Adamites, of whom the inspired writer of Genesis does not speak, for the only reason that their existence did not bear upon the eternal salvation of the children of Adam. Furthermore, a minute study of the first chapters of Genesis has proved to me the existence of two successive creations separated by untold ages, of which the second is only, so to speak, the adaptation of a corner of the earth to the needs of Adam and his posterity.

He paused, then he continued in a low voice and with a solemnity truly religious:

"I, Martial Safrac, unworthy priest, doctor of theology, submissive as an obedient child to the authority of our Holy Mother the Church, I assert with absolute certainty—yielding all due submission to our holy father the Pope and the Councils—that Adam, who was created in the image of God, had two wives, of whom Eve was the second."

These singular words drew me little by little out of myself and filled me with a curious interest. I therefore felt something of disappointment when M. Safrac, planting his elbows on the table, said to me:

"Enough on that subject. Some day, perhaps, you will read my book, which will enlighten you on this point. I was obliged, in obedience to strict duty, to submit the work to Monseigneur, and to beg his Grace's approval. The manuscript is at present in the archbishop's hands, and any minute I

may expect a reply which I have every reason to
believe will be favourable. My dear child, try
those mushrooms out of our own woods, and this na-
tive wine of ours, and acknowledge that this is the
second promised land, of which the first was only
the image and the forecast."

From this time on our conversation, grown more
familiar, ranged over our common recollections.

"Yes, my child," said M. Safrac, "you were my
favourite pupil, and God permits preferences if they
are founded on impartial judgment. So I decided
at once that there was in you the making of a man
and a Christian. Not that great imperfections
were not in evidence. You were irresolute, uncertain, and easily disconcerted. Passions, so far la-
tent, smouldered in your soul. I loved you because
of your great restlessness, as I did another of my
pupils for quite opposite qualities. I loved Paul
d'Ervy for his unswerving steadfastness of mind
and heart."

At this name I blushed and turned pale and with
difficulty suppressed a cry, and when I tried to answer I found it impossible to speak. M. Safrac appeared not to notice my distress.

"If I remember aright, he was your best friend,"
he added. "You have remained intimate ever
since, have you not? I know he has started on a

diplomatic career, and a great future is predicted
for him. I hope that in happier times than the
present he may be entrusted with office at the Holy
See. In him you have a faithful and devoted
friend."

" My father," I replied, with a great effort, "to-
morrow I will speak to you of Paul d'Ervy and
of another person."

M. Safrac pressed my hand. We separated, and
I went to the room which had been prepared for
me. In my bed, fragrant with lavender, I dreamed
that I was once again a child, and that as I knelt in
the college chapel I was admiring the blonde and
ecstatic women with which the gallery was filled,
when suddenly out of a cloud over my head I
seemed to hear a voice say:

"Ary, you believe that you love them in God, but
it is God you love in them."

The next morning when I woke I found M. Safrac
standing at the side of my bed.

"Come, Ary, and hear the Mass which I am about
to celebrate for your intention. After the Holy
Sacrifice I shall be ready to listen to what you have
to say."

The Church of Artigues was a little sanctuary in
the Norman style which still flourished in Aquitaine
in the twelfth century. Restored some twenty

years ago, it had received the addition of a bell-tower which had not been contemplated in the original plan. At any rate, poverty had safeguarded its pure bareness. I tried to join in the prayers of the celebrant as much as my thoughts would permit, and then I returned with him to the presbytery. Here we breakfasted on a little bread and milk, after which we went to M. Safrac's room.

He drew a chair to the fireplace, over which hung a crucifix, and invited me to be seated, and seating himself beside me he signed to me to speak. Outside the snow fell. I began as follows:

"My father, it is ten years ago since I left your care and entered the world. I have preserved my faith, but, alas, not my purity. But it is unnecessary to remind you of my life; you know it, you my spiritual guide, the only keeper of my conscience. Moreover, I am in haste to arrive at the event which has convulsed my being. Last year my family had decided that I must marry, and I myself had willingly consented. The young girl destined for me united all the advantages of which parents are usually in search. More than that, she was pretty; she pleased me to such a degree that instead of a marriage of convenience I was about to make a marriage of affection. My offer was accepted, and we were betrothed. The happiness and peace of my life seemed assured when I received a letter from Paul d'Ervy who had returned from Constantinople and announced his arrival in Paris. He expressed a great desire to see me. I hurried to him and announced my marriage. He congratulated me heartily.

" 'My dear old boy,' he said, 'I rejoice in your happiness.'

"I told him that I counted on him to be my witness and he willingly consented. The date of my wedding was fixed for May 15, and he was not obliged to return to his post until the beginning of June.

" 'How lucky that is,' I said to him. 'And you?'

" 'Oh, I,' he replied, with a smile which expressed in turn joy and sorrow, 'I—what a change! I am mad—a woman—Ary. I am either very fortunate or very unfortunate! What name can one give to a happiness gained by an evil action? I have betrayed, I have broken the heart of a good friend . . . I carried off—yonder—in Constantinople——"

M. Safrac interrupted me:

"My son, leave out of your narrative the faults of others and name no one."

I promised to obey, and continued as follows:

"Paul had hardly ceased speaking when a woman entered the room. Evidently it was she; dressed in a long blue *peignoir*, she seemed to be at home. I will describe to you in one word the terrible impression she produced on me: she did not seem *natural*. I realise how vague is this expression and how inadequately it explains my meaning. But perhaps it will become more intelligible in the course of my story. But, indeed, in the expression of her golden eyes, that seemed at times to throw out sparks of light, in the curve of her enigmatical mouth, in the substance of her skin, at once brown and yet luminous, in the play of the angular and yet harmonious lines of her body, in the ethereal lightness of her footsteps, even in her bare arms, to which invisible wings seemed attached, and, finally, in her ardent and magnetic personality, I felt an indescribable something foreign to the nature of humanity; an indescribable something inferior and yet superior to the woman God has created in his formidable goodness, so that she should be our companion in this earthly exile. From the moment I saw her one feeling alone overmastered my soul and pervaded it; I felt a profound revulsion from everything that was not this woman.

"Seeing her enter, Paul frowned slightly, but changing his mind, he made an effort to smile.

" 'Leila, I wish to present to you my best friend.'

"Leila replied:

" 'I know M. Ary.'

"These words could not but seem strange as we had certainly never seen each other before; but the voice with which they were uttered was stranger still.

"If crystal could utter thought, so it would speak.

" 'My friend Ary,' continued Paul, 'is to be married in six weeks.'

"At these words Leila looked at me and I saw distinctly that her golden eyes said 'No!'

"I went away greatly disturbed, nor did my friend show the slightest desire to detain me. All that day I wandered aimlessly through the streets, my heart empty and desolate; then, towards night, finding myself in front of a florist's shop, I remembered my *fiancée,* and went in to get her a spray of white lilac. I had hardly taken hold of the flowers when a little hand tore them out of my grasp, and I saw Leila, who turned away laughing. She wore a short grey dress and a jacket of the same colour and a small round hat. I must confess that this costume of a Parisian dressed for walking was most unbecoming to her fairy-like beauty and seemed a kind of disguise. And yet, seeing her so, I felt that I loved

her with an undying love. I tried to rejoin her, but
I lost her among the crowd and the carriages.

"From this time on I seemed to cease to live. I
called several times at Paul's without seeing Leila
again. He always received me in a friendly manner, but he never spoke of her. We had nothing to
say to each other, and I was sad when we parted.
At last, one day, the footman said that his master
was out. He added 'Perhaps you would like to see
Madame?' I replied 'Yes.' O, my father, what
tears of blood can ever atone for this little word!
I entered. I found her in the drawing-room, half
reclining on a couch, in a dress as yellow as gold,
under which she had drawn her little feet. I saw
her—but, no, I saw nothing. My throat was suddenly parched, I could not utter a word. A fragrance of myrrh and aromatic perfumes which
emanated from her seemed to intoxicate me with
languor and longing, as if at once all the odours of
the mystic East had penetrated my quivering nostrils. No, this was certainly not a natural woman,
for nothing human seemed to emanate from her.
Her face expressed no emotion, either good or bad,
beyond a voluptuousness at once sensual and divine.
She doubtless noticed my suffering, for she asked
with a voice as clear as the ripple of a mountain
brook:

186

" 'What ails you?'

"I threw myself in tears at her feet and cried, 'I love you madly!'

"She opened her arms; then enfolding me with a lingering glance of her candid and voluptuous eyes:

" 'Why have you not told me this before?'

"Indescribable moment! I held Leila in my arms. It seemed as if we two together had been transported to Heaven and filled all its spaces. I felt myself become the equal of God, and my breast seemed to enfold all the beauty of earth and the harmonies of nature—the stars and the flowers, the forests that sing, the rivers and the deep seas. I had enfolded the infinite in a kiss. . . ."

At these words Monsieur Safrac, who had listened to me for some moments with growing impatience rose, and standing before the fireplace, lifted his cassock to his knees to warm his legs and said with a severity which came near being disdain:

"You are a wretched blasphemer, and instead of despising your crimes, you only confess them because of your pride and delight in them. I will listen no more."

At these words I burst into tears and begged his forgiveness. Recognising that my humility was sincere, he desired me to continue my confession on condition that I realised my own self-abasement.

I continued my story as follows, determined to make it as brief as possible:

"My father, I was torn by remorse when I left Leila. But, from the following day on, she came to me, and then began a life which tortured me with joy and anguish. I was jealous of Paul, whom I had betrayed, and I suffered cruelly.

"I do not believe that there is a more debasing evil than jealousy, nor one which fills the soul with more degrading thoughts. Even to console me Leila scorned to lie. Besides, her conduct was incomprehensible. I do not forget to whom I am speaking, and I shall be careful not to offend the ears of the most revered of priests. I can only say that Leila seemed ignorant of the love she permitted. But she had enveloped my whole being in the poison of sensuality. I could not exist without her, and I trembled at the thought of losing her.

"Leila seemed absolutely devoid of what we call moral sense. You must not, however, think that she was either wicked or cruel. On the contrary, she was gentle and compassionate. Nor was she without intelligence, but her intelligence was not of the same nature as ours. She said little, and she refused to reply to any questions that were asked her about her past. She was ignorant of all that we know.   On the other hand, she knew many things of which we are ignorant.

"Educated in the East, she was familiar with all sorts of Hindoo and Persian legends, which she would repeat with a certain monotonous cadence and with an infinite grace.   Listening to her as she described the charming dawn of the world, one would have said she had lived in the youth of creation.   This I once said to her.

" 'It is true, I am old,' " she answered smiling.

M. Safrac, still standing in front of the fireplace, had for some time bent towards me in an attitude of keen attention.

"Continue," he said.

"Often, my father, I questioned Leila about her religion.   She replied that she had none, and that she had no need of one; that her mother and sisters were the daughters of God, but that they were not bound to Him by any creed.   She wore a medallion about her neck filled with a little red earth which she said she had piously gathered because of her love for her mother.

Hardly had I uttered these words when M. Safrac, pale and trembling, sprang forward, and, seizing my arm, *shouted:*

"She told the truth!   I know now.   I know who

this creature was, Ary! Your instinct did not deceive you. It was not a woman. Continue, continue, I implore."

"My father, I have nearly finished. Alas, for
Leila's love, I had broken my solemn plighted troth,
I had betrayed my best friend. I had affronted
God. Paul, having heard of Leila's faithlessness,
became mad with grief. He threatened her with
death, but she replied gently:

" 'Kill me, my friend; I long to die, but I cannot.'

"For six months she gave herself to me; then one
morning she said that she was about to return to
Persia, and that she would never see me again. I
wept, I moaned, I raved: 'You have never loved
me!'

" 'No, my friend,' she replied gently. 'And yet
how many women who have loved you no better
have denied you what you received from me! You
still owe me some gratitude. Farewell.'

"For two days I was plunged in alternate fury
and apathy. Then remembering the salvation of
my soul, I hurried to you, my father. Here I am.
Purify me, uplift me, strengthen my heart, for I
love her still."

I ceased. M. Safrac, his hand raised to his forehead, remained lost in thought. He was the first to
break the silence.

THE DAUGHTER OF LILITH

"My son, this confirms my great discovery. What you tell me will confound the vainglory of our modern sceptics. Listen to me. We live to-day in the midst of miracles as did the first-born of men. Listen, listen! Adam, as I have already told you, had a first wife whom the Bible does not make mention of, but of whom the Talmud speaks. Her name was Lilith. Created, not out of one of his ribs, but from this same red earth out of which he himself had been kneaded, she was not flesh of his flesh. She voluntarily separated from him. He was still living in innocence when she left him to go to those regions where long years afterwards the Persians settled, but which at this time were inhabited by the pre-Adamites, more intelligent and more beautiful than the sons of men. She therefore had no part in the transgression of our first father, and was unsullied by that original sin. Because of this she also escaped from the curse pronounced against Eve and her descendants. She is exempt from sorrow and death; having no soul to be saved, she is incapable of virtue or vice. Whatever she does, she accomplishes neither good nor evil. The daughters that were born to her of some mysterious wedlock are immortal as she is, and free as she is both in their deeds and thoughts, seeing that they can neither gain nor lose in the sight of

God. Now, my son, I recognise by indisputable signs that the creature who caused your downfall, this Leila, was a daughter of Lilith. Compose yourself to prayer. To-morrow I will hear you in confession."

He remained silent for a moment, then drawing a paper out of his pocket, he continued:

"Late last night, after having wished you good night, the postman, who had been delayed by the snow, brought me a very distressing letter. The senior vicaire informs me that my book has been a source of grief to Monseigneur, and has already overshadowed the spiritual joy with which he looked forward to the festival of our Lady of Mount Carmel. The work, he adds, is full of foolhardy doctrines and opinions which have already been condemned by the authorities. His Grace could not approve of such unwholesome lucubrations. This, then, is what they write to me. But I will relate your story to Monseigneur. It will prove to him that Lilith exists and that I do not dream."

I implored Monsieur Safrac to listen to me a moment more.

"When she went away, my father, Leila left me a leaf of cypress on which certain characters which I cannot decipher had been traced with the point of a style. It seems to be a kind of amulet."

THE DAUGHTER OF LILITH

Monsieur Safrac took the light film which I held out to him and examined it carefully.

"This," he said, "is written in Persian of the best period and can be easily translated thus:

"THE PRAYER OF LEILA, DAUGHTER OF LILITH

"*My God, promise me death, so that I may taste of life. My God, give me remorse, so that I may at last find happiness. My God, make me the equal of the daughters of Eve.*"

LESLIE WOOD

HERE was music and private theatricals at Madame N——'s reception in the Boulevard Malesherbes.

Whilst on the outskirts of a display of bare shoulders the younger men at the doorway were suffocating in the stifling, scented air, we older guests, not without grumbling, were keeping ourselves cool in a little *salon* from which we could see nothing, and to which the voice of Mademoiselle Réjane only penetrated like the slightly metallic sound of a dragon-fly's flight. From time to time we could hear the laughter and applause burst forth in the sweltering room, and we were disposed to extend a mild tolerance to the entertainment we did not share. We were exchanging fairly amusing trivialities, when one of the company, a genial deputy, Monsieur B——, remarked—

"Did you know that Wood was here?"

At this statement each in turn exclaimed—

"Wood? Leslie Wood? It's impossible. It is ten years since he was seen in Paris. Nobody knows what's become of him."

"The story goes that he has established a black republic on the shores of the Victoria Nyanza."

"What a tale! You know, of course, that he is fabulously wealthy, and that he is a past master in achieving the impossible. Well, he is living in Ceylon, in a fairy palace, in the midst of enchanted gardens, where the bayadères never cease dancing night and day."

"How can any one believe such balderdash? The truth is, that Leslie Wood has gone off with a Bible and a carbine to convert the Zulus."

Monsieur B—— interrupted in an undertone—

"There he is; there, do you see?"

And he drew our attention by a slight movement of the head and eyes to a man leaning against the doorway, dominating by his lofty stature the heads of the crowd huddled in front of him. He seemed engrossed in the performance.

That athletic carriage, the ruddy face with the white whiskers, the penetrating eyes and calm gaze, they could belong to no one else but Leslie Wood.

Recalling the inimitable letters which for ten years he contributed to the *World*, I said to Monsieur B——

"That man is the foremost journalist of our time."

"You may possibly be right," replied B——.

"At any rate, I am ready to assert that for twenty years past no one has known Europe as thoroughly as Leslie Wood."

Baron Moïse, who was following our talk, shook his head.

"You don't know the real Wood. I know him myself, though. He was before all things a financier. He had a better grasp of the money market than any one I know. What are you laughing at, Princess?"

Lolling expansively on the sofa, and in gloomy depression at being unable to smoke a cigarette, the Princess Zévorine had smiled.

"You neither of you understand Mr. Wood— neither of you," she said. "He was always a mystic and a lover, never anything else."

"I can't agree to that," replied Baron Moïse. "But I should be very glad to know where this devil of a fellow has been spending the best ten years of his life."

"And at what period do you place those best ten years of life?"

"Between the fiftieth and sixtieth years; a man's position is made by then, and he has nothing to do but enjoy his existence."

"Baron, you can question Wood himself. He is coming towards us."

The applause, this time rising to a furious pitch like the fall of a heavy body or the banging of doors, announced the close of the performance. The black-coated contingent leaving the doorways clear overflowed into the smaller *salon,* and as the company made their way in couples in the direction of the buffet, Leslie Wood approached us.

He shook hands with undemonstrative cordiality.

"An apparition! an apparition!" exclaimed Baron Moïse.

"Oh!" rejoined Wood, "one can't reappear from any very remote quarter. The world is small."

"Do you know what the Princess is saying about you, my dear Wood? She declares that you are nothing but a mystic. Now is that true?"

"Well it depends on what you mean by mystic."

"The word is self-explanatory. A mystic is one who is preoccupied with the concerns of the next world. Now you are too well acquainted with the affairs of this world to trouble yourself about the next."

At these words Wood slightly contracted his eyebrows.

"You are quite in the wrong, Moïse. The affairs of the other world are of far, far greater importance than those of the world we live in, Moïse."

"What a man he is, this good Wood of ours!"

197

exclaimed the Baron, with a sneer. "He is positively witty!"

The Princess replied very seriously—

"Mr. Wood, tell me that you are not witty. I thoroughly detest witty men."

Upon this she rose, and said—

"Mr. Wood, will you take me to the buffet?"

An hour later, when Monsieur G—— was holding both men and women spell-bound with his songs, I came across Leslie Wood and the Princess Zévorine again, alone in front of the deserted buffet.

The Princess was speaking with almost vehement enthusiasm of Count Tolstoi, whose friend she was. She described this great man who had descended to the lowliest life, donning the dress, and with it the spirit of the moujik, and using his hands which had indited literary masterpieces in the manufacture of shoes for the poor.

To my great surprise, Wood was expressing approbation of a kind of life so completely opposed to common sense. In his slightly panting voice, to which the beginnings of asthma had given a singular sweetness, he said—

"Yes, Tolstoi is right. The whole of philosophy is contained in that phrase: 'May the will of God be done!' He has realized that all the woes of humanity are the outcome of the exercise of human

will as distinct from the will divine. My only fear
is that he may impair so noble a doctrine by fantastic
and extravagant additions."

"Oh!" returned the Princess in a subdued voice,
and hesitating a little, "the Count's teaching is only
extravagant upon one point; that is, in inculcating
the extension of the rights and duties of husbands to
an extremely advanced period of their lives, and im-
posing on the saints of these latter days the fruitful
old age of the patriarchs."

Wood, himself elderly, replied with a restrained
exaltation—

"And that again is excellent, very saintly even.
Physical and natural love is becoming to all God's
creatures, and so long as it does not involve either
dissension or restlessness, it maintains that divine
simplicity, that saintly fleshliness without which there
is no salvation. Asceticism is nothing but pride and
rebellion. We must always bear in mind the example of that holy man Boaz, and let us remember
that the Bible calls love the bread of old age."

Then, all of a sudden, transported, illuminated,
transfigured, ecstatic, and invoking with eyes and
arms and his whole soul some invisible presence, he
murmured—

"Annie! Annie! Annie, my best beloved, it is

199

true, is it not, that our Lord desires his saints, whilst they are men and women, to love one another humbly, even as the beasts of the field?"

Upon this he fell exhausted into an arm-chair. A terrific inhalation shook his broad chest, and in this condition his appearance was fuller of vitality than ever, like those machines that appear more formidable when they are out of gear. The Princess Zévorine, without any show of astonishment, wiped his forehead with her handkerchief and gave him a glass of water, which he drank.

For my part I was dumfounded. In this clairvoyant I was unable to recognize the man who in his study, littered with blue-books, had so many times conversed with me with the utmost clear-headedness upon Oriental affairs, the Treaty of Frankfort, and critical situations on the money market. As I allowed the Princess to observe my uneasiness, she said, with a shrug of the shoulders—

"It is easy to see you are French! You look upon every one as a madman who does not think exactly what you think yourself. You need not be uneasy; our friend Mr. Wood is level-headed enough, perfectly level-headed. Let us go and listen to G——."

When I had conducted the Princess to the principal *salon,* I prepared to leave. In the antechamber I found Wood putting on his overcoat. He did not appear to feel any ill effects from his attack.

"My dear fellow," he said, "I think we are neighbours. I suppose you are still living on the Quai Malaquais, and I have taken up my quarters in a hotel in the Rue des Saints Péres. In dry weather like this it is a pleasure to go on foot. If you are willing we will stroll along together and chat."

I agreed readily. On the doorstep he offered me a cigar, and held out a pocket electric torch for me to light it by.

"I find it very convenient," he said, and proceeded to explain the principle of it very lucidly.

I recognized the Wood of old times again. We moved on perhaps a hundred paces along the street chatting on indifferent subjects. Then suddenly my companion put his hand quietly on my shoulder.

"My dear friend," he began, "some of the things I said this evening cannot have failed to surprise you. You would probably like me to explain them."

"I was intensely interested, my dear Wood, pray do."

"I will do so willingly. I have the greatest admiration of your character. We may not regard life from the same point of view. But you are not one of those who repel an idea because it is new, and that is a disposition sufficiently rare, in France especially."

"I fancy, however, my dear Wood, that for liberty of thought——"

"Oh! no, you are not, like the English, a race of theologians. But enough of that. I want to tell you in as few words as possible the history of my convictions. When you knew me fifteen years ago I was the correspondent of the London *World*. With us journalism is a more lucrative profession, and is held in higher esteem than with you. My appointment was a good one, and I fancy I reaped the greatest possible advantages from it. I am familiar with business transactions, and I carried through some very profitable ones, and in a few years I achieved two very desirable things: influence and fortune. You are aware that I am a practical man.

"I have never worked without a goal in view. And, above all things, I aimed at attaining the supreme goal of life. Fairly exhaustive theological studies undertaken in my youth had convinced me that that goal lay outside the sphere of this terrestrial life. But I was yet in doubt as to the practical means of attaining it. As a result, I suffered cruelly.

Uncertainty is absolutely insupportable to a man of my temperament.

"In this state of mind I turned my attention seriously to the psychical researches of Sir William Crookes, one of the most distinguished members of our Royal Society. I knew him personally, and needed no assurance that he was both a man of learning and a gentleman. He was at that time giving his attention to the case of a young woman endowed with psychic powers of an altogether uncommon nature, and, like Saul of old, he was fortunate enough to evoke the presence of an indisputable disembodied spirit.

"A charming woman, who had passed through the experience of earthly life and was now living the life beyond the tomb, lent herself to the experiments of the eminent spiritualist, and submitted to every test he could exact from her within the limits of decorum. I considered that investigations such as this, bearing on the point at which terrestrial existence borders on extra-terrestrial existence, would lead me, if I followed them step by step, to the discovery of that which it is above all necessary to know, that is to say, the true aim of life. But it was not long before I was disappointed in my hopes. The researches of my respected friend, although conducted with a precision which left nothing to be desired, did not result

203

in a theological and moral conviction sufficiently un-equivocal.

"Moreover, Sir William was suddenly deprived of the co-operation of the incomparable dead lady who had so graciously attended several of his spirit-ualistic séances.

"Discouraged by the incredulity of the public, and irritated by the sallies of his colleagues, he ceased to give any information relative to his psychic experi-ences. I communicated my discomfiture to the Reverend Mr. B——, with whom I had been on friendly terms from the time of his return from South Africa, where he had laboured as an evangelist in a devoted and systematic fashion truly worthy of old England.

"Mr. B—— is, of all men, the one who has at all times exercised the most powerful and decisive in-fluence over me."

"He is very intellectual, then?" I asked.

"His knowledge of doctrine is profound," replied Wood. "But better than all else he has a strong character, and you are aware, my dear fellow, that it is by force of character that men are swayed. My mischances occasioned no surprise to him; he attrib-uted them to my lack of method, and, above all, to the pitiable moral infirmity I had shown on this oc-casion.

" 'Scientific experiments,' he declared, 'can never lead to discoveries in any other domain than that of science. How is it you did not understand this? Leslie Wood, you have been strangely heedless and frivolous. The Apostle Paul has told us that the Spirit searcheth all things. If we would discover spiritual truths we must set our feet on the spiritual path.'

"These words produced a profound impression on me.

" 'How then,' I asked, 'shall I enter on the spiritual path?'

" 'Poverty and simplicity must be your guides!' Mr. B—— replied. 'Sell your goods and give the purchase money to the poor. You are renowned. Conceal yourself. Pray, and devote yourself to works of charity. Put on a spirit of simplicity and a pure soul and you will attain truth.'

"I resolved to follow out these precepts to the letter. I sent in my resignation as correspondent to the *World*. I realized my investments, which were in great part in commercial enterprises, and, fearing to repeat the sin of Ananias and Sapphira, I conducted this delicate operation in such a way as not to risk the loss of a penny of the capital which was no longer my own. Baron Moïse, who kept an eye on my negotiations, conceived an almost religious rev-

erence for my financial genius. By direction of Mr.
B——, I handed over to the treasurer of the *Evangelical Society* the sums I had realized, and when I
expressed to that eminent theologian my delight at
being poor—

" 'Have a care,' said he, 'that in your poverty you
do not indulge in exaltation at your prowess. It
will serve you but ill to strip yourself outwardly if
within your own breast you cherish a golden idol.
Be humble!' "

Leslie Wood had reached this point in his narrative when we arrived at the Pont Royal. The Seine,
upon whose surface the lights threw flickering re-
flections, flowed beneath the arches with a dull moan.

"I shall have to cut my story short," Wood began
once more. "Each episode of my new life would
occupy a whole night to recount. Mr. B——, to
whom I was as obedient as a child, sent me to the
Basutos, commissioned to fight against the slave
trade. There I lived under a tent alone with that
hardy bedfellow whose name is danger, and through
fever and drought became aware of the presence of
God.

"At the end of five years Mr. B—— recalled me
to England. On the steamer I met a young girl.
What a haunting face she had! She was a vision a
thousand times more radiant than the phantom

presence which appeared to Sir William Crookes!

"She was the orphan daughter of a colonel in the Indian army and she was poor. She had no particular beauty of features. Her pale complexion and emaciated face indicated suffering; but her eyes expressed all that one can imagine of heaven; her body seemed to glow gently with an inward light. How I loved her! At sight of her I fathomed the hidden meaning of all creation! That simple young girl with one glance revealed to me the secret of the harmony of the spheres!

"Ah! she was simple, very simple, my monitress, my well-loved lady, sweet Annie Fraser! In her translucent soul I could read the sympathy she felt for me. One night, one serene night, when we were alone together on the deck of the ship in the presence of the seraphic company of the stars, which throbbed in chorus in the sky, I took her hand and said—

" 'Annie Fraser, I love you. I believe that it would be good for us both for you to become my wife, but I am debarred from planning my own future in order that God may dispose of it as He sees fit. May it be His will to unite us! I have surrendered my own will into the hands of Mr. B———. When we reach England we will go together in search of him; will you, Annie Fraser? And if he gives his sanction we will marry.'

"She gave her consent. For the remainder of the voyage we read the Bible together.

"Immediately on our arrival in London I accompanied my fellow passenger to Mr. B——'s, and told him what the love of this young girl meant to me, and with what clear insight it inspired me.

"Mr. B—— gazed for a long time on her with kindliness.

" 'You may marry,' he said at length. 'The Apostle Paul has declared that the husband is sanctified by the wife, and the wife by the husband. But let your union resemble those held in honour amongst Christians in the primitive Church! Let it remain purely spiritual, and see that the angel's sword lies between you in your bed. Go, now, and remain humble and secluded, and let not the world hear your name.'

"I married Annie Fraser, and I need scarcely tell you that we complied rigidly with the condition imposed on us by Mr. B——. For four years I delighted in that brotherly and sisterly union.

"By grace of simple little Annie Fraser I advanced in the knowledge of God. There was nothing now that could cause us suffering.

"Annie was ill, and her strength declined, and we repeated joyfully in union, 'May the will of God be done on earth as it is in heaven!'

"After four years of this life together, there came a day, a Christmas day, when Mr. B—— summoned me to him.

" 'Leslie Wood,' he said, 'I have put you to the proof for your soul's sake. But it would be to fall into papistical error to believe that the union of His creatures after the flesh is displeasing to God. Twice He blessed both animals and mankind in pairs, in the earthly Paradise, and in the ark of Noah. Go, and live henceforth with your wife, Annie Fraser, as a husband with his wife.'

"When I arrived home, Annie, my well-loved Annie, was dead. . . .

"I own my weakness. It was with my lips and not with my heart that I pronounced the words, 'O God, Thy will be done!' and thinking upon Mr. B——'s tardy removal of the restrictions upon our love, I felt my mouth full of bitterness, and as it were ashes in my heart.

"So it was with a forlorn soul that I knelt down at the foot of the bed where, beneath a cross of roses, silent and white and with the faint violets of death on her cheeks, my Annie slept her last sleep.

"O thou of little faith! thou didst bid her adieu and remain a whole week plunged in barren sorrow that approached despair. How much rather shouldst thou, on the contrary, have rejoiced, both in body and soul! . . .

"On the night of the eighth day, as I was weeping, my forehead bowed upon the cold and empty bed, I had a sudden conviction that the beloved was near me in my chamber.

"Nor was I deceived. When I raised my head I saw Annie, smiling and radiant, holding out her arms to me. But how find words for what remains to tell? How express the ineffable? And is it permissible to reveal such mysteries of love?

"Clearly when Mr. B—— said to me 'Live with Annie as a husband with his wife!' he knew that love is stronger than death.

"Learn, then, my friend, that from that hour of forgiveness and joy my Annie has returned nightly to my side distilling celestial odours."

He spoke with appalling exaltation.

We had slackened our pace. He stopped in front of a hotel of Moorish exterior.

"This is where I live," he said. "Do you see that window on the second floor with the light in it? She is waiting for me."

He left me abruptly.

Eight days later I learned from the newspapers of the sudden death of Leslie Wood, former correspondent of the *World*.

FIVE FAIR LADIES

OF PICARDY, OF POITOU, OF TOURAINE, OF
LYONS, AND OF PARIS

NE day the Capuchin, Brother Jean Chavaray, meeting my good master the Abbé Coignard in the cloister of "The Innocents," fell into talk with him of the Brother Olivier Maillard, whose sermons, edifying and macaronic, he had lately been reading.

"There are good bits to be found in these sermons," said the Capuchin, "notably the tale of the five ladies and the go-between . . ." You will readily understand that Brother Olivier, who lived in the reign of Louis XI and whose language smacks of the coarseness of that age, uses a different word. But our century demands a certain politeness and decency in speech; wherefore I employ the term I have, to wit, *go-between.*

"You mean," replied my good master, "to signify by the expression a woman who is so obliging as to play intermediary in matters of love and love-making. The Latin has several names for her,—

as *lena, conciliatrix,* also *internuntia libidinum,* am-
bassadress of naughty desires. These prudish
dames perform the best of services; but seeing they
busy themselves therein for money, we distrust their
disinterestedness. Call yours a *procuress,* good
Father, and have done with it; 'tis a word in common use, and has a not unseemly sound."

"So I will, Monsieur l'Abbé," assented Brother
Jean Chavaray. "Only don't say *mine,* I pray,
but the Brother Olivier's. A procuress then, who
lived on the Pont des Tournelles, was visited one
day by a knight, who put a ring into her hands.
'It is of fine gold,' he told her, 'and hath a balass
ruby mounted in the bezel. An you know any dames
of good estate, go say to the most comely of them
that the ring is hers if she is willing to come to see
me and do at my pleasure.'

"The procuress knew, by having seen them at
Mass, five ladies of an excellent beauty,—natives
the first of Picardy, the second of Poitou, the third
of Touraine, another from the good city of Lyons,
and the last a Parisian, all dwelling in the Cité or
its near neighbourhood.

"She knocked first at the Picard lady's door. A
maid opened, but her mistress refused to have one
word to say to her visitor. She was an honest
woman.

"The procuress went next to see the lady of Poitiers and solicit her favours for the gallant knight. This dame answered her:

" 'Prithee, go tell him who sent you that he is come to the wrong house, and that I am not the woman he takes me for.'

"She too is an honest woman; yet less honest than the first, in that she tried to appear more so.

"The procuress then went to see the lady from Tours, made the same offer to her as to the other, and showed her the ring.

" 'I faith,' said the lady, 'but the ring is right lovely.'

" ' 'Tis yours, an you will have it.'

" 'I will not have it at the price you set on it. My husband might catch me, and I should be doing him a grief he doth not deserve.'

"This lady of Touraine is a harlot, I trow, at bottom of her heart.

"The procuress left her and went straight to the dame of Lyons, who cried:

" 'Alack! my good friend, my husband is a jealous wight, and he would cut the nose off my face to hinder me winning any more rings at this pretty tilting.'

"This dame of Lyons, I tell you, is a worthless good-for-naught.

"Last of all the procuress hurried to the Parisian's. She was a hussy, and answered brazenly:

" 'My husband goes Wednesday to his vineyards; tell the good sir who sent you I will come that day and see him.'

"Such, according to Brother Olivier, from Picardy to Paris, are the degrees from good to evil amongst women. What think you of the matter, Monsieur Coignard?"

To which my good master made answer:

" 'Tis a shrewd matter to consider the acts and impulses of these petty creatures in their relations with Eternal Justice. I have no lights thereanent. But methinks the Lyons dame who feared having her nose cut off was a more good-for-nothing baggage than the Parisian who was afraid of nothing."

"I am far, very far, from allowing it," replied Brother Jean Chavaray. "A woman who fears her husband may come to fear hell fire. Her Confessor, it may be, will bring her to do penance and give alms. For, after all, that is the end we must come at. But what can a poor Capuchin hope to get of a woman whom *nothing* terrifies?"

CRAINQUEBILLE

I

N every sentence pronounced by a judge in the name of the sovereign people, dwells the whole majesty of justice. The august character of that justice was brought home to Jérôme Crainquebille, costermonger, when, accused of having insulted a policeman, he appeared in the police court. Having taken his place in the dock, he beheld in the imposing sombre hall magistrates, clerks, lawyers in their robes, the usher wearing his chains, *gendarmes,* and, behind a rail, the bare heads of the silent spectators. He, himself, occupied a raised seat, as if some sinister honour were conferred on the accused by his appearance before the magistrate. At the end of the hall, between two assessors, sat the Président Bourriche. The palm-leaves of an officer of the Academy decorated his breast. Over the tribune were a bust representing the Republic and a crucifix, as if to indicate that all laws divine and human were suspended over Crainquebille's head. Such symbols naturally in-

spired him with terror. Not being gifted with a philosophic mind, he did not inquire the meaning of the bust and the crucifix; he did not ask how far Jesus and the symbolical bust harmonized in the Law Courts. Nevertheless, here was matter for reflection; for, after all, pontifical teaching and canon law are in many points opposed to the constitution of the Republic and to the civil code. So far as we know the Decretals have not been abolished. To-day, as formerly, the Church of Christ teaches that only those powers are lawful to which it has given its sanction. Now the French Republic claims to be independent of pontifical power. Crainquebille might reasonably say:

"Gentlemen and magistrates, in so much as President Loubet has not been anointed, the Christ, whose image is suspended over your heads, repudiates you through the voice of councils and of Popes. Either he is here to remind you of the rights of the Church, which invalidate yours, or His presence has no rational signification."

Whereupon President Bourriche might reply:

"Prisoner Crainquebille, the kings of France have always quarrelled with the Pope. Guillaume de Nogaret was excommunicated, but for so trifling a reason he did not resign his office. The Christ of the tribune is not the Christ of Gregory VII or of

Boniface VIII. He is, if you will, the Christ of
the Gospels, who knew not one word of canon law,
and had never heard of the holy Decretals."

Then Crainquebille might not without reason
have answered:

"The Christ of the Gospels was an agitator.
Moreover, he was the victim of a sentence, which
for nineteen hundred years all Christian peoples
have regarded as a grave judicial error. I defy
you Monsieur le Président, to condemn me in His
name to so much as forty-eight hours' imprison-
ment."

But Crainquebille did not indulge in any considerations either historical, political or social. He
was wrapped in amazement. All the ceremonial,
with which he was surrounded, impressed him with
a very lofty idea of justice. Filled with reverence,
overcome with terror, he was ready to submit to
his judges in the matter of his guilt. In his own
conscience he was convinced of his innocence; but
he felt how insignificant is the conscience of a costermonger in the face of the panoply of the law,
and the ministers of public prosecution. Already
his lawyer had half persuaded him that he was not
innocent.

A summary and hasty examination had brought
out the charges under which he laboured.

II

CRAINQUEBILLE'S MISADVENTURE

P and down the town went Jérôme Crainquebille, costermonger, pushing his barrow before him and crying: "Cabbages! Turnips! Carrots!" When he had leeks he cried: "Asparagus!" For leeks are the asparagus of the poor. Now it happened that on October 20, at noon, as he was going down the Rue Montmartre, there came out of her shop the shoemaker's wife, Madame Bayard. She went up to Crainquebille's barrow and scornfully taking up a bundle of leeks, she said:

"I don't think much of your leeks. What do you want a bundle?"

"Sevenpence halfpenny, mum, and the best in the market!"

"Sevenpence halfpenny for three wretched leeks?"

And disdainfully she cast the leeks back into the barrow.

Then it was that Constable 64 came and said to Crainquebille:

"Move on."

Moving on was what Crainquebille had been doing from morning till evening for fifty years. Such an order seemed right to him, and perfectly in accordance with the nature of things. Quite prepared to obey, he urged his customer to take what she wanted.

"You must give me time to choose," she retorted sharply.

Then she felt all the bundles of leeks over again. Finally, she selected the one she thought the best, and held it clasped to her bosom as saints in church pictures hold the palm of victory.

"I will give you sevenpence. That's quite enough; and I'll have to fetch it from the shop, for I haven't anything on me."

Still embracing the leeks, she went back into the shop, whither she had been preceded by a customer, carrying a child.

Just at this moment Constable 64 said to Crainquebille for the second time:

"Move on."

"I'm waiting for my money," replied Crainquebille.

"And I'm not telling you to wait for your money; I'm telling you to move on," retorted the constable grimly.

Meanwhile, the shoemaker's wife in her shop was fitting blue slippers on to a child of eighteen months, whose mother was in a hurry. And the green heads of the leeks were lying on the counter.

For the half century that he had been pushing his barrow through the streets, Crainquebille had been learning respect for authority. But now his position was a peculiar one: he was torn asunder between what was his due and what was his duty. His was not a judicial mind. He failed to understand that the possession of an individual's right in no way exonerated him from the performance of a social duty. He attached too great importance to his claim to receive sevenpence, and too little to the duty of pushing his barrow and moving on, for ever moving on. He stood still.

For the third time Constable 64 quietly and calmly ordered him to move on. Unlike Inspector Montauciel, whose habit it is to threaten constantly but never to take proceedings, Constable 64 is slow to threaten and quick to act. Such is his character. Though somewhat sly he is an excellent servant and a loyal soldier. He is as brave as a lion and as gentle as a child. He knows naught save his official instructions.

"Don't you understand when I tell you to move on?"

To Crainquebille's mind his reason for standing still was too weighty for him not to consider it sufficient. Wherefore, artlessly and simply he explained it:

"Good Lord! Don't I tell you that I am waiting for my money."

Constable 64 merely replied:

"Do you want me to summons you? If you do you have only to say so."

At these words Crainquebille slowly shrugged his shoulders, looked sadly at the constable, and then raised his eyes to heaven, as if he would say:

"I call God to witness! Am I a law-breaker? Am I one to make light of the by-laws and ordinances which regulate my ambulatory calling? At five o'clock in the morning I was at the market. Since seven, pushing my barrow and wearing my hands to the bone, I have been crying: 'Cabbages! Turnips! Carrots!' I am turned sixty. I am worn out. And you ask me whether I have raised the black flag of rebellion. You are mocking me and your joking is cruel."

Either because he failed to notice the expression on Crainquebille's face, or because he considered it no excuse for disobedience, the constable inquired curtly and roughly whether he had been understood.

Now, just at that moment the block of traffic in the Rue Montmartre was at its worst. Carriages, drays, carts, omnibuses, trucks, jammed one against the other, seemed indissolubly welded together. From their quivering immobility proceeded shouts and oaths. Cabmen and butchers' boys grandiloquent and drawling insulted one another from a distance, and omnibus conductors, regarding Crainquebille as the cause of the block, called him "a dirty leek."

Meanwhile, on the pavement the curious were crowding round to listen to the dispute. Then the constable, finding himself the centre of attention, began to think it time to display his authority:

"Very well," he said, taking a stumpy pencil and a greasy notebook from his pocket.

Crainquebille persisted in his idea, obedient to a force within. Besides, it was now impossible for him either to move on or to draw back. The wheel of his barrow was unfortunately caught in that of a milkman's cart.

Tearing his hair beneath his cap he cried:

"But don't I tell you I'm waiting for my money! Here's a fix! *Misère de misère! Bon sang de bon sang!*"

By these words, expressive rather of despair than of rebellion, Constable 64 considered he had been insulted. And, because to his mind all insults must necessarily take the consecrated, regular, traditional, liturgical, ritual form so to speak of *Mort aux vaches*,* thus the offender's words were heard and understood by the constable.

"Ah! You said: *Mort aux vaches*. Very good. Come along."

Stupefied with amazement and distress, Crainquebille opened his great rheumy eyes and gazed at Constable 64. With a broken voice proceeding now from the top of his head and now from the heels of his boots, he cried, with his arms folded over his blue blouse:

"I said '*Mort aux vaches*'? I? . . . Oh!"

The tradesmen and errand boys hailed the arrest with laughter. It gratified the taste of all crowds for violent and ignoble spectacles. But there was one serious person who was pushing his way through the throng; he was a sad-looking old man, dressed in black, wearing a high hat; he went up to the constable and said to him in a low voice very gently and firmly:

"You are mistaken. This man did not insult you."

"Mind your own business," replied the police-

*It is impossible to translate this expression. As explained on p. 231, it means "down with spies," the word spies being used to indicate the police.

man, but without threatening, for he was speaking to a man who was well dressed.

The old man insisted calmly and tenaciously. And the policeman ordered him to make his declaration to the Police Commissioner.

Meanwhile Crainquebille was explaining:

"Then I did say *'Mort aux vaches!'* Oh! . . ."

As he was thus giving vent to his astonishment, Madame Bayard, the shoemaker's wife, came to him with sevenpence in her hand. But Constable 64 already had him by the collar; so Madame Bayard, thinking that no debt could be due to a man who was being taken to the police-station, put her sevenpence into her apron pocket.

Then, suddenly beholding his barrow confiscated, his liberty lost, a gulf opening beneath him and the sky overcast, Crainquebille murmured:

"It can't be helped!"

Before the Commissioner, the old gentleman declared that he had been hindered on his way by the block in the traffic, and so had witnessed the incident. He maintained that the policeman had not been insulted, and that he was labouring under a delusion. He gave his name and profession: Dr. David Matthieu, chief physician at the Ambroise-Paré Hospital, officer of the Legion of Honour. At another time such evidence would have been sufficient for the Commissioner. But just then men of science were regarded with suspicion in France.

Crainquebille continued under arrest. He passed the night in the lock-up. In the morning he was taken to the Police Court in the prison van.

He did not find prison either sad or humiliating. It seemed to him necessary. What struck him as he entered was the cleanliness of the walls and of the brick floor.

"Well, for a clean place, yes, it is a clean place. You might eat off the floor."

When he was left alone, he wanted to draw out his stool; but he perceived that it was fastened to the wall. He expressed his surprise aloud:

"That's a queer idea! Now there's a thing I should never have thought of, I'm sure."

Having sat down, he twiddled his thumbs and remained wrapped in amazement. The silence and the solitude overwhelmed him. The time seemed long. Anxiously he thought of his barrow, which had been confiscated with its load of cabbages, carrots, celery, dandelion and corn-salad. And he wondered, asking himself with alarm: "What have they done with my barrow?"

On the third day he received a visit from his lawyer, Maître Lemerle, one of the youngest members of the Paris Bar, President of a section of La Ligue de la Patrie Française.

Crainquebille endeavoured to tell him his story; but it was not easy, for he was not accustomed to conversation. With a little help he might perhaps have succeeded. But his lawyer shook his head doubtfully at everything he said; and, turning over his papers, muttered:

"Hm! Hm! I don't find anything about all this in my brief."

Then, in a bored tone, twirling his fair moustache he said:

"In your own interest it would be advisable, perhaps, for you to confess. Your persistence in absolute denial seems to me extremely unwise."

And from that moment Crainquebille would have made confession if he had known what to confess.

III

CRAINQUEBILLE BEFORE THE MAGISTRATES

RESIDENT BOURRICHE devoted six whole minutes to the examination of Crainquebille. This examination would have been more enlightening if the accused had replied to the questions asked him. But Crainquebille was unaccustomed to discussion; and in such a company his lips were sealed by reverence and fear. So he was silent: and the President answered his own question; his replies were staggering. He concluded: "Finally, you admit having said, *'Mort aux vaches.'*"

"I said, *'Mort aux vaches!'* because the policeman said, *'Mort aux vaches!'* so then I said *'Mort aux vaches!'*"

He meant that, being overwhelmed by the most unexpected of accusations, he had in his amazement merely repeated the curious words falsely attributed to him, and which he had certainly never pronounced. He had said, *"Mort aux vaches!"* as he

227

might have said, "I capable of insulting any one! how could you believe it?"

President Bourriche put a different interpretation on the incident.

"Do you maintain," he said, "that the policeman was, himself, the first to utter the exclamation?"

Crainquebille gave up trying to explain. It was too difficult.

"You do not persist in your statement. You are quite right," said the President.

And he had the witness called.

Constable 64, by name Bastien Matra, swore he spoke the truth and nothing but the truth. Then he gave evidence in the following terms:

"I was on my beat on October 20, at noon, when I noticed in the Rue Montmartre a person who appeared to be a hawker, unduly blocking the traffic with his barrow opposite No. 328. Three times I intimated to him the order to move on, but he refused to comply. And when I gave him warning that I was about to charge him, he retorted by crying: *'Mort aux vaches!'* Which I took as an insult."

This evidence, delivered in a firm and moderate manner, the magistrates received with obvious approbation. The witnesses for the defence were Madame Bayard, shoemaker's wife, and Dr. David

Matthieu, chief physician to the Hospital Ambroise
Paré, officer of the Legion of Honour. Madame
Bayard had seen nothing and heard nothing. Dr.
Matthieu was in the crowd which had gathered
round the policeman, who was ordering the costermonger to move on. His evidence led to a new
episode in the trial.

"I witnessed the incident," he said, "I observed
that the constable had made a mistake; he had
not been insulted. I went up to him and called
his attention to the fact. The officer insisted on
arresting the costermonger, and told me to follow
him to the Commissioner of Police. This I did.
Before the Commissioner, I repeated my declaration."

"You may sit down," said the President.
"Usher, recall witness Matra."

"Matra, when you proceeded to arrest the accused, did not Dr. Matthieu point out to you that
you were mistaken?"

"That is to say, Monsieur le Président, that he
insulted me."

"What did he say?"

"He said, '*Mort aux vaches!*'"

Uproarious laughter arose from the audience.

"You may withdraw," said the President hur-
riedly.

And he warned the public that if such unseemly demonstrations occurred again he would clear the court. Meanwhile, Counsel for the defence was haughtily fluttering the sleeves of his gown, and for the moment it was thought that Crainquebille would be acquitted.

Order having been restored, Maître Lemerle rose. He opened his pleading with a eulogy of policemen: "those unassuming servants of society who, in return for a trifling salary, endure fatigue and brave incessant danger with daily heroism. They were soldiers once, and soldiers they remain; soldiers, that word expresses everything. . . ."

From this consideration Maître Lemerle went on to descant eloquently on the military virtues. He was one of those, he said, who would not allow a finger to be laid on the army, on that national army, to which he was so proud to belong.

The President bowed. Maître Lemerle happened to be lieutenant in the Reserves. He was also nationalist candidate for Les Vieilles Haudriettes. He continued:

"No, indeed, I do not esteem lightly the invaluable services unassumingly rendered, which the valiant people of Paris receive daily from the guardians of the peace. And had I beheld in Crainquebille, gentlemen, one who had insulted an ex-soldier, I should never have consented to represent him before you. My client is accused of having said: *'Mort aux vaches!'* The meaning of such an expression is clear. If you consult *Le Dictionnaire de la Langue Verte* (slang) you will find: *'Vachard* a sluggard, an idler, one who stretches himself out lazily like a cow instead of working. *Vache,* one who sells himself to the police; spy.' *Mort aux vaches* is an expression employed by certain people. But the question resolves itself into this: how did Crainquebille say it? And, further, did he say it at all? Permit me to doubt it, gentlemen.

"I do not suspect Constable Matra of any evil intention. But, as we have said, his calling is arduous. He is sometimes harassed, fatigued, overdone. In such conditions he may have suffered from an aural hallucination. And, when he comes and tells you, gentlemen, that Dr. David Matthieu, officer of the Legion of Honour, chief physician at the Ambroise-Paré Hospital, a gentleman and a prince of science, cried: *'Mort aux vaches,'* then we are forced to believe that Matra is obsessed, and if the term be not too strong, suffering from the mania of persecution.

"And even if Crainquebille did cry: *'Mort aux vaches,'* it remains to be proved whether such words

231

on his lips can be regarded as an offence. Crainquebille is the natural child of a costermonger, depraved by years of drinking and other evil courses. Crainquebille was born alcoholic. You behold him brutalized by sixty years of poverty. Gentlemen you must conclude that he is irresponsible."

Maître Lemerle sat down. Then President Bourriche muttered a sentence condemning Jérôme Crainquebille to pay fifty francs fine and to go to prison for a fortnight. The magistrates convicted him on the strength of the evidence given by Constable Matra.

As he was being taken down the long dark passage of the Palais, Crainquebille felt an intense desire for sympathy. He turned to the municipal guard who was his escort and called him three times:

"'Cipal! . . . 'cipal! . . . Eh! 'cipal!" And he sighed:

"If anyone had told me only a fortnight ago that this would happen!"

Then he reflected:

"They speak too quickly, these gentlemen. They speak well, but they speak too quickly. You can't make them understand you. . . . 'cipal, don't you think they speak too quickly?"

But the soldier marched straight on without replying or turning his head.

Crainquebille asked him:

"Why don't you answer me?"

The soldier was silent. And Crainquebille said bitterly:

"You would speak to a dog. Why not to me? Do you never open your mouth? Is it because your breath is foul?"

IV

AN APOLOGY FOR PRESIDENT BOURRICHE

FTER the sentence had been pronounced, several members of the audience and two or three lawyers left the hall. The clerk was already calling another case. Those who went out did not reflect on the Crainquebille affair, which had not greatly interested them; and they thought no more about it. Monsieur Jean Lermite, an etcher, who happened to be at the Palais, was the only one who meditated on what he had just seen and heard. Putting his arm on the shoulder of Maître Joseph Aubarrée, he said:

"President Bourriche must be congratulated on having kept his mind free from idle curiosity, and from the intellectual pride which is determined to know everything. If he had weighed one against the other the contradictory evidence of Constable Matra and Dr. David Matthieu, the magistrate would have adopted a course leading to nothing but doubt and uncertainty. The method of exam-

ining facts in a critical spirit would be fatal to the
administration of justice. If the judge were so imprudent as to follow that method, his sentences
would depend on his personal sagacity, of which he
has generally no very great store, and on human
infirmity which is universal. Where can he find a
criterion? It cannot be denied that the historical
method is absolutely incapable of providing him
with the certainty he needs. In this connexion you
may recall a story told of Sir Walter Raleigh.

" 'One day, when Raleigh, a prisoner in the
Tower of London, was working, as was his wont,
at the second part of his "History of the World,"
there was a scuffle under his window. He went
and looked at the brawlers; and when he returned
to his work, he thought he had observed them very
carefully. But on the morrow, having related the
incident to one of his friends who had witnessed
the affair and had even taken part in it, he was
contradicted by his friend on every point. Reflecting, therefore, that if he were mistaken as to events
which passed beneath his very eyes, how much
greater must be the difficulty of ascertaining the
truth concerning events far distant, he threw the
manuscript of his history into the fire.'

"If the judges had the same scruples as Sir
Walter Raleigh, they would throw all their notes

235

into the fire. But they have no right to do so. They would thus be flouting justice; they would be committing a crime. We may despair of knowing, we must not despair of judging. Those who demand that sentences pronounced in Law Courts should be founded upon a methodical examination of facts, are dangerous sophists, and perfidious enemies of justice both civil and military. President Bourriche has too judicial a mind to permit his sentences to depend on reason and knowledge, the conclusions of which are eternally open to question. He founds them on dogma and moulds them by tradition, so that the authority of his sentences is equal to that of the Church's commandments. His sentences are indeed canonical. I mean that he derives them from a certain number of sacred canons. See, for example, how he classifies evidence, not according to the uncertain and deceptive qualities of appearances and of human veracity, but according to intrinsic, permanent and manifest qualities. He weighs them in the scale, using weapons of war for weights. Can anything be at once simpler and wiser? Irrefutable for him is the evidence of a guardian of the peace, once his humanity be abstracted, and he conceived as a registered number, and according to the categories of an ideal police. Not that Matra (Bastien), born at Cinto-

Monte in Corsica, appears to him incapable of error. He never thought that Bastien Matra was gifted with any great faculty of observation, nor that he applied any secret and vigorous method to the examination of facts. In truth it is not Bastien Matra he is considering, but Constable 64. A man is fallible, he thinks. Peter and Paul may be mistaken. Descartes and Gassendi, Leibnitz and Newton, Bichat and Claude Bernard were capable of error. We may all err and at any moment. The causes of error are innumerable. The perceptions of our senses and the judgment of our minds are sources of illusion and causes of uncertainty. We dare not rely on the evidence of a single man: *Testis unus, testis nullus.* But we may have faith in a number. Bastien Matra, of Cinto-Monte, is fallible. But Constable 64, when abstraction has been made of his humanity, cannot err. He is an entity. An entity has nothing in common with a man, it is free from all that confuses, corrupts and deceives men. It is pure, unchangeable and unalloyed. Wherefore the magistrates did not hesitate to reject the evidence of the mere man, Dr. David Matthieu, and to admit that of Constable 64, who is the pure idea, an emanation from divinity come down to the judgment bar.

"By following such a line of argument, President

Bourriche attains to a kind of infallibility, the only kind to which a magistrate may aspire. When the man who bears witness is armed with a sword, it is the sword's evidence that must be listened to, not the man's. The man is contemptible and may be wrong. The sword is not contemptible and is always right. President Bourriche has seen deeply into the spirit of laws. Society rests on force; force must be respected as the august foundation of society. Justice is the administration of force. President Bourriche knows that Constable 64 is an integral part of the Government. The Government is immanent in each one of its officers. To slight the authority of Constable 64 is to weaken the State. To eat the leaves of an artichoke is to eat the artichoke, as Bossuet puts it in his sublime language. (*Politique tirée de l'Ecriture sainte, passim.*)

"All the swords of the State are turned in the same direction. To oppose one to the other is to overthrow the Republic. For that reason, Crainquebille, the accused, is justly condemned to a fortnight in prison and a fine of fifty francs, on the evidence of Constable 64. I seem to hear President Bourriche, himself, explaining the high and noble consideration which inspired his sentence. I seem to hear him saying:

" 'I judged this person according to the evidence of Constable 64, because Constable 64 is the emanation of public force. And if you wish to prove my wisdom, imagine the consequences had I adopted the opposite course. You will see at once that it would have been absurd. For if my judgments were in opposition to force, they would never be executed. Notice, gentlemen, that judges are only obeyed when force is on their side. A judge without policemen would be but an idle dreamer. I should be doing myself an injury if I admitted a policeman to be in the wrong. Moreover, the very spirit of laws is in opposition to my doing so. To disarm the strong and to arm the weak would be to subvert that social order which it is my duty to preserve. Justice is the sanction of established injustice. Was justice ever seen to oppose conquerors and usurpers? When an unlawful power arises, justice has only to recognize it and it becomes lawful. Form is everything; and between crime and innocence there is but the thickness of a piece of stamped paper. It was for you, Crainquebille, to be the strongest. If, after having cried: *"Mort aux vaches!"* you had declared yourself emperor, dictator, President of the Republic or even town councillor, I assure you you would not have been sentenced to pass a fortnight in

prison, and to pay a fine of fifty francs. I should
have acquitted you. You may be sure of that.'

"Such would have doubtless been the words of
President Bourriche; for he has a judicial mind,
and he knows what a magistrate owes to society.
With order and regularity he defends social principles. Justice is social. Only wrong-headed persons would make justice out to be human and reasonable. Justice is administered upon fixed rules,
not in obedience to physical emotions and flashes of
intelligence. Above all things do not ask justice
to be just, it has no need to be just since it is justice,
and I might even say that the idea of just justice
can have only arisen in the brains of an anarchist.
True, President Magnaud pronounces just sentences; but if they are reversed, that is still justice.

"The true judge weighs his evidence with weights
that are weapons. So it was in the Crainquebille
affair, and in other more famous cases."

Thus said Monsieur Jean Lermite as he paced
up and down the Salle des Pas Perdus.

Scratching the tip of his nose, Maître Joseph
Aubarrée, who knows the Palais well, replied:

"If you want to hear what I think, I don't believe that President Bourriche rose to so lofty a
metaphysical plane. In my opinion, when he received as true the evidence of Constable 64, he

merely acted according to precedent. Imitation lies at the root of most human actions. A respectable person is one who conforms to custom. People are called good when they do as others do."

CRAINQUEBILLE SUBMITS TO THE
LAWS OF THE REPUBLIC

AVING been taken back to his prison, Crainquebille sat down on his chained stool, filled with astonishment and admiration. He, himself, was not quite sure whether the magistrates were mistaken. The tribunal had concealed its essential weakness beneath the majesty of form. He could not believe that he was in the right, as against magistrates whose reasons he had not understood: it was impossible for him to conceive that anything could go wrong in so elaborate a ceremony. For, unaccustomed to attending Mass or frequenting the Elysée, he had never in his life witnessed anything so grand as a police court trial. He was perfectly aware that he had never cried *"Mort aux vaches!"* That for having said it he should have been sentenced to a fortnight's imprisonment seemed to him an august mystery, one of those articles of faith to which believers adhere without understanding them, an obscure, striking, adorable and terrible revelation.

This poor old man believed himself guilty of having mystically offended Constable 64, just as the little boy learning his first Catechism believes himself guilty of Eve's sin. His sentence had taught him that he had cried: *"Mort aux vaches!"* He must, therefore have cried *"Mort aux vaches!"* in some mysterious manner, unknown to himself. He was transported into a supernatural world. His trial was his apocalypse.

If he had no very clear idea of the offence, his idea of the penalty was still less clear. His sentence appeared to him a solemn and superior ritual, something dazzling and incomprehensible, which is not to be discussed, and for which one is neither to be praised nor pitied. If at that moment he had seen President Bourriche, with white wings and a halo round his forehead, coming down through a hole in the ceiling, he would not have been surprised at this new manifestation of judicial glory. He would have said: "This is my trial continuing!"

On the next day his lawyer visited him:

"Well, my good fellow, things aren't so bad after all! Don't be discouraged. A fortnight is soon over. We have not much to complain of."

"As for that, I must say the gentlemen were very kind, very polite: not a single rude word. I shouldn't have believed it. And the *cipal* was wearing white gloves. Did you notice?"

"Everything considered, we did well to confess."

"Perhaps."

"Crainquebille, I have a piece of good news for you. A charitable person, whose interest I have elicited on your behalf, gave me fifty francs for you. The sum will be used to pay your fine."

"When will you give me the money?"

"It will be paid into the clerk's office. You need not trouble about it."

"It does not matter. All the same I am very grateful to this person." And Crainquebille murmured meditatively: "It's something out of the common that's happening to me."

"Don't exaggerate, Crainquebille. Your case is by no means rare, far from it."

"You couldn't tell me where they've put my barrow?"

VI

CRAINQUEBILLE IN THE LIGHT OF
PUBLIC OPINION

FTER his discharge from prison, Crainquebille trundled his barrow along the Rue Montmartre, crying: "Cabbages, turnips, carrots!" He was neither ashamed nor proud of his adventure. The memory of it was not painful. He classed it in his mind with dreams, travels and plays. But, above all things, he was glad to be walking in the mud, along the paved streets, and to see overhead the rainy sky as dirty as the gutter, the dear sky of the town. At every corner he stopped to have a drink; then, gay and unconstrained, spitting in his hands in order to moisten his horny palms, he would seize the shafts and push on his barrow. Meanwhile a flight of sparrows, as poor and as early as he, seeking their livelihood in the road, flew off at the sound of his familiar cry: "Cabbages, turnips, carrots!" An old house wife, who had come up, said to him as she felt his celery:

"What's happened to you, Père Crainquebille?

We haven't seen you for three weeks. Have you been ill? You look rather pale."

"I'll tell you, M'ame Mailloche, I've been doing the gentleman."

Nothing in his life changed, except that he went oftener to the pub, because he had an idea it was a holiday and that he had made the acquaintance of charitable folk. He returned to his garret rather gay. Stretched on his mattress he drew over him the sacks borrowed from the chestnut-seller at the corner which served him as blankets and he pondered: "Well, prison is not so bad; one has everything one wants there. But all the same one is better at home."

His contentment did not last long. He soon perceived that his customers looked at him askance.

"Fine celery, M'ame Cointreau!"

"I don't want anything."

"What! nothing! do you live on air then?"

And M'ame Cointreau without deigning to reply returned to the large bakery of which she was the mistress. The shopkeepers and caretakers, who had once flocked round his barrow all green and blooming, now turned away from him. Having reached the shoemaker's, at the sign of l'Ange Gardien, the place where his adventures with justice had begun, he called:

CRAINQUEBILLE

"M'ame Bayard, M'ame Bayard, you owe me sevenpence halfpenny from last time."

But M'ame Bayard, who was sitting at her counter, did not deign to turn her head.

The whole of the Rue Montmartre was aware that Père Crainquebille had been in prison, and the whole of the Rue Montmartre gave up his acquaintance. The rumour of his conviction had reached the Faubourg and the noisy corner of the Rue Richer. There, about noon, he perceived Madame Laure, a kind and faithful customer, leaning over the barrow of another costermonger, young Martin. She was feeling a large cabbage. Her hair shone in the sunlight like masses of golden threads loosely twisted. And young Martin, a nobody, a good-for-nothing, was protesting with his hand on his heart that there were no finer vegetables than his. At this sight Crainquebille's heart was rent. He pushed his barrow up to young Martin's, and in a plaintive broken voice said to Madame Laure: "It's not fair of you to forsake me."

As Madame Laure herself admitted, she was no duchess. It was not in society that she had acquired her ideas of the prison van and the police-station. But can one not be honest in every station in life? Every one has his self-respect; and one does not like to deal with a man who has just

247

come out of prison. So the only notice she took of Crainquebille was to give him a look of disgust. And the old costermonger resenting the affront shouted:

"Dirty wench, go along with you."

Madame Laure let fall her cabbage and cried:

"Eh! Be off with you, you bad penny. You come out of prison and then insult folk!"

If Crainquebille had had any self-control he would never have reproached Madame Laure with her calling. He knew only too well that one is not master of one's fate, that one cannot always choose one's occupation, and that good people may be found everywhere. He was accustomed discreetly to ignore her customers' business with her; and he despised no one. But he was beside himself. Three times he called Madame Laure drunkard, wench, harridan. A group of idlers gathered round Madame Laure and Crainquebille. They exchanged a few more insults as serious as the first; and they would soon have exhausted their vocabulary, if a policeman had not suddenly appeared, and at once, by his silence and immobility, rendered them as silent and as motionless as himself. They separated. But this scene put the finishing touch to the discrediting of Crainquebille in the eyes of the Faubourg Montmàrtre and the Rue Richer.

VII

RESULTS

THE old man went along mumbling: "For certain she's a hussy, and none more of a hussy than she."

But at the bottom of his heart that was not the reproach he brought against her. He did not scorn her for being what she was. Rather he esteemed her for it, knowing her to be frugal and orderly. Once they had liked to talk together. She used to tell him of her parents who lived in the country. And they had both resolved to have a little garden and keep poultry. She was a good customer. And then to see her buying cabbages from young Martin, a dirty, good-for-nothing wretch; it cut him to the heart; and when she pretended to despise him, that put his back up, and then . . . !

But she, alas! was not the only one who shunned him as if he had the plague. Every one avoided him. Just like Madame Laure, Madame Cointreau the baker, Madame Bayard of l'Ange Gardien scorned and repulsed him. Why! the whole of society refused to have anything to do with him.

So because one had been put away for a fortnight one was not good enough even to sell leeks! Was it just? Was it reasonable to make a decent chap die of starvation because he had got into difficulties with a copper? If he was not to be allowed to sell vegetables then it was all over with him. Like a badly doctored wine he turned sour. After having had words with Madame Laure he now had them with every one. For a mere nothing he would tell his customers what he thought of them and in no ambiguous terms, I assure you. If they felt his wares too long he would call them to their faces chatterer, soft head. Likewise at the wine-shop he bawled at his comrades. His friend, the chestnut-seller, no longer recognized him; old Père Crainquebille, he said, had turned into a regular porcupine. It cannot be denied: he was becoming rude, disagreeable, evil-mouthed, loquacious. The truth of the matter was that he was discovering the imperfections of society; but he had not the facilities of a Professor of Moral and Political Science for the expression of his ideas concerning the vices of the system and the reforms necessary; and his thoughts evolved devoid of order and moderation.

Misfortune was rendering him unjust. He was taking his revenge on those who did not wish him ill and sometimes on those who were weaker than he. One day he boxed Alphonse, the wine-seller's little boy, on the ear, because he had asked him what it was like to be sent away. Crainquebille struck him and said:

"Dirty brat! it's your father who ought to be sent away instead of growing rich by selling poison."

A deed and a speech which did him no honour; for, as the chestnut-seller justly remarked, one ought not to strike a child, neither should one reproach him with a father whom he has not chosen.

Crainquebille began to drink. The less money he earned the more brandy he drank. Formerly frugal and sober he himself marvelled at the change.

"I never used to be a waster," he said. "I suppose one doesn't improve as one grows old."

Sometimes he severely blamed himself for his misconduct and his laziness:

"Crainquebille, old chap, you ain't good for anything but liftin' your glass."

Sometimes he deceived himself and made out that he needed the drink.

"I must have it now and then; I must have a drop to strengthen me and cheer me up. It seems as if I had a fire in my inside; and there's nothing like the drink for quenching it."

251

It often happened that he missed the auction in the morning and so had to provide himself with damaged fruit and vegetables on credit. One day, feeling tired and discouraged, he left his barrow in its shed, and spent the livelong day hanging round the stall of Madame Rose, the tripe-seller, or lounging in and out of the wine-shops near the market. In the evening sitting on a basket, he meditated and became conscious of his deterioration. He recalled the strength of his early years: the achievements of former days, the arduous labours and the glad evenings: those days quickly passing, all alike and fully occupied; the pacing in the darkness up and down the Market pavement, waiting for the early auction; the vegetables carried armfuls and artistically arranged in the barrow; the piping hot black coffee of Mère Théodore swallowed standing, and at one gulp; the shafts grasped vigorously; and then the loud cry, piercing as cock crow, rending the morning air as he passed through the crowded streets. All that innocent, rough life of the human pack-horse came before him. For half a century, on his travelling stall, he had borne to townsfolk worn with care and vigil the fresh harvest of kitchen gardens. Shaking his head he sighed:

"No! I'm not what I was. I'm done for.

The pitcher goes so often to the well that at last it comes home broken. And then I've never been the same since my affair with the magistrates. No, I'm not the man I was."

In short he was demoralized. And when a man reaches that condition he might as well be on the ground and unable to rise. All the passers-by tread him under foot.

VIII

THE FINAL RESULT

POVERTY came, black poverty. The old costermonger who used to come back from the Faubourg Mont-martre with a bag full of five-franc pieces, had not a single coin now. Winter came. Driven out of his garret, he slept under the carts in a shed. It had been raining for days; the gutters were overflowing, and the shed was flooded.

Crouching in his barrow, over the pestilent water, in the company of spiders, rats and half-starved cats, he was meditating in the gloom. Having eaten nothing all day and no longer having the chestnut-seller's sacks for a covering, he recalled the fort-night when the Government had provided him with food and clothing. He envied the prisoner's fate. They suffer neither cold nor hunger, and an idea oc-curred to him:

"Since I know the trick why don't I use it?"

He rose and went out into the street. It was a little past eleven. The night was dark and chill.

'A drizzling mist was falling colder, and more penetrating than rain. The few passers-by crept along under the cover of the houses.

Crainquebille went past the Church of Saint-Eustache and turned into the Rue Montmartre. It was deserted. A guardian of the peace stood on the pavement, by the apse of the church. He was under a gas-lamp, and all around fell a fine rain looking reddish in the gaslight. It fell on to the policeman's hood. He looked chilled to the bone; but, either because he preferred to be in the light or because he was tired of walking he stayed under the lamp, and perhaps it seemed to him a friend, a companion. In the loneliness of the night the flickering flame was his only entertainment. In his immobility he appeared hardly human. The reflection of his boots on the wet pavement, which looked like a lake, prolonged him downwards and gave him from a distance the air of some amphibious monster half out of water. Observed more closely he had at once a monkish and a military appearance. The coarse features of his countenance, magnified under the shadow of his hood, were sad and placid. He wore a thick moustache, short and grey. He was an old copper, a man of some two-score years. Crainquebille went up to him softly, and in a weak hesitating voice, said: *"Mort aux vaches!"*

Then he waited the result of those sacred words. But nothing came of them. The constable remained motionless and silent, with his arms folded under his short cloak. His eyes were wide open; they glistened in the darkness and regarded Crainquebille with sadness, vigilance and scorn.

Crainquebille, astonished, but still resolute, muttered:

"*Mort aux vaches!* I tell you."

There was a long silence in the chill darkness and the falling of the fine penetrating rain. At last the constable spoke:

"Such things are not said. . . . For sure and for certain they are not said. At your age you ought to know better. Pass on."

"Why don't you arrest me?" asked Crainquebille.

The constable shook his head beneath his dripping hood:

"If we were to take up all the addle-pates who say what they oughn't to, we should have our work cut out! . . . And what would be the use of it?"

Overcome by such magnanimous disdain, Crainquebille remained for some time stolid and silent, with his feet in the gutter. Before going, he tried to explain:

"I didn't mean to say: *Mort aux vaches!* to you.

It was no more for you than for another. It was only an idea."

The constable replied sternly but kindly:

"Whether an idea or anything else it ought not to be said, because when a man does his duty and endures much, he ought not to be insulted with idle words. . . . I tell you again to pass on."

Crainquebille, with head bent and arms hanging limp plunged into the rain and the darkness.

LAETA ACILIA

AETA ACILIA lived in Marseilles during the reign of the Emperor Tiberius. She had been married for several years to a Roman noble named Helvius, but she had no children, though she longed passionately to become a mother. One day as she went to the temple to pray to the gods she found the entrance crowded by a band of men, half naked, emaciated and devoured by leprosy and ulcers. She paused in terror on the lowest step of the temple. Laeta Acilia was not without compassion. She pitied the poor creatures, but she was afraid of them. Nor had she ever seen beggars as wild looking as those who at this moment crowded before her, livid, lifeless, their empty wallets flung at their feet. She grew pale and held her hand to her heart; she could neither advance nor escape, and she felt her limbs giving way under her when a woman of striking beauty detached herself from these unfortunates and came towards her.

"Fear nothing, young woman," and the unknown spoke in a voice both grave and tender, "the men you see here are not cruel. They are the bearers not of falsehood and evil, but of truth and love. We have come from Judaea, where the Son of God has died and risen again. When He ascended to the right hand of His Father those who believed in Him suffered cruel wrongs. Stephen was stoned by the people. As for us, the priests placed us on board a ship without sails or rudder, and we were delivered over to the waters of the sea to the end that we should perish. But the God who loved us in His mortal life mercifully led us to the harbour of this town. Alas! the people of Marseilles are avaricious, idolatrous and cruel. They permit the disciples of Jesus to die of hunger and cold. And had we not taken refuge in this temple, which they deem sacred, they would already have dragged us to their gloomy prisons. And yet it would have been well had they welcomed us, since we bring good tidings."

Having thus spoken the stranger held out her hand towards her companions and pointed to each in turn.

"That old man, lady," she said, "who turns on you his serene gaze, that is Cedon, he whom, though blind from birth, the Master healed. Cedon now sees with equal clearness things both visible and invisible. That other old man, whose beard is as white as the snow on the mountains, is Maximin. This man, still so young, and who yet seems so weary, is my brother. He was possessed of great wealth in Jerusalem. Near him stand Martha my sister and Mantilla, the faithful servant who in happier days gathered olives on the hillsides of Bethany."

"And you," asked Laeta Acilia, "you whose voice is so soft and whose face is so beautiful, what is your name?"

The Jewess replied:

"I am called Mary Magdalen. I divined by the gold embroidery on your raiment, and the unconscious pride of your bearing, that your are the wife of one of the principal citizens of this town. For this reason I have approached you to the end that you may move the heart of your husband on behalf of the disciples of Jesus Christ. Say to this rich man: 'Lord, they are naked, let us clothe them; they are anhungered, and thirsty; let us give them bread and wine, and God will restore to us in His Kingdom what was borrowed from us in His name.' "

Laeta Acilia replied:

"Mary, I will do as you ask. My husband is named Helvius; he is of noble rank and one of the richest citizens of the town; never for long does he refuse what I desire, for he loves me. Your companions have now ceased, O Mary, to fill me with fear. I shall even dare to pass close to them, though their limbs are polluted by ulcers, and I shall go to the temple to pray to the immortal gods to grant my wish. Alas; hitherto they have refused."

Mary, with arms outstretched, barred her way.

"Beware, lady," she cried, "of worshipping vain idols. Do not demand of images of stone words of hope and life. There is only one God, and with my hair I have wiped His feet."

At these words the flashing of her eyes, dark as the sky in a storm, mingled with tears, and Laeta Acilia said to herself:

"I am pious, and I faithfully perform the cere-monies religion demands, but in this woman there is a strange feeling of a love divine."

Mary Magdalen continued in ecstasy: "He was the God of Heaven and earth, and He uttered His parables seated on the bench by the threshold, under the shade of the old fig-tree. He was young and beautiful. He would have been glad to be loved. When he came to supper in my sister's house I sat at His feet, and the words flowed from His lips like the waters of a torrent. And when my sister complained of my sloth, saying: 'Master, tell her it is but right that she should aid me to prepare the supper,' He smiled and made excuse for me, and permitted me to remain seated at His feet, and said that I had chosen the good part.

"One would have thought to see Him that He was but a young shepherd from the mountains, and yet His eyes flashed flames like those that issued from the brow of Moses. His gentleness was like the peace of night and His anger was more terrible than a thunderbolt. He loved the humble and the little ones. Along the roadside the children ran towards Him and clung to His garments. He was the God of Abraham and Jacob, and with the same hands that had created the sun and the stars, He caressed the cheeks of the newly born whom their happy mothers held out to Him from the thresholds of their cottages. He was himself as simple as a child, and He raised the dead to life. Here among my companions you see my brother whom He raised from the dead. Behold, lady! Lazarus bears on his face the pallor of death, and in his eyes is the horror of one who has seen hell."

But for some moments past Laeta Acilia had ceased to listen.

She raised towards the Jewess her candid eyes and her small, smooth forehead.

"Mary," she said, "I am a pious woman, attached to the faith of my fathers. Unbelief is evil for our

sex. And it does not beseem the wife of a Roman
noble to accept new fashions in religions. And yet
I must confess that there are some charming gods in
the East. Your God, Mary, seems one of these.
You have told me that He loves little children, and
that He kisses them as they lie in the arms of their
young mothers. By that I see that He is a God
who is favourable to women, and I regret that He
is not held in esteem among the aristocracy and the
official classes, or I would gladly bring him offerings
of honey-cakes. But, listen, Mary the Jewess, appeal to Him, you whom He loves, and demand of
Him for me that which I dare not demand myself,
which my goddesses have refused."

Laeta Acilia uttered these words with hesitation.
She paused and blushed.

"What is it," Mary Magdalen asked eagerly,
"and what desire, lady, has your unsatisfied soul?"

Gaining courage little by little, Laeta Acilia
replied:

"Mary, you are a woman, and though I know
you not, I yet may confide to you a woman's secret.
During the six years that I have been married I
have not had a child, and that is a great sorrow to
me; I need a child to love; the love in my heart for
the little creature I am awaiting, and who yet may
never come, is stifling me. If your God, Mary

Magdalen, grants me through your intercession what my goddesses have denied me, I shall say that He is a good God, and I will love Him and I will make my friends love Him. And like us they are young and rich, and they belong to the first families of the town."

Mary Magdalen replied gravely:

"Daughter of the Romans, when you shall have received that for which you ask, may you remember this promise that you have made to the servant of Jesus."

"I shall remember," she replied. "In the mean-time take this purse, Mary, and divide the money it contains among your companions. Farewell, I shall return to my house. As soon as I arrive I will send baskets full of bread and meat for you and your friends. Tell your brother and your sister and your friends that they may without fear leave the sanctuary where they have taken refuge and go to some inn on the outskirts of the town. Helvius, who has great influence in the town, will prevent any one molesting them. May the gods protect you, Mary Magdalen! When it shall please you to see me again ask of the passers-by for the house of Laeta Acilia; any of the citizens will be able to show you the way without trouble."

T was six months later that Laeta Acilia, lying on the purple couch in the courtyard of her house, crooned a little song that had no sense and which her mother had sung before her. The water sang gaily in the fountain out of whose shallow basin rose young Tritons in marble, and the balmy air gently stirred the murmuring leaves of the old plane-tree. Tired, languid, happy, heavy as a bee leaving the orchard, the young woman crossed her arms over her rounded body, and, having ceased her song, glanced about her and sighed in the fulness of pride.

At her feet her black, white and yellow slaves were busy with needle, shuttle and spindle, vying with each other as they worked at the garments for the expected infant. Laeta stretched out her hand and took a little cap which an old slave laughingly offered her. She placed it on her closed hand and laughed in turn. It was a little cap of purple and gold, silver and pearls, and splendid as the dreams of a poor African slave.

At that moment a stranger entered this interior

court. She was clothed in a seamless garment of one piece, in colour like the dust of the roads. Her long hair was covered with ashes, but her face, worn by tears, still shone with glory and beauty.

The slaves, mistaking her for a beggar, were about to drive her away when Laeta Acilia, recognising her at the first glance, rose and ran towards her.

"Mary, Mary," she cried, "it is true that you were the favourite of a god. He whom you loved on earth has heard you in Heaven, and through your intercession He has granted my prayer. See," she added, and she showed her the little cap which she still held in her hand, "how happy I am and how grateful to you."

"I knew it," replied Mary Magdalen "and I have come, Laeta Acilia, to instruct you in the truth of Jesus Christ."

Thereupon the Marseillaise dismissed her slaves, and offered the Jewess an ivory armchair with cushions embroidered in gold. But Mary Magdalen, pushing it back with disgust, seated herself on the ground with feet crossed in the shade of the great plane-tree stirred by the murmuring breeze.

"Daughter of the Gentiles," she said, "you have not despised the disciples of the Lord. For this reason I will teach you to know Jesus as I know

266

Him, to the end that you shall love Him as I love Him. I was a sinner when I saw for the first time the most beautiful of the sons of men."

Thereupon she told how she had thrown herself at the feet of Jesus in the house of Simon the Leper, and how she had poured over the Master's adored feet all the ointment of spikenard contained in the alabaster vase. She repeated the words the gentle Master had uttered in reply to the murmurs of His rough disciples.

"Why do you reprove this woman?" He had said. "That which she has done is well done. For the poor ye have always with you, but Me ye have not always. She has with forethought anointed My body for My burial. I tell you in truth that in the whole world, wherever the Gospel is preached, shall be told what she has done, and she shall be praised."

She then described how Jesus had cast out the seven devils that had raged within her.

She added:

"Since then, enraptured and consumed by all the joys of faith and love, I have lived in the shadow of the Master as in a new Eden."

She told her of the lilies of the fields upon which they had gazed together, and of that infinite happiness, the happiness born of faith alone. Then she

267

described how He had been betrayed and put to death for the salvation of His people. She recalled the ineffable scenes of the passion, the burial and the resurrection.

"It was I," she cried, "it was I who of all was the first to see Him. I found two angels clad in white seated, one at the head, the other at the feet, where we had laid the body of Jesus. And they said to me: 'Woman, why weepest thou?' 'I weep because they have taken away my Lord, and I know not where they have laid Him.

"O joy! Jesus came towards me, and at first I thought He was the gardener. But he called me 'Mary' and I recognised His voice. I cried 'Master' and held out my arms, but He replied gently, 'Touch me not, for I am not yet ascended to my Father.' "

As she listened to this narrative Laeta Acilia lost little by little her sense of joy and contentment. Recalling the past and examining her own life, it seemed to her very monotonous in comparison to the life of the woman who had loved a god. Young and pious and a patrician, her own red-letter days were those on which she had eaten cakes with her girl friends. Visits to the circus, the love of Helvius and her needle-work also counted in her life. But what were these all in comparison to the scenes with which Mary Magdalen kindled her senses and her soul? She left her heart stifling with bitter jealousy and vague regrets.

She envied this Jewess, whose radiant beauty still glowed under the ashes of penitence, her divine adventures, and even her sorrows.

"Begone, Jewess!" she cried, forcing back her tears with her hands. "Begone! But a moment since I was so contented, I believed myself so happy. I did not know that there were other joys than those which were mine. I knew of no other love than that of my good Helvius, and I knew of no other holy joy than to celebrate the mysteries of the goddesses in the manner of my mother and of my grandmother. O, now I understand! Wicked woman, you wished to make me discontented with the life I have led. But you have not succeeded! Why have you come to tell me of your love for a visible God? Why do you boast before me of having seen the resurrection of the Master since I shall not see Him? You even hoped to spoil the joy that is mine in bearing a child. It was wicked! I refuse to know your God. You have loved Him too much! To please Him one is obliged to fall prostrate and dishevelled at His feet. That is not an attitude which beseems the wife of a noble! Helvius would be annoyed did I worship in such a way. I will have nothing to do with a religion that disarranges one's hair! No indeed, I will not allow the little child I bear in my bosom to know your Christ! Should this poor little creature be a daughter she shall learn to love the little goddesses of baked clay that are not larger than my finger, and with these she can play without fear. These are the proper divinities for mothers and children. You are very audacious to boast of your love affairs and to ask me to share them. How could your God be mine? I have not led the life of a sinner, I have not been possessed of seven devils, nor have I frequented the highways. I am a respectable woman. Begone!"

And Mary Magdalen, perceiving that proselytising was not her vocation, retired to a wild cavern since called the Holy Grotto. The sacred historians believe unanimously that Laeta Acilia was not converted to the faith of Christ until many years after this interview which I have faithfully recorded.

A NOTE ON A POINT OF EXEGESIS

HAVE been reproached for having in this story confused Mary of Bethany, sister of Martha, and Mary Magdalen. I must confess at once that the Gospel seems to make of Mary who poured the perfume of spïkenard over the feet of Jesus and of Mary to whom the Master said: *"Noli me tangere,"* two women absolutely distinct. Upon this point I am willing to make amends to those who have done me the honour to blame me.

Among the number is a princess who belongs to the Orthodox Greek Church. This does not in the least surprise me. The Greeks have always distinguished between the two Marys. It was not the same in the Western Church. On the contrary, the identity of the sister of Martha and Magdalen the sinner was early acknowledged.

The texts lend themselves but ill to this interpretation, but texts never present difficulties to any one but the pundits; the poetry of the people is more subtle than science: it can never be held in check, and it overcomes the obstacles which prove a stumbling block to criticism. By a happy turn of the imagination popular fancy has welded the two Marys together and thus created the marvellous type of Mary Magdalen. It has been made sacred by legend, and it is the legend which has inspired my little story. In this I consider myself above reproach. Nor is that all! I am able, even, to in-voke the authority of the learned, and I may, with-out vanity, say that the Sorbonne is on my side. The Sorbonne declared on December 1, 1521, that there is but one Mary.

EDMÉE, OR CHARITY WELL BESTOWED

ORTEUR, the founder of *l'Etoile*, the political and literary editor of *La Revue Nationale* and of *Le Nouveau Siècle Illustré*, Horteur, having received me in his editorial room, from the depths of his editorial arm-chair addressed me thus:

"My good Martean, write me a story for the special number of *Le Nouveau Siècle*. Three hundred lines for New Year's Day. Something amusing with a high society atmosphere."

I told Horteur that that was not in my line, at least not in the sense in which he understood it, but that I was prepared to write him a story.

"I should like it to be entitled," he said, "a tale for the rich."

"I should prefer a tale for the poor."

"That is what I mean. A tale to inspire the rich with pity for the poor."

"But that is precisely what I object to. I do not want the rich to have pity on the poor."

"Curious!"

"No, it is not curious, but scientific. In my opinion the pity of the rich for the poor is an insult and a denial of human brotherhood. If you wish me to address the rich I shall say: 'Spare the poor your pity: they have no use for it. Wherefore pity and not justice? You have an account with them. Settle it. This is no question of sentiment. It is a matter of economics. If that which you are pleased to give them is calculated to prolong their poverty and your wealth, the gift is iniquitous and the tears you mingle with it will not render it just. "You must make restitution," as the attorney said to the judge after good Brother Maillard's sermon. You give alms in order to avoid making restitution. You give a little in order to keep much, and you gloat over it. For a like reason the tyrant of Samos threw his ring into the sea. But the Nemesis of the gods declined to receive the offering. A fisherman brought back the tyrant his ring in a fish's belly. And Polycrates was despoiled of all his wealth.' "

"You are joking."

'I am not joking. I want to make the rich understand that they are benevolent on the cheap, that their generosity costs them little, that they only make the creditor curl his lip, and that such is not the way to conduct business. It is an opinion which may be of use to them."

"And these are the ideas you propose to express in *Le Nouveau Siècle* in order to increase the circulation! Not a bit of it my friend! Not a bit of it!"

"Why do you insist on the rich man assuming towards the poor an attitude different from that which he assumes towards the rich and powerful? He pays the rich what he owes them, and if he owe them nothing he pays them nothing. That is honest. If he be honest let him do the same for the poor. And do not say that the rich owe the poor nothing. I do not believe that a single rich man thinks so. It is upon the extent of the debt that opinions begin to differ. And no one is in a hurry to solve the problem. It is thought better to leave the matter vague. Every one is aware that he is in debt. But what he owes is uncertain, and so from time to time a little is paid on account. That is called philanthropy, and it is profitable."

"But, my dear fellow, there is no common sense in what you have been saying. Possibly I am more of a Socialist than you, but I am practical. To relieve suffering, to prolong a life, to redress some particle of social injustice is to attain a result. The little good one does is at any rate done. It is not everything but it is something. If the story I ask you to write goes home to the hearts of a hundred of my rich subscribers and induces them to give it will be so much won from evil and suffering. Thus little by little the lot of the poor is rendered bearable."

"Is it good for the lot of the poor to be bearable? Poverty is indispensable to wealth and wealth to poverty. These two evils beget one another and foster one another. The condition of the poor does not need to be improved, but to be suppressed. I will not encourage the rich to give alms, because their alms are poisoned, because their alms do good to the giver and harm to the receiver, because in short, wealth being itself hard and cruel it must not put on the deceitful appearance of kindness. Since you wish me to write a story for the rich, I will say to them: 'Your poor are your dogs whom you feed in order that they may bite. Your bedesmen become the hounds of the propertied classes who bay at the proletariat. The rich give only to those who ask. The workers ask nothing, and they receive nothing.'"

"But the infirm, the aged and the orphaned? . . ."

"They have the right to live. For them I would not excite pity, I would appeal to justice."

"All this is mere theorizing! To return to reality, you will write me a New Year's Story, and you may introduce a suggestion of Socialism. Socialism is quite fashionable. It is even distinction. Of course I am not referring to the Socialism of Guesde or of Jaurès, but to a moderate Socialism such as men of the world intelligently and rightly oppose to collectivism. Have some young faces in your story. It will be illustrated and readers like pictures to be pleasing. Bring a young girl on the scene, a charming young girl. It will not be difficult."

"No, it is not difficult."

"Could you not introduce a little chimney-sweep? I have an illustration ready, a coloured engraving, which represents a young girl giving alms to a little chimney-sweep on the steps of the Madeleine. This would be an opportunity for using it. . . . It is cold, the snow is falling: the pretty girl is dropping a coin into the chimney-sweep's hand. Can you see it?"

"I see it."

"You will develop that theme."

"I will develop it. The little sweep, in a transport of gratitude throws his arms round the girl's neck. She happens to be the daughter of the Comte de Linotte. He gives her a kiss, imprinting on the charming child's cheek a little round O of soot. A perfectly enchanting little O, quite round and quite black. He loves her. Edmée (her name is Edmée) is not indifferent to so sincere and ingenuous an attachment. . . . I fancy the idea is sufficiently pathetic."

"Yes. You will be able to make something of it."

"You encourage me to continue. On her return to her sumptuous home in the Boulevard Malesherbes, for the first time in her life Edmée is reluctant to wash her face: she would like to preserve the imprint of those lips on her cheek. Meanwhile the little sweep has followed her to her door. Rapt in ecstasy he stands beneath the adorable young girl's window. . . . Will that do?"

"Why, yes!"

"I continue. The next morning, lying on her little white bed, Edmée sees the little sweep coming down the chimney. Without any ado he throws himself on the charming child and covers her with little round O's of soot. I omitted to tell you that he is extremely handsome. While thus delightfully occupied he is surprised by the Comtesse de Linotte. She screams, she calls for help. But so absorbed is he that he neither sees nor hears."

"My dear Marteau. . . ."

"So absorbed is he that he neither sees nor hears. The Comte hastens into the room. He has the soul of a true aristocrat. He takes up the little sweep by the seat of his breeches . . . and throws him out of the window——"

"My dear Marteau. . . ."

"I hasten to conclude. . . . Nine months later the little sweep married the high-born maiden. And it was high time too. Such was the result of charity well bestowed."

"My dear Marteau, you have amused yourself long enough at my expense."

"Not a bit of it. I must finish. Having married Mademoiselle de Linotte, the little sweep became a papal count and was ruined on the Turf. To-day he is a stove dealer at Montparnasse in the Rue de la Gaîté. His wife keeps his shop and sells stoves at eighteen francs apiece payable in eight months."

"My dear Marteau it isn't the least bit funny."

"Beware, my dear Horteur. What I have just told you is really Lamartine's *Chute d'un Ange* and Alfred de Vigny's *Eloa*. And, taking it all round, it is better than your tearful tales, which make folk believe that they are very kind when they are not kind at all, that they do good when they do nothing of the sort, that it is easy for them to be benevolent when it is the most difficult thing in the world. My story is moral. Moreover it is optimistic and ends well. For, in her shop in the Rue de la Gaîté, Edmée found the happiness which in amusements and festivities she would have sought in vain, had she been married to a diplomat or an officer. . . . My dear editor, are we agreed: Will you have *Edmée, or Charity well Bestowed* for the *Nouveau Siècle Illustré?*"

"You ask me that in all seriousness? . . ."

"In all seriousness I ask you. If you will not have my story, I will publish it elsewhere."

"Where?"

"In some high class journal."

"I dare you to do so."

"You will see."

The *Figaro*, under the editorship of Monsieur de Rodays, published *Edmée ou La Charité bein placée.* It was, so to speak, offered as a New Year's gift to the readers of that paper.

MADEMOISELLE DE DOUCINE'S NEW YEAR'S PRESENT

O N January 1st, in the forenoon, the good M. Chanterelle sallied out on foot from his hôtel in the Faubourg Saint-Marcel. He felt the cold and was a poor walker; so it was a real penance to him to face the chilly air and the bleak streets which were full of half-melted snow. He had refused to take his couch by way of mortifying the flesh, having grown very solicitous since his illness about the salvation of his soul. He lived in retirement, aloof from all society and company, and paid no visits save to his niece, Mademoiselle de Doucine, a little girl of seven.

Leaning on his walking-cane, he made his way painfully to the Rue Saint-Honoré and entered the shop of Madame Pinson at the sign of the *Panier Fleuri*. Here was displayed an abundant stock of children's toys to tempt customers seeking presents for this New Year's Day of 1696. You could scarce move for the host of mechanical figures of dancers and tipplers, birds in the bush that clapped their wings and sang, cabinets full of wax puppets, soldiers in white and blue ranged in battle array, and dolls dressed some as fine ladies, others as servant wenches, for the inequality of stations, established by God himself among mankind, appeared even in these innocent mannikins.

M. Chanterelle chose a doll. The one he selected was dressed like the Princess of Savoy on her arrival in France, on November 4th. The head was a mass of bows and ribbons; she wore a very stiff corsage, covered with gold filigrees, and a brocade petticoat with an overskirt caught up by pearl clasps.

M. Chanterelle smiled to think of the delight such a lovely doll would give Mademoiselle de Doucine, and when Madame Pinson handed him the Princess of Savoy wrapped up in silk paper, a gleam of sensuous satisfaction flitted over his kind face, pinched as it was with illness, pale with fasting and haggard with the fear of hell.

He thanked Madame Pinson courteously, clapped the Princess under his arm and walked away, dragging his leg painfully, towards the house where he knew Mademoiselle de Doucine was waiting for him to attend her morning levée.

At the corner of the Rue de l'Arbre-Sec, he met M. Spon, whose great nose divided almost his lace cravat.

"Good morning, Monsieur Spon," he greeted him. "I wish you a happy New Year, and I pray God everything may turn out according to your wishes."

"Oh! my good sir, don't say that," cried M. Spon. " 'Tis often for our chastisement that God grants our wishes. *Et tribuit eis petitionem eorum.*"

" 'Tis very true," returned M. Chanterelle, "we do not know our own best interests. I am an example myself, as I stand before you. I thought at first that the complaint I have suffered from for the last two years was a curse; but I see now it is a blessing, since it has removed me from the abominable life I was leading at the play-houses and in society. This complaint, which tortures my limbs and is like to turn my brain, is a signal token of God's goodness toward me. But, sir, will you not do me the favor to accompany me as far as the Rue du Roule, whither I am bound, to carry a New Year's gift to my niece Mademoiselle de Doucine?"

At the words M. Spon threw up his arms and gave a great cry of horror.

"What!" he exclaimed. "Can it be M. Chanterelle I hear say such things,—and not some profligate libertine? Is it possible, sir, that living as you do a religious and retired life, I see you

283

all in a moment plunge into the vices of the day?"

"Alack! I did not think I was plunging into vice," faltered M. Chanterelle, trembling all over. "But I sorely lack a lump of guidance. Is it so great a sin then to offer a doll to Mademoiselle de Doucine?"

"Yes, a great and terrible sin," replied M. Spon. "And what you are offering this innocent child to-day is meeter to be called an idol, a devilish simulacrum, than a doll. Are you not aware, sir, that the custom of New Year's gifts is a foul super-stition and a hideous survival of Paganism?"

"No, I did not know that," said M. Chanter-elle.

"Let me tell you, then," resumed M. Spon, "that this custom descends from the Romans, who seeing something divine in all beginnings, held the begin-ning of the year holy also. Hence, to act as they did is to do idolatry. You make New Year's of-ferings, sir, in imitation of the worshippers of the God Janus. Be consistent, and like them conse-crate to Juno the first day of every month."

M. Chanterelle, hardly able to keep his feet, begged M. Spon to give him his arm, and while they moved on, M. Spon proceeded in the same vein: .

"Is it because the Astrologers have fixed on the first of January for the beginning of the year that you deem yourself obliged to make presents on that day? Pray, what call have you to revive at that precise date the affection of your friends. Was their love dying then with the dying year? And will it be so much worth the having when you have reanimated it by dint of cajolements and baneful gifts?"

"Sir," returned the good M. Chanterelle, leaning on M. Spon's arm and trying hard to make his tottering steps keep pace with his impetuous companion's, "sir, before my sickness, I was only a miserable sinner, taking no heed but to treat my friends with civility and govern my behaviour by the principles of honesty and honour. Providence hath deigned to rescue me from this abyss, and I direct my conduct since my conversion by the admonitions the Director of my conscience gives me. But I have been so light-minded and thoughtless as not to seek his advice on this question of New Year's gifts. What you tell me of them, sir, with the authority of a man alike admirable for sober living and sound doctrine, amazes and confounds me."

"Nay! that is indeed what I meant to do," resumed M. Spon,—"to confound you, and to illumine you, not indeed by my own lights, which burn feebly, but by those of a great Doctor. Sit down on that wayside post."

And pushing M. Chanterelle into the archway of a carriage gate, where he made himself as easy as circumstances allowed, M. Spon drew from his pocket a little parchment-bound book, which he opened, and after hunting through the pages, lighted on a passage which he proceeded to read out loud amid a gaping circle of chimney-sweeps, chamber-maids, and scullions who had collected at the re-sounding tones of his voice:

"'We who hold in abhorrence the festivals of the Jews, and who would deem strange and out-landish their Sabbaths and New Moons and other Holy Days erst loved of the Almighty, we deal familiarly with the Saturnalia and the Calends of January, with the Matronalia and the Feast of the Winter Solstice; New Year's gifts and foolish presents fill all our thoughts; merrymakings and junketings are in every house. The Heathens guard their religion better; they are heedful to observe none of our Feasts, for fear of being taken for Christians, while we never hesitate to make ourselves look like Heathens by celebrating their Ceremonial Days.'

"You hear what I say," went on M. Spon.

" 'Tis Tertullian speaks in this wise and from the depths of Africa displays before your eyes, sir, the odiousness of your behaviour. He it is upbraids you, declaring how 'New Year's gifts and foolish presents fill all your thoughts. You keep holy the feasts of the Heathen.' I have not the honour to know your Confessor. But I shudder, sir, to think of the way he neglects his duty toward you. Tell me this, can you rest assured that at the day of your death, when you come to stand before God, he will be at your side, to take upon him the sins he hath suffered you to fall into?"

After haranguing in this sort, he put back his book in his pocket and marched off with angry strides, followed at a distance by the astonished chimney-sweeps and scullions.

The good M. Chanterelle was left sitting alone on the post with the Princess of Savoy, and thinking how he was risking the eternal pains of hell fire for giving a doll to Mademoiselle de Doucine, his niece, he fell to pondering the unfathomable mysteries of Religion.

His legs, which had been tottery for several months, refused to carry him, and he felt as unhappy as ever a well-meaning man possibly can in this world.

He had been sitting stranded in this distressful mood on his post for some minutes when a Capuchin friar stepped up and addressed him:

"Sir, will you not give New Year's presents to the Little Brethren who are poor, for the love of God?"

"Why! what! good Father," M. Chanterelle burst out, "you are a man of religion, and you ask me for New Year's gifts?"

"Sir," replied the Capuchin, "the good St. Francis bade his sons make merry with all simplicity. Give the Capuchins wherewith to make a good meal this day, that they may endure with cheerfulness the abstinence and fasting they must observe all the rest of the year,—barring, of course, Sundays and Feast Days."

M. Chanterelle gazed at the holy man with wonder:

"Are you not afraid, Father, that this custom of New Year's gifts is baneful to the soul?"

"No, I am not afraid."

"The custom comes to us from the Pagans."

"The Pagans sometimes followed good customs. God was pleased to suffer some faint rays of his light to pierce the darkness of the Gentiles. Sir, if you refuse to give *us* presents, never refuse a boon to our poor little ones. We have a home for foundlings. With this poor crown I shall buy each child a little paper windmill and a cake. They will owe you the only pleasure perhaps of all their life; for they are not fated to have much joy in the world. Their laughter will go up to heaven; when children laugh, they praise the Lord."

M. Chanterelle laid his well-filled purse in the poor friar's palm and got him down from his post, saying over softly to himself the word he had just heard:

"When children laugh, they praise the Lord."

Then his soul was comforted and he marched off with a firmer step to carry the Princess of Savoy to Mademoiselle de Doucine, his niece.

THE MIRACLE OF THE GREAT
ST. NICOLAS

T. NICOLAS, Bishop of Myra in Lycia, lived in the time of Constantine the Great. The most ancient and weighty of those authors who have mentioned him celebrate his virtues, his labours, and his worth: they give abundant proofs of his sanctity; but none of them records the miracle of the salting-tub. Nor is it mentioned in the Golden Legend. This silence is important: still one does not willingly consent to throw doubt upon a fact so widely known, which is attested by the ballad which all the world knows:

> "There were three little children
> In the fields they went to glean."

This famous text expressly states that a cruel pork-butcher put the innocents "like pigs into the salting-vat." That is to say, he apparently preserved them, cut into pieces, in a bath of brine. This is, to be sure, how pork is cured: but one is surprised to read further on that the three little

children remained seven years in pickle, whereas it is
usual to begin withdrawing the pieces of flesh from
the tub, with a wooden fork, at the end of about
six weeks. The text is explicit: according to the
elegy, it was seven years after the crime that St.
Nicolas entered the accursed hostelry. He asked
for supper. The landlord offered him a piece of
ham:

> " 'Wilt eat of ham? 'Tis dainty food.'
> ' I'll have no ham: it is not good.'
> ' Wilt eat a piece of tender veal?'
> ' I will not make of that my meal.
> Young salted flesh I want, and that
> Has lain seven years within the vat.'
> Whenas the butcher heard this said
> Out of the door full fast he fled."

The Man of God immediately resuscitated the
tender victims by the laying of hands on the salting-
tub.

Such is, in substance, the story of the old
anonymous rhyme. It bears the inimitable stamp
of honesty and good faith. Scepticism seems ill-
inspired when it attacks the most vital memories of
the popular mind. It is not without a lively
satisfaction that I have found myself able to recon-

cile the authority of the ballad with the silence
of the ancient biographers of the Lycian pontiff.
I am happy to proclaim the result of my long meditations and scholastic researches. The miracle of
the salting-tub is true, in so far as essentials are
concerned, but it was not the blessed Bishop of Myra
who performed it; it was another St. Nicolas, for
there were two: one, as we have already stated,
Bishop of Myra in Lycia; the other more recent,
Bishop of Trinqueballe in Vervignole. For me was
reserved the task of distinguishing between them.
It was the Bishop of Trinqueballe who rescued the
three little boys from the salting-tub. I shall establish the fact by authentic documents, and no one
will have occasion to deplore the end of a legend.

I have been fortunate enough to recover the entire history of the Bishop Nicolas and the children
whom he resuscitated. I have fashioned it into
a narrative which will be read, I hope, with both
pleasure and profit.

CHAPTER I

ICOLAS, a scion of an illustrious family of Vervignole, showed marks of sanctity from his earliest childhood, and at the age of fourteen vowed to consecrate himself to the Lord. Having embraced the ecclesiastical profession, he was raised, while still young, by popular acclamation and the wish of the Chapter, to the see of St. Cromadaire, the apostle of Vervignole, and first Bishop of Trinqueballe. He exercised his pastoral ministry with piety, governed his clergy with wisdom, taught the people, and feared not to remind the great of Justice and Moderation. He was liberal, profuse in almsgiving, and set aside for the poor the greater part of his wealth.

His castle proudly lifted its crenelated walls and pepper-pot roofs from the summit of a hill overlooking the town. He made of it a refuge where all who were pursued by the secular arm might find a place of refuge. In the lower hall, the largest to be seen in all Vervignole, the table laid for meals was so long that those who sat at one end saw it lose itself in the distance in an indistinct point, and

when the torches upon it were lighted it recalled
the tail of the comet which appeared in Vervignole
to announce the death of King Comus. The holy
St. Nicolas sat at the upper end. There he entertained the principal folk of the town and of the
kingdom, and a multitude of clergy and laymen.
But on his right there was always reserved a seat
for the poor man who might come begging for his
bread at the door.

Children, particularly, aroused the solicitude of
the good St. Nicolas. He delighted in their innocence, and he felt for them with the heart of a
father and the bowels of a mother. He had the
virtues and morals of an apostle. Yearly, in the
dress of a simple monk, with a white staff in his
hand, he would visit his flock, desirous of seeing
everything with his own eyes; and in order that no
adversity or disorder should escape his notice he
would traverse, accompanied by a single priest, the
wildest parts of his diocese, crossing, in winter,
the flooded rivers, climbing mountains, and plunging
into the thick forests.

One day, having ridden since dawn upon his
mule, in company with the Deacon Modernus,
through gloomy woods haunted by the lynx and
the wolf, and the ancient pines bristling on the sum-

mits of the Marnouse mountains, the man of God made his way at the fall of night into some thorny thickets through which his mount with difficulty forced a winding path. The Deacon Modernus followed him with much difficulty on his mule, which carried the baggage.

Overcome with hunger and fatigue, the man of God said to Modernus:

"Let us halt here, my son, and if you still have a little bread and wine we will sup here, for I feel that I hardly have the strength to proceed further, and you, although the younger, must be nearly as tired as I."

"Monseigneur," answered Modernus, "there remains neither a drop of wine nor a crumb of bread; for, by your orders, I gave all to some people on the road, who had less need of it than ourselves."

"Without a doubt," replied the Bishop, "had there been a few scraps left in your wallet we should have eaten them with pleasure, for it is fitting that those who govern the Church should be nourished on the leavings of the poor. But since you have nothing left it is because God has desired it so, and He has surely desired it for our good and profit. It is possible that He will for ever hide from us the reason of this favour: perhaps, on the other hand,

He will quickly make it manifest. Meanwhile, I think the only thing left for us is to push on until we find some arbutus berries and blackberries for our own nourishment, and some grass for our mules, and, being thus refreshed, to lie down upon a bed of leaves."

"As you please, Monseigneur," answered Modernus, pricking his mount.

They travelled all night, and a part of the following morning; then, having climbed a fairly steep ascent, they suddenly found themselves at the border of the wood, and beheld at their feet a plain covered by a yellowish sky, and crossed by four white roads, which lost themselves in the mist. They took that to the left, an old Roman road, formerly frequented by merchants and pilgrims, but deserted since the war had laid waste this part of Vervignole. Dense clouds were gathering in the sky, across which birds were flying; a stifling atmosphere weighed down upon the dumb, livid earth. Lightning flashed on the horizon. They urged on their wearied mules. Suddenly a mighty wind bent the tops of the trees, making the boughs crack and the battered foliage moan. The thunder muttered, and heavy drops of rain began to fall.

As they made their way through the storm, the

lightning flashing about them, along a road which had become a torrent, they perceived, by the light of a flash, a house outside which there hung a branch of holly, a sign of hospitality.

The inn appeared deserted; nevertheless, the host advanced towards them, a man fierce yet humble, with a great knife in his belt, and asked what they wished for.

"A lodging, and a scrap of bread, with a drop of wine," answered the Bishop, "for we are weary and benumbed with cold."

While the host was fetching wine from the cellar, and Modernus was taking the mules to the stable, St. Nicolas, sitting at the hearth beside a dying fire, cast a glance round the smoky room. Dust and dirt covered the benches and casks; spiders spun their webs between the worm-eaten joists, whence hung scanty bunches of onions. In a dark corner the salt-ing-tub displayed its iron-hooped belly.

In those days the demons used to take a hand in domestic life in a far more intimate fashion than they do to-day. They haunted houses, concealed in the salt-box, the butter-tub, or some other hid-ing-place; they spied upon the people of the house, and watched for the opportunity to tempt them and lead them into evil. Then, too, the angels made more frequent appearances among Christian folk.

Now a devil, as big as a hazel-nut, who was hidden among the burning logs, spoke up and said to the holy Bishop:

"Look at that salting-tub, Father; it is well worth a look. It is the best salting-tub in the whole of Vervignole. It is, indeed, the model and paragon of salting-tubs. When the master here, Seigneur Garum, received it from the hands of a skilful cooper he perfumed it with juniper, thyme, and rosemary. Seigneur Garum has not his equal in bleeding the meat, boning it, and cutting it up, carefully, thoughtfully, and lovingly, and steeping it in salted liquors by which it is preserved and embalmed. He is without a rival for seasoning, concentrating, boiling down, skimming, straining, and decanting the pickle. Taste his mild-cured pork, father, and you will lick your fingers: taste his mild-cured pork, Nicolas, and you will have something to say about it."

But in these words, and above all in the voice that uttered them (it grated like a saw), the holy Bishop recognized an evil spirit. He made the sign of the Cross, whereupon the little devil exploded with

298

a horrible noise and a very bad smell, just like a chestnut thrown into the fire without having had its skin split.

And an angel from Heaven appeared, resplendent in light, and said to Nicolas:

"Nicolas, beloved of the Lord, you must know that three little children have been in that salting-tub for seven years; Garum, the innkeeper, cut up these tender infants, and put them in salt and pickle. Arise, Nicolas, and pray that they may come to life again. For, if you intercede for them, O Pontiff, the Lord, who loves you, will restore them to life."

During this speech Modernus entered the room, but he did not see the angel, nor did he hear him, for he was not sufficiently holy to be able to communicate with the heavenly spirits.

The angel further said:

"Nicolas, son of God, lay your hands on the salting-tub, and the three children will be resuscitated."

The blessed Nicolas, filled with horror, pity, zeal, and hope, gave thanks to God, and when the innkeeper reappeared with a jug in either hand, the Saint said to him in a terrible voice:

"Garum, open the salting-tub!"

Whereupon, Garum, overcome by fear, dropped both his jugs.

And the saintly Bishop Nicolas stretched out his hands, and said:

"Children, arise!"

At these words, the lid of the salting-tub was lifted up, and three young boys emerged.

"Children," said the Bishop, "give thanks to God, who through me, has raised you from out the salting-tub."

And turning towards the innkeeper, who was trembling in every limb, he said:

"Cruel man, recognize the three children whom you shamefully put to death. May you loathe your crime, and repent, that God may pardon you!"

The innkeeper, filled with terror, fled into the storm, amidst the thunder and lightning.

CHAPTER II

T. NICOLAS embraced the three children and gently questioned them about the miserable death which they had suffered. They related that Garum, having approached them while they were gleaning in the fields, had lured them into his inn, had made them drink wine, and had cut their throats while they slept.

They still wore the rags in which they had been clothed on the day of their death, and they retained, after their resurrection, a wild and timid air. The sturdiest of the three, Maxime, was the son of a half-witted woman, who followed the soldiers to war, mounted on an ass. One night he fell from the pannier in which she carried him, and was left abandoned by the roadside. From that time forward he had lived solely by theft. The feeblest, Robin, could hardly recall his parents, peasants in the highlands, who being too poor or too avaricious to support him had deserted him in the forest. The third, Sulpice, knew nothing of his birth, but a priest had taught him his alphabet.

301

The storm had ceased; in the buoyant, limpid air the birds were calling loudly to one another. The smiling earth was green. Modernus having fetched the mules, Bishop Nicolas mounted his, and carried Maxime wrapped in his cloak: the deacon took Sulpice and Robin upon his crupper, and they set off toward the city of Trinqueballe.

The road unfolded itself between fields of corn, vineyards, and meadows. As they went along the great Saint Nicolas who already loved the children with all his heart, examined them on subjects suitable to their age, and asked them easy questions such as: "How much is five times five?" or "What is God?" He obtained no satisfactory answers. But, far from shaming them for their ignorance, he thought only of gradually dissipating it by the application of the best pedagogic methods.

"Modernus," he said, "we will teach them firstly the truths necessary for salvation, and secondly the liberal arts, especially music, so that they may sing the praises of the Lord. It will also be expedient to teach them rhetoric, philosophy, and the history of men, plants, and animals. I desire that they shall study, in their habits and their structure, the animals, all of whose organs, in their wonderful perfection, attest the glory of the Creator."

Scarcely had the venerable Pontiff concluded this speech when a peasant woman passed along the road, dragging by the halter an old mare so heavily laden with branches cut with their leaves on that her knees were trembling, and she stumbled at every step.

"Alas," sighed the great St. Nicolas, "here is a poor horse carrying more than its burden. He has unfortunately fallen into the hands of unjust and hard-hearted masters. One should not overload any creature, not even beasts of burden."

At these words the three boys burst out laughing. The Bishop having asked why they laughed so loudly:

"Because——" said Robin.

"That is——" said Sulpice.

"We laughed," said Maxime, "because you mistook a mare for a horse. Can't you see the difference? It is very plain to me. Don't you know anything about animals?"

"I think," said Modernus, "the first thing is to teach these children manners."

At every town, borough, village, hamlet or castle by which he passed, St. Nicolas showed the people the children rescued from the salting-tub, and related the great miracle performed by God, on his intercession; whereupon they were all very joyful, and blessed him. Informed by messengers and travellers of so prodigious an occurrence, the entire population of Trinqueballe came out to meet their pastor, unrolling precious carpets and scattering flowers in his path. The citizens, their eyes wet with tears, gazed at the three victims who had escaped from the salting-tub, and cried: "The Lord be praised!" But the poor children knew no better than to laugh and stick out their tongues; this caused further wonder and compassion, as being a palpable proof of their innocence and misfortune.

The saintly Bishop Nicolas had an orphan niece, Mirande by name, who had just reached her seventh year, and was dearer to him than the light of his eyes. A worthy widow by name Basine was rearing her in piety, good manners, and ignorance of evil. The three miraculously saved children were confided to the care of this lady. She was not lacking in judgment. She quickly saw that Maxime had courage, Robin prudence, and Sulpice the power of reflection. She devoted herself to confirming these good qualities, which, by the corruption common to the whole human race, tended unceasingly to become perverted and distorted; for Robin's cautiousness turned easily into hypocrisy, and mostly hid a greedy covetousness; Maxime was subject to fits of rage, and Sulpice frequently and obstinately expressed false ideas in very important matters. However, they were but mere children who went bird's-nesting, stole the garden fruit, tied cooking-pots to dogs' tails, put ink in the holy water font, and cow-itch in Modernus' bed.

At night, wrapped in white sheets and walking on stilts, they would go into the gardens, and frighten into a swoon the serving-maids belated in their lovers' arms. They would cover the seat which Madame Basine was wont to use with bristling spikes, and when she sat down they would delight in her sufferings, observing the confusion with which she openly applied a heedful and comforting hand to the damaged spot, for she would not for all the world have been lacking in modesty.

In spite of her age and virtues, this lady inspired them with neither love nor fear. Robin called her an old goat, Maxime an old she-ass, and Sulpice, the ass of Balaam. They teased little Mirande in all sorts of ways; they would dirty her pretty clothes by making her fall face downward on the stones. Once they pushed her head right up to the neck into a barrel of treacle. They taught her to sit astride railings, and to climb trees, contrary to the decorum of her sex; they taught her words and manners that smacked of the inn and the salting-tub. Following their example, she called Madame Basine "an old goat," and even, taking the part for the whole, "old goat's rump." But she remained completely innocent. The purity of her soul was unchangeable.

"I am fortunate," said the holy Bishop Nicolas, "in that I rescued these children from the salting-tub, to make them good Christians. They will become faithful servants of God, and their merits will be accounted to me."

Now, by the third year after their resurrection, when they were already tall and well-made, on a day of spring, as they were all playing in the field beside the river, Maxime in a moment of facetiousness, and natural high spirits, threw the Deacon Modernus into the water. Hanging on to the branch of a willow-tree, Modernus called for help. Robin ran up, made as though to draw him out by the hand, took off his ring, and fled.

Meanwhile, Sulpice, sitting motionless on the bank with his arms crossed, said:

"Modernus is making a bad end. I can see six devils, in the form of flittermice, ready to seize his soul as it comes out of his mouth."

When this serious affair was reported to him by Madame Basine and Modernus, the holy Bishop was much afflicted and fell a-sighing.

"These children," he said, "were reared in suffering, by unworthy parents. The excess of their misfortunes has caused the deformity of their characters. We must redress their wrongs by enduring patience, and persevering kindness."

"Monseigneur," answered Modernus, who was chattering with fever in his dressing-gown, and sneezing under his nightcap, for his bath had given him a cold, "it is possible that their wickedness is derived from the wickedness of their parents. But how do you explain, father, the fact that neglect has produced in each of them different and, so to speak, contrary vices, and that the desertion and destitution into which they were thrown before they were put in the salting-tub has made one avaricious, a second violent, and the third a visionary? And in your place, my Lord, I should feel most uneasy about the last."

"Each of these children," answered the Bishop, "has yielded in his weak spot. Ill-treatment has deformed their souls in those portions that offered the least resistance. Let us straighten them out with a thousand precautions, for fear of increasing

307

the evil instead of diminishing it. Mildness, clemency, and forbearance are the only means which should ever be employed for the improvement of men, heretics of course excepted."

"No doubt, Monseigneur, no doubt," said Modernus, sneezing three times. "But you cannot have a good education without chastisement, nor discipline without discipline. I know what I am about. If you do not punish these three little ragamuffins, they will grow up worse than Herod. I assure you I am right."

"Modernus could not be mistaken," said Madame Basine.

The Bishop did not answer. With the widow and the Deacon, he paced the length of a hawthorn hedge, which breathed forth an agreeable fragrance of honey and bitter almonds. In a slight hollow, where the soil received the water from a neighbouring spring, he stopped before a bush, whose twisted, close-packed branches were covered with gleaming, clean-cut leaves and white clusters of flowers.

"Look," he said, "at this leafy, fragrant shrub, this lovely may, this noble thorn-bush, so strong and vigorous. Observe that it is in more abundant leaf, and more glorious with bloom, than all the other thorns in the hedge. But notice also that the pale bark of its branches bears only a few thorns, which are weak and soft and blunt. What is the reason of this? It is because, growing in a rich, moist soil, quiet and secure in the wealth which sustains its life, it has utilized all the juices of the earth to augment its power and its glory, and being too strong to dream of arming against its feeble enemies, it has devoted itself entirely to the joys of its magnificent and delicious fertility. Now come a few steps up this rising path, and look at this other hawthorn, which having with difficulty issued from a dry, stony soil, languishes, deficient in both wood and leaves, and has had no other thought during its hard life than to defend itself against the innumerable enemies that threaten the weak. It is nothing but a bundle of thorns. It has employed the little sap which it received in fashioning innumerable spears, broad at the base, hard and sharp, which but ill restore confidence to its apprehensive weakness. It has nothing left over for fruitful and fragrant blossom. My friends, we are like the hawthorns. The care given to our childhood makes us better. Too harsh an upbringing hardens us."

CHAPTER III

HEN Maxime was approaching his seventeenth year he filled the holy Bishop Nicolas with grief and the diocese with scandal by forming and training a company of rogues of his own age, with a view of kidnapping the girls of a village called Grosses-Nates, situated at a distance of four leagues from Trinqueballe. The expedition was marvellously successful. The ravishers entered the village by night, clasping to their bosoms the dishevelled virgins, who vainly uplifted to heaven their burning eyes and imploring hands. But when the fathers, brothers, and betrothed of these ravished maidens sought them out, they refused to return to the place of their birth, alleging that they felt too deeply shamed, and preferred to hide their dishonour in the arms that had caused it. Maxime, who, for his share, had taken the three most beautiful, was living in their company in a little manor dependent upon the episcopal See. In the absence of their ravisher, the Deacon Modernus arrived, by order of the Bishop, to knock at their door, answering that he came to set them free.

They refused to open; and when he represented to them the abomination of their lives they dropped upon his head a crockful of dish-water, with the crock, by which his skull was fractured.

Armed with a gentle severity, the holy Bishop reproached Maxime for this violence and disorder:

"Alas," he said, "did I draw you from out of the salting-box to the ruin of the virgins of Vervignole?"

And he reproached him with the magnitude of his offence. But Maxime shrugged his shoulders, and turned his back, without making any reply.

At that moment King Berlu, in the fourteenth year of his reign, was assembling a powerful army to fight the Mambournians, the determined enemies of his kingdom, who, having entered Vervignole, were ravaging and depopulating the richest provinces of that great country.

Maxime left Trinqueballe without saying good-bye to a soul. When he was some leagues distant from the town, seeing in a field a mare of moderate quality, except that she was blind in one eye and lame, he jumped on her back and galloped off. On the following morning, accidentally meeting a farm lad who was taking a great plough horse to water, he immediately dismounted, bestrode the great horse, and ordered the lad to mount the blind mare, and to follow him, saying that he would take him for his squire should he prove satisfactory. Thus equipped Maxime presented himself to King Berlu, who accepted his services. He became in a very short time one of Vervignole's greatest captains.

Meanwhile, Sulpice was giving the holy Bishop cause for perhaps more cruel, and certainly more momentous, uneasiness; for if Maxime sinned grievously, he sinned without malice, and offending God without thought, and, so to speak, unknowingly. But Sulpice set himself to do evil with a greater and more unusual malignity. Being destined from early youth for the Church he assiduously studied letters, both sacred and profane; but his soul was a corrupted vessel, wherein Truth was turned into Error. He sinned in spirit; he erred in matters of faith with surprising precocity. At an age when people have as yet no ideas at all, he overflowed with wrong ones. A thought occurred to him which was doubtless suggested by the devil. In a field belonging to the Bishop he gathered a multitude of boys and girls of his own age and, climbing into a tree, he exhorted them to leave their fathers and mothers to follow Jesus Christ, and to go in parties through the country-side, burning priories and presbyteries in order to lead the Church back into evangelical poverty. This youthful mob, led away by emotion, followed the sinner along the roads of Vervignole, singing canticles, burning barns, pillaging chapels, and devastating the ecclesiastical lands. Many of these crazy creatures perished of fatigue, hunger, and cold, or were killed by villagers. The episcopal palace re-echoed with the complaints of the priest-hood and the lamentations of mothers.

The pious Bishop Nicolas sent for the originator of these disorders. With extreme mildness, and infinite sadness, he reproached him for having mis-used the Word for the misleading of souls, and reminded him that God had not picked him out of the salting-tub in order that he should attack the property of our Holy Mother, the Church.

"Consider, my son," he said, "the greatness of your offence. You appear before your pastor charged with turmoil, sedition, and murder."

But young Sulpice, maintaining a horrid calm, answered with a voice full of assurance, that he had not sinned, neither had he offended God; but, on the contrary, he had acted in accordance with the bidding of Heaven, for the good of the Church. And he professed before the dismayed Bishop the false doctrines of the Manicheans, the Arians, the Nestorians, the Sabellians, the Vaudois, the Albigenses, and the Bégards. So eager was he to embrace these monstrous errors that he did not see how they contradicted one another, and were mutually devoured in the bosom that cherished and revived them.

The pious Bishop endeavoured to lead Sulpice back into the right path, but he failed to overcome the unhappy lad's obstinacy.

Having dismissed him, he knelt and prayed.

"I thank thee, O Lord, for having sent me this young man, as a whetstone on which to sharpen my patience and my charity."

While two of the children he had rescued from the salting-tub were causing him so much pain, St. Nicolas was obtaining some consolation from the third. Robin showed himself neither violent in his actions nor arrogant in his thoughts. He had not the sturdy, ruddy appearance of Maxime; nor the grave, audacious manner of Sulpice. Small, thin, yellow, lined, and shrunken, of humble, obsequious and reverential bearing, he devoted himself to assisting the Bishop and clergy, helping the clerks to keep the accounts of the episcopal revenues, and making complicated calculations with the assistance of balls threaded on rods; he even multiplied and divided numbers in his head, without the use of slate or pencil, with a rapidity and accuracy that would have been admired even in a past master of money and finance. For him it was a pleasure to keep the books of the Deacon Modernus, who, growing old, used to muddle the figures and fall asleep at his desk. To oblige the Bishop, and obtain money for him, he spared neither trouble nor fatigue. From the Lombards, he learnt how to calculate both the simple and compound interest on a sum of money for a day, week, month, or year; he feared not to visit the filthy Jews in the black lanes of the Ghetto, in order to learn, by mingling with them, the standard of metals, the price of precious stones, and the art of clipping coin. Ultimately, with a little store which he had accumulated by marvellous industry in Vervignole, in Mondousiana, and even in Mambournia, he attended the fairs, tournaments, pardons, and jubilees, to which people of all conditions flocked from all parts of Christendom: peasants, burghers, clerics, and *seigneurs;* there he changed their money, and every time he returned a little richer than he had departed. Robin did not spend the money he had made, but brought it to the Bishop.

St. Nicolas was extremely hospitable, and very liberal in almsgiving. He spent all his property and that of the Church in making gifts to pilgrims and assisting the unfortunate. Thus he continually found himself short of money; and he was much obliged to Robin for the skill and energy with which the young treasurer obtained the sums which he required. The condition of penury in which the holy Bishop had placed himself owing to his magnificence and liberality was greatly aggravated by the condition of the times. The war which was ravaging Vervignole also ruined the Church in Trinqueballe. The soldiery who were fighting in the country-side about the town pillaged the farms, levied contributions on the peasantry, drove out the religious orders, and burned the castles and abbeys.

The clergy and the faithful could no longer contribute to the expenses of their creed, and thousands of peasants, fleeing from the free-booters, came daily to beg their bread at the door of the episcopal palace. For their sakes, the good St. Nicolas felt the poverty which he had never felt for his own. Fortunately, Robin was always ready to lend him money, which the holy pontiff naturally agreed to return in more prosperous times.

Alas, the war was now raging throughout the kingdom, from north to south, from east to west, attended by its two inseparable companions, famine and pestilence. The peasantry turned robbers, and the monks followed the armies. The inhabitants of Trinqueballe, having neither wood for firing, nor bread to eat, died like flies at the approach of winter. Wolves entered the outlying parts of the town, devouring little children. At this sad juncture, Robin came to inform the Bishop that not only was he unable to provide any further sum of money, however small, but that being unable to obtain anything from his debtors, and being pressed by his creditors, he had been compelled to hand over all his assets to the Jews.

He brought this distressing news to his benefactor with the obsequious politeness which was usual to him; but he appeared a great deal less afflicted than he might have been in this grievous extremity. As a matter of fact, he was hard put to it to conceal, under a long face, his joyous feelings and his lively satisfaction. The parchment of his dry, humble, yellow eyelids ill concealed the light of joy which shone from his sharp eyes.

Sadly stricken, St. Nicolas remained quiet and serene under the blow.

"God will soon re-establish our declining affairs," he said. "He will not permit the house which He has built to be overthrown."

"That is true," said Modernus, "but you may be sure that Robin, whom you drew out of the salting-tub, has made an arrangement with the Lombards of Pont-Vieux and the Jews of the Ghetto to despoil you, and that he is retaining the lion's share of the plunder."

Modernus spoke the truth. Robin had lost no money. He was richer than ever, and had just been appointed treasurer to the King.

CHAPTER IV

T this time Mirande was nearing the close of her seventeenth year. She was beautiful, and well grown. An air of purity, innocence, and artlessness hung round her like a veil. The length of her eyelashes, which barred her blue eyes, and the childlike smallness of her mouth, gave the impression that evil could never find means to enter into her. Her ears were so tiny, so fine, so finished and so delicate, that the least modest of men could never have dared to breathe into them any but the most innocent of speeches. In the whole of Vervignole no virgin inspired so much respect, and none had greater need to do so, for she was marvellously simple, credulous, and defenceless.

The pious Bishop Nicolas, her uncle, cherished her more dearly every day, and was more deeply attached to her than one should be to any of God's creatures. He loved her, undoubtedly, in God; but he also loved her for herself; he took great delight in her, and he loved to love her; it was his only weakness. The Saints themselves are not

319

always able to cut through all the ties of the flesh. St. Nicolas loved his niece, with a pure love, but not without gratification of the senses. On the day following that on which he had learned of Robin's bankruptcy, he went to see Mirande in order to hold pious converse with her, as was his duty, for he stood in the place of a father to her, and had taken charge of her education.

She lived in the upper town, near the Cathedral in a house called "The House of the Musicians," because there were to be seen on its front men and animals playing on divers instruments. There were, notably, an ass playing a flute, and a philosopher, recognizable by his long beard and ink-horn, clashing cymbals. Every one explained these figures according to his fancy. It was the finest dwelling-house in the town.

The Bishop found his niece crouching on the floor, with dishevelled hair, her eyes glittering with tears, by the side of an empty, open coffer, in a room full of confusion.

He inquired of her the reason of this affliction, and of the disorder that prevailed around her. Turning upon him her despairing gaze, she told him with a thousand sighs that Robin, the Robin who had escaped from the salting-tub, the darling Robin, having many a time told her that if she ever wanted a dress, an ornament or a jewel, he would gladly lend her the money wherewith to buy it, she had frequently had recourse to his kindness, which appeared inexhaustible; but that very morning a Jew called Seligmann had come to her with four sheriff's officers, had presented the notes, signed by herself, which she had given Robin, and as she had not the money to pay them he had taken away all the clothes, head-dresses and jewels which she possessed.

"He has taken," she sobbed, "my bodices and petticoats of velvet, brocade and lace; my diamonds, my emeralds, my sapphires, my jacinths, my amethysts, my rubies, my garnets, and my turquoises; he has taken my great diamond cross, with angels' heads in enamel, my large necklace, consisting of two table diamonds, three cabochons, and six knots each of four pearls; he has taken my great collar of thirteen table diamonds, and twenty hanging pearls!"

And without saying more she wept bitterly into her handkerchief.

"My daughter," answered the saintly Bishop, "a Christian virgin is sufficiently adorned when she wears modesty for a necklace, and chastity for a

girdle. None the less, as the scion of a most noble
and most illustrious family it was right that you
should wear diamonds and pearls. Your jewels
were the treasury of the poor, and I deplore the
fact that they should have been snatched from you."

He assured her that she would certainly recover
them, either in this world or the next; he said
everything possible to assuage her regret, and soothe
her sorrow, and he comforted her. For she had a
tender soul, which longed for consolation. But he
himself left her full of affliction.

On the following day, as he was about to celebrate
Mass in the cathedral, the holy Bishop saw coming
towards him, in the sacristy, the three Jews,
Seligmann, Issachar, and Meyer, who, wearing
green hats and fillets upon their shoulders, very
humbly presented him the notes which Robin had
made over to them. As the venerable pontiff could
not pay them, they called up twenty porters, with
baskets, sacks, picklocks, carts, cords, and ladders,
and commenced to pick the locks of the wardrobes,
coffers, and tabernacles. The holy man cast on
them a look which would have destroyed three
Christians. He threatened them with the penalties
of sacrilege, both in this world and the next, he
pointed out that their mere presence in the house

of the God, whom they had crucified, called down
the fire of heaven upon their heads.   They listened
with the calm of people for whom anathema, rep-
robation, malediction, and execration were their
daily bread.   He then prayed to them, besought
them, and promised to pay as soon as he could,
twofold, threefold, tenfold, a hundredfold, the
debt which they had acquired.   They excused
themselves politely for being unable to postpone
the little transaction.   The Bishop threatened to
sound the tocsin, to rouse against them the people
who would kill them like dogs for profaning, violating, and stealing the miraculous images and holy
relics.   They smilingly pointed to the sheriff's
officers, who were guarding them.   They were
protected by King Berlu, for they lent him money.

At this sight the holy Bishop, recognizing that
resistance would be rebellion, and remembering
Him who replaced the ear of Malchus, remained
inert and speechless, and bitter tears dropped from
his eyes.   Seligmann, Issachar, and Meyer took
away the golden shrines enriched with precious
stones, enamels and cabochons, the reliquaries in
the form of chalices, lanterns, naves, and towers,
the portable altars of alabaster encased in gold and
silver, the coffers enamelled by the skilful craftsmen

of Limoges and the Rhine, the altar-crosses, the
Gospels bound in carved ivory and antique cameos,
the desks ornamented with festoons of trailing
vines, the consular registers, the pyxes, the can-
delabra and candlesticks, the lamp, of which they
blew out the sacred flame, and spilt the blessed oil
on the tiles, the chandeliers like enormous crowns,
the chaplets with beads of pearl and amber, the
eucharistic doves, the ciboria, the chalices, the
patens, the kisses of peace, incense boxes and flagons, the innumerable ex-votos—hands, arms, legs,
eyes, mouths, and hearts, all of silver—the nose of
King Sidoc, the breast of Queen Blandine, and the
head in solid gold of Saint Cromadaire, the first
apostle of Vervignole, and the blessed patron of
Trinqueballe. They even carried off the miraculous image of St. Gibbosine, whom the people of
Vervignole had never invoked in vain in time of pestilence, famine, or war. This very ancient and venerable image was made of leaves of beaten gold
nailed upon a core of cedar-wood, and was covered
with precious stones of the bigness of ducks' eggs,
which emitted fiery rays of red, blue, yellow and
violet and white. For the past three hundred
years her enamelled eyes, wide open in her golden
face, had compelled such respect from the inhabit-

ants of Trinqueballe that they saw her in their dreams, splendid and terrible, threatening them with the direst penalties if they failed to supply her with sufficient quantities of virgin wax and crown-pieces. St. Gibbosine groaned, trembled, and tottered on her pedestal, and allowed herself to be carried away without resistance, out of the basilica to which, from time immemorial, she had drawn innumerable pilgrims.

After the departure of these sacrilegious thieves the holy Bishop Nicolas ascended the steps of the despoiled altar, and consecrated the blood of our Lord in an old silver chalice, of German origin, thin and deeply dented. He prayed for the afflicted, and in particular for Robin, whom, by the will of God, he had rescued from the salting-box.

CHAPTER V

SHORTLY after this, King Berlu defeated the Mambournians in a great battle. He was, at first, unaware of the fact, for armed conflicts always present a great confusion, and during the last two hundred years the Vervignolians had lost the habit of victory. But the precipitate and disordered flight of the Mambournians informed him of his advantage. Instead of fighting a rearguard action he pursued the enemy, and regained half his kingdom. The victorious army entered the city of Trinqueballe, all beflagged and beflowered in its honour, and in that illustrious capital of Vervignole it committed a great number of rapes, thefts, murders, and other cruelties, burnt several houses, sacked the churches, and took from the cathedral all that the Jews had left there, which, truth to tell, was not much.

Maxime, who having become a knight and commander of eighty lances, had largely contributed to the victory, was one of the first to enter the city, and repaired straightway to the House of the Musicians, where dwelt the beautiful Mirande, whom he had not seen since his departure for the war. He found her in her bower, plying her distaff, and fell upon her with such impetuosity that the young lady lost her innocence without, so to speak, realizing that she had done so. And when, having recovered from her surprise, she exclaimed: "Is it you, Seigneur Maxime? What are you doing here?" and was preparing as in duty bound to resist her aggressor, he was quietly walking down the street, readjusting his armour and ogling the girls.

Possibly she would have entirely overlooked this offence, had it not been that some time later she found that she was about to become a mother. Captain Maxime was then fighting in Mambournia. All the town knew her shame: she confided it to the great St. Nicolas, who, on learning this astonishing news, lifted his eyes to heaven, and said:

"Lord, did you rescue this man from the salting-tub only as a ravening wolf to devour my sheep? Your wisdom is adorable; but your ways are dark, and your designs mysterious."

And in that same year, on the Sunday of Mid-Lent, Sulpice threw himself at the feet of the holy Bishop, saying:

"From my earliest youth, my keenest wish has been to consecrate myself to the Lord. Allow me, father, to embrace the monastic state, and to make my profession in the monastery of the mendicant friars of Trinqueballe."

"My son," answered the good St. Nicolas, "there is no worthier condition than that of the monk. Happy is he who in the shade of the cloister takes shelter from the tempests of the age. But of what avail to flee the storm if the storm is within one-self? Of what avail to affect an outward show of humility, if one's bosom contains a heart full of pride? What shall you profit by donning the livery of obedience if your soul be in revolt? I have seen you, my son, fall into more errors than Sabellius, Arius, Nestorius, Eutyches, Manes, Pelagius, and Pachosius combined, and revive, before your twentieth year, twelve centuries of peculiar opinions. It is true that you have not been very obstinate in any of them, but your successive recantations appear to betray less submission to our Holy Mother the Church than eagerness to rush from one error to another, to leap from Manicheeism to Sabellianism, and from the crime of the Albigenses to the ignominies of the Vaudois."

Sulpice listened to this discourse with a contrite heart, a simplicity of mind and submissiveness, that drew tears from the great St. Nicolas.

"I deplore, repudiate, condemn, reprove, detest, execrate, and abominate my errors, past, present, and future." he said. "I submit myself to the Church fully and entirely, totally and generally, purely and simply; and I have no belief but her belief, no faith but her faith, no knowledge but her knowledge: I neither see, hear, nor feel, save only through her. She might tell me that the fly which has but now settled on the nose of the Deacon Modernus was a camel, and I should incontinently, without dispute, contest, murmur, resistance, hesitation or doubt, believe, declare, proclaim, and confess, under torture and unto death, that it was a camel that settled on the nose of the Deacon Modernus. For the Church is the Fountain of Truth, and I am nought by myself but a vile receptacle of Error."

"Take care, my father," said Modernus. "Sulpice is capable of overdoing submission to the Church even to the point of Heresy. Do you not see that he submits with frenzy, in transports and swooning? Is wallowing in submission a good way of submitting? He is annihilating himself; he is committing suicide."

But the Bishop reprimanded his deacon for holding such ideas, which were contrary to charity, and sent the postulant to the noviciate of the mendicant friars of Trinqueballe.

Alas, at the end of a year those priests, till then so quiet and humble, were torn by frightful schisms, plunged into a thousand errors against the Catholic truth, their days filled with disorder, and their souls with sedition! Sulpice inspired the brothers with this poison. He sustained against his superiors that there was no longer any true Pope, since miracles no longer accompanied the elections of the Sovereign Pontiffs; nor, rightly speaking, any Church, since Christians had ceased to live the life of the apostles and the first of the faithful; that there was no purgatory; that it was not necessary to confess to a priest if one confessed to God; that men do wrong in making use of moneys of gold and silver, for they should share in common the fruits of the earth. These abominable maxims, which he forcibly sustained, were combated by some, and adopted by others, causing horrible scandals. A little later Sulpice taught the doctrine of perfect purity, which nothing can soil, and the good brothers' monastery became like a cage of monkeys. This pestilence did not remain confined within the walls of a monastery. Sulpice went preaching through the city; his eloquence, the internal fire by which he was consumed, the simplicity of his life, and his unshakable courage touched all hearts.

On hearing the voice of the reformer, the ancient city, evangelized by St. Cromadaire, and enlightened by St. Gibbosine, fell into disorder and dissolution; every sort of extravagance and impiety was committed there, by day and by night. In vain did the great St. Nicolas warn his flock by exhortations, threats, and fulminations. The evil increased unchecked, and it was sad to see the contagion spreading itself among the well-to-do townsfolk, the lords, and the clergy, as much as and more than among the poor artisans and the small tradesfolk.

One day when the man of God was lamenting the deplorable state of the church of Vervignole in the cloister of the cathedral, his meditations were disturbed by strange shrieks, and he saw a woman, stark naked, walking on all fours, with a peacock's feather for a tail. As she came nearer, she barked, sniffed, and licked the ground. Her fair head was covered with mud, and her whole body was a mass of filth. In this unhappy creature the holy Bishop Nicolas recognized his niece Mirande.

"What do you there, my daughter?" he cried. "Why are you naked, and wherefore do you walk on your hands and knees? Have you no shame?"

"No, uncle, I am not ashamed," sweetly replied Mirande. "I should, on the contrary, be ashamed of any other gesture, or method of progression. If one wishes to please God, it is thus that one should behave. The holy Brother Sulpice taught me to conduct myself thus, in order to resemble the beasts, who are nearer to God than is Man, in that they have not sinned. So long as I am in the state in which you see me, there will be no danger of my sinning. I have come, uncle, to beg you in all love and charity to do likewise; for unless you do you cannot be saved. Remove, I beg, your clothes, and adopt the posture of the animals, in whom God joyfully sees His image which has not been distorted by sin. I give you this advice by order of the holy brother Sulpice, and consequently by order of God Himself, for the holy brother is in the Lord's secrets. Strip yourself naked, uncle, and come with me, so that we may show ourselves to the people for their edification."

"Can I believe my eyes and ears?" gasped the holy Bishop, whose voice was stifled by sobs. "I had a niece blooming in beauty, virtue, and piety; the three children whom I rescued from the salting-tub have reduced her to the miserable condition in which I now see her. The first has despoiled

332

her of all her property, an abundant source of alms, and the patrimony of the poor; the second has robbed her of her honour, and the third has turned her into a heretic."

He threw himself on the flagstones, embracing his niece, begging her to renounce so evil a way of life, and adjuring her to reclothe herself, and walk on her feet like a human being, ransomed by the blood of Jesus Christ.

But she replied only by sharp yelps and lamentable shrieks.

Before long the town of Trinqueballe was filled with naked men and women, walking on all fours and barking; they called themselves the Edenites, and their ambition was to lead back the world to the times of perfect innocence, before the unfortunate creation of Adam and Eve.

The Reverend Father Gilles Caquerole, a Dominican, inquisitor of the faith in the city, university, and ecclesiastical province of Trinqueballe, became uneasy concerning this novelty, and proceeded to look into it minutely. In the most urgent fashion, by letters under his seal, he invited the Bishop Nicolas, in co-operation with himself, to arrest, imprison, interrogate, and sentence these enemies of

God, and especially their principal leaders, the Franciscan monk, Sulpice, and a dissolute woman named Mirande. The great St. Nicolas burned with an ardent zeal for the unity of the Church and the destruction of heresy, but he dearly loved his niece. He hid her in the episcopal palace, and refused to hand her over to the inquisitor Caquerole, who denounced him to the Pope as an abettor of disorder and the propagator of a new and very detestable heresy. The Pope enjoined Nicolas to no longer withhold the guilty one from her legitimate judges. Nicolas eluded the injunction, protested his obedience, and did not obey. The Pope fulminated against him in the Bull *Maleficus pastor,* in which the venerable pontiff was accused of being a disobedient member of the Church, a heretic, or one smelling of heresy, a keeper of concubines, a committer of incest, a corrupter of the people, an old woman and a meddling old fool, and was passionately admonished.

In this way the Bishop did himself a great deal of harm without any benefit to his beloved niece. King Berlu, having been threatened with excommunication if he did not lend his secular arm to the Church in pursuit of the Edenites, sent some men-at-arms to the episcopal palace of Trinqueballe. They tore Mirande from her asylum: she was brought before the inquisitor Caquerole, thrown into a deep dungeon, and fed upon bread which the jailers' dogs had refused; but what afflicted her most was that she was forcibly compelled to don an old frock and a hood, and that she could no longer be certain of not sinning.

The monk Sulpice escaped the investigations of the Holy Office and succeeded in reaching Mambournia, and found an asylum in a monastery of that kingdom, where he established new sects even more pernicious than the previous one.

Nevertheless, heresy, fortified by persecution, and exulting in danger, now spread its ravages over the whole of Vervignole. All over the kingdom there were seen in the fields thousands of naked men and women, nibbling the grass, bleating, lowing, roaring, neighing, and contending at night with sheep, cattle, and horses for the use of stable and manger. The inquisitor informed the Holy Father of these horrible scandals, and warned him that so long as the Protector of the Edenites, the odious Nicolas, remained seated on the throne of St. Cromadaire, the evil could only continue to increase. Conformably with this advice the Pope hurled against the Bishop, like a thunderbolt, the Bull *Deterrima quondam,* by which he deprived him of all his ecclesiastical functions, and cut him off from the communion of the faithful.

CHAPTER VI

RUSHED by the Vicar of Jesus Christ, steeped in bitterness, overwhelmed by affliction, the holy Nicolas stepped down without regret from his illustrious seat, and departed, no more to return thither, from the city of Trinqueballe, which for thirty years had witnessed his pontifical virtues and apostolic labours. There is in western Vervignole a lofty mountain, whose peaks are covered with perpetual snow; from its flanks there descend, in spring, the foaming sonorous cascades that fill the valley torrents with a water as blue as the sky. There, in a region where grow the larch, the arbutus, and the hazel, some hermits supported themselves on berries and milk. This mountain is called that of the Saviour. It was here that St. Nicolas resolved to take refuge, and, far from the world, to weep for his sins and those of man.

As he was climbing the mountain in search of some wild spot where he might establish his habitation, having emerged above the clouds which are almost always gathered about the flanks of the peak, he saw upon the threshold of a hut an old man sharing his bread with a tame hind. His hair fell over his forehead, and nothing could be perceived of his face but the tip of his nose and a long white beard.

The holy Nicolas greeted him with these words:

"Peace be with you, brother."

"It delights to dwell upon this mountain," answered the recluse.

"I also," replied the holy Nicolas, "have come hither to end, in calm, days which have been disturbed by the tumult of the times and the malignity of men."

As he was speaking in this wise, the hermit gazed at him attentively.

"Are you not," he said at length, "the Bishop of Trinqueballe, that Nicolas whose works and virtues are extolled by men?"

When, by a sign, the holy pontiff admitted that he was that man, the hermit threw himself at his feet.

"Monseigneur, to you I owe the saving of my soul, if, as I hope, my soul is saved."

Nicolas raised him with kindness, and asked him:

THE MIRACLE OF ST. NICOLAS

"My brother, how have I had the happiness to work for your salvation?"

"Twenty years ago," replied the recluse, "when I was an innkeeper at the edge of a wood, on a deserted road, I saw one day, in a field, three little children gleaning. I lured them to my house, gave them wine to drink, cut their throats in their sleep, cut them up into small pieces, and salted them. On seeing them emerge from the salting-tub I was frozen with terror; owing to your exhortations my heart melted; I experienced a salutary repentance, and, fleeing from men, I came to this mountain, where I consecrated my days to God. He bestowed His peace upon me."

"What," cried the holy Bishop, "you are that cruel Garum, guilty of so heinous a crime! I praise God that he has accorded you a peaceful heart, after the horrible murder of three children, whom you put in the salting-tub like pigs; but as for me, alas! for having drawn them out of it my life has been filled with tribulations, my soul steeped in bitterness, and my Bishopric laid wholly desolate. I have been deposed, excommunicated by the common Father of the Faithful. Why have I been so cruelly punished for what I did?"

"Let us worship God," said Garum, "and let us not ask His motives."

The great St. Nicolas, with his own hands, built a hut near that of Garum, and there, in prayer and penitence, he ended his days.

GESTAS

" 'Gestas,' dixt li Signor, 'entrez en Paradis.' "

"Gestas, dans nos anciens mystères, c'est le nom du larron crucifié à la droite de Jésus-Christ" (AugustinThierry, *la Rédemption de Larmor*).[1]

OLKS say that we have amongst us at this very day a sad rogue named Gestas, who writes the sweetest songs in the world. It was written on his flat-featured face that he would be a sinner after the flesh, and towards evening evil exultation shines in his green eyes. He is no longer young. The protuberances on his skull have taken on the lustre of copper; the long hair falling about his neck has taken a greenish tinge. Nevertheless he is ingenuous, and has kept fast hold on the naive faith of his childhood. When he is not in hospital he occupies a little room in some squalid hotel between the Panthéon and the Jardin des Plantes. There, in the old impoverished quarter, every stone is familiar with his tread, the gloomy byways are

---

[1] " 'Gestas,' said the Lord, 'enter into Paradise.' "
"Gestas, in our ancient mystery plays, was the name of the thief who was crucified on the right hand of Jesus Christ" (Augustin Thierry, *The Redemption of Larmor*).

341

tolerant of him, and one of these narrow lanes is entirely after his own heart; for, lined though it is with dram shops and boosing kens, it boasts on the corner of one of the houses an image of the Virgin in a blue niche behind bars. Of an evening he progresses from café to café, and at station after station, with pious orderliness, he takes his beer or his spirits: the exacting duties of the devotee of debauchery call for method and regularity. The night is far gone when, without knowing how, he once more reaches his den, and by a daily miracle discovers the sacking bed, upon which he falls fully dressed. There with clenched fists he sleeps the sleep of the vagabond and the child. But that sleep is brief.

As soon as dawn casts its pale radiance upon the window, and between the curtains darts its luminous shafts into the attic, Gestas opens his eyes, rises, shakes himself like an ownerless dog awakened by a kick, hurries down the long, spiral staircase, and once more sets his eyes delightedly on the street, the kind street which is so indulgent to the vices of the lowly and the poor. His eyelids wink at the clear light of the early morning; the nostrils, which recall Silenus, inhale the clean air. Vigorous and upright, one leg stiffened by rheumatism of long standing, he goes on his way leaning on his dog-wood stick, the

ferrule of which he has worn out with twenty years
of wandering. But in his nocturnal adventures he
has never lost either his pipe or his stick. And at the
beginning of the day his appearance is that of a man
perfectly simple and perfectly happy. Which is
what he actually is. His greatest joy in life, which
he buys at the sacrifice of sleep, is to go from bar to
bar in the morning drinking white wine with the
workmen. It is an innocent sort of tippling: the
transparent wine, in the pale light of early morning,
amongst the white blouses of the masons; there you
have a symphony in whites which enchants this soul,
of which vice has not yet subdued the candour.

Now one spring morning when he had sauntered
in this fashion from his lodging as far as *The Little
Moor,* Gestas had the satisfaction of seeing the
door, over which appeared a Saracen's head in cast
iron, gay with paint, thrown open as he came up, and
so he reached the tin counter in the company of
friends with whom he had no acquaintance: a gang
of workmen from La Creuse, who clinked their
glasses, talked of their own part of the country, and
indulged in boasting after the manner of the twelve
peers of Charlemagne. They drank a glass and
cracked a crust; when one of them thought of a good
thing he laughed very loudly at it, and so that his
comrades might understand it the better gave them

a good thump or two on the back with his fist. The older men, however, dispatched their potations slowly and silently. When these had all departed to their work, Gestas, the last left, quitted *The Little Moor* and made his way to *The Juicy Quince*, with the lance-headed railings of which he was familiar. Here, again, in excellent company, he had a drink, and even offered a glass to two mistrustful but mild guardians of the peace. After this he visited a third bar, the ancient wrought-iron sign of which represents two little men staggering under an enormous bunch of grapes, and there he was served by the lovely Madame Trubert, famous all the quarter through for her prudence, her strength, and her jollity. Then as he neared the fortifications he had yet another drink at the distillery where, in the shadow, the gleaming copper taps of the barrels attract the eye; and still another at the general shop where the green shutters were still fast closed between the two boxes of laurels; after which he returned to the most populous districts and ordered *vermouth* and the brandy known as marc in various cafés. Eight o'clock struck. He walked very erect, with a steady, rigid, solemn gait; he was astonished when women, running to buy provisions, with bare head and their hair twisted in a knot low on the neck, ran against him with their heavy baskets, or

when he came into collision with some small girl
grasping an enormous loaf in her arms. Still, at
times, if he crossed the road the milkman's cart, with
its clinking, rattling tin cans, would pull up so close
to him that he could feel the horse's warm breath
on his cheek. But he continued his way unhasting
and careless of the imprecations of the rustic milk-
vendor. His gait, secure of support from his dog-
wood stick, was calm and haughty. But internally
the old man was staggering. Nothing was left of
his early morning gaiety. The lark, whose joyous
trills had thrilled through him with his earliest sips
of the pale-hued wine, had sped away at a single
flight, and now his soul was a murky rookery, where
crows croaked hoarsely upon inky trees. He was
mortally sad. A great disgust of himself welled up
in his heart. The voice of his repentance, his shame,
cried out in him: "Hog, hog! What a hog you
are!" And he marvelled at that clear, angry voice,
that superb angel's voice, which spoke mysteriously
within himself, repeating: "Hog! hog! What a
hog you are!" A yearning desire for innocence and
purity woke in him. He wept; great tears fell down
on his goat-like beard. He wept over himself.
Obedient to the words of his Master, who said,
"Weep for yourselves and for your children, O
daughters of Jerusalem," he shed the bitter dew

from his downcast eyes upon the body he had delivered up to the seven deadly sins, and upon the
obscene fancies born of his drunkenness.   The faith
of his childhood revived in him, and spread out fresh
vigorous tendrils.   From his lips pathetic prayers
flowed forth.   He said under his breath: "O God,
grant me to become once more even as the little child
which once was I!"   At the moment he offered up
this simple petition he realized that he was standing
under a church porch.

It was an old church, once white and comely beneath its lacework of stone, which time and the hand
of man had marred.   Now it had become as black
as the Shulamite, and its beauty could only appeal to
the hearts of poets; it was a church "little and poor
and old," like the mother of François Villon, who
perchance in her day came to kneel in its precincts,
and saw on the walls, nowadays whitewashed, that
painted paradise, the harps of which she believed she
could hear, and that inferno where the damned suffered fiery torment, which caused the worthy soul to
be much afraid.   Gestas entered into the House of
God.   He saw no one within, not even any one to
offer him holy water, not even a poor woman like the
mother of François Villon.   Ranged in seemly order
in the nave, a congregation of chairs alone bore wit-

ness to the faith of the parishioners, and seemed to sustain public worship.

In the cool, moist shade afforded by the vaulting Gestas turned to his right towards the aisle where, close to the porch, before a statue of the Virgin, a pyramidal frame of iron displayed its pointed teeth, on which, however, not a single taper now burned. Then as he gazed on the image, white, pink, and blue in colour, smiling from the midst of little gold and silver hearts hung up as votive offerings, he bent his stiff old legs, wept tears like St. Peter, and sobbed out tender, disconnected words: "Holy Virgin, Mother, Mary, Mary, your child, your child, Mother!" But very speedily he rose up again, took several rapid steps, and stopped in front of a confessional. Framed of oak, darkened by the passage of time, oiled as are the beams of an olive press, this confessional had the irreproachable, homely, intimate appearance of an old linen cupboard. On its panels religious symbols carved in shell-like lozenges and rusticated work called up the memory of the townswomen of the olden time, who had come hither to bow their caps with lofty erections of lace and lave their housewifely souls in this type of the cleansing piscina. Where they had set their knees Gestas set his, and with lips close up to the wooden

347

grating called in a hushed voice: "Father! father!"
As no one answered his call he knocked very gently
with his finger on the wicket.

"Father! father!"

He wiped his eyes so as to see better through the
holes in the grating, and thought he could make out
through the dimness the white surplice of a priest.

He repeated—

"Father! father! pray listen to me. I am in need
of confession, I must cleanse my soul; it is black and
dirty; it disgusts me; it turns my stomach. Quick,
father, the bath of repentance, the bath of pardon,
the bath of Jesus. At the thought of my impurities
my heart comes into my mouth, and I am ready to
spew with disgust at my uncleanness. The bath,
the bath of cleansing!"

Then he waited. Now fancying he perceived a
hand, which made a sign to him from the depths of
the confessional, now failing to discover in the alcove
anything more than an empty seat, a long time
passed. He remained motionless, his knees glued
to the wooden step, his gaze intent on the wicket,
whence he awaited the outpouring of pardon, peace,
refreshment, health, innocence, reconciliation with
God and himself, heavenly joy, submission to the
divine love, the sovereign good. At intervals he
murmured tender supplications—

348

"Monsieur le curé, father, monsieur le curé! I thirst! give me to drink, give me that which is yours to give, the water of innocence, a white robe, and wings for my poor soul. Give me penitence and pardon!"

Receiving no reply, he knocked still harder at the grating, and said aloud—

"Confession, I beg of you!"

At last he lost patience, and rising, showered heavy blows with his dog-wood stick on the walls of the confessional, shouting—

"Ho, there, monsieur le curé! Ho, there, monsieur le vicaire!"

And in proportion as he raised his voice he knocked more loudly. The blows fell furiously on the confessional, causing clouds of dust to arise from it, and only evoking in reply to his violence the vibration of its worm-eaten old planks.

The verger, who was sweeping out the sacristy, ran forward with his sleeves turned up on hearing the noise. When he saw the man with the stick he stopped short for a moment, and then advanced towards him with the cautious reserve common to the officials who have grown white in the service of this lowliest of police. Arrived within earshot he demanded—

"What is it you want?"

349

"I want to confess."

"Folks don't come to confess at an hour like this."

"I want to confess."

"Be off with you!"

"I want to see the curé."

"For what purpose?"

"To make my confession."

"The curé can't be seen just now."

"The senior vicaire, then."

"Nor he either. Now off you go."

"The second vicaire, the third vicaire, the fourth vicaire, the youngest vicaire."

"Be off with you."

"Ah, then! would you let me die unshriven? It's worse than it was in '93, it seems! . . . Any little vicaire. How will it hurt you if I make my confession to some little vicaire not any taller than my arm? Take word to some priest that he must come to hear my confession. I'll undertake to disclose to him a batch of sins rarer, more extraordinary, more interesting, you may take my word for it, than all those his chattering women penitents can trot out before him. You can tell him that he is wanted for a really fine confession."

"Get away now!"

"But won't you understand, you old Barabbas,

you? I tell you that I wish to reconcile myself
with the good God—by God, I do!"

Although he did not rejoice in the majestic stature of the verger of a rich parish, this official staff-
bearer was vigorous enough. He took our poor
Gestas by the shoulders and hurled him outside the
doors.

Gestas, once in the street, had only one idea in
his brain, which was to get back into the church by
one of the side doors, so as, if possible, to steal a
march on the verger from behind, and perhaps lay
hands on some underling vicaire who would consent to hear his confession.

Unhappily for the success of this manœuvre, the
church was surrounded on all sides by old houses,
and Gestas was soon hopelessly entangled, without
hope of delivery, in an inextricable maze of streets,
lanes, courts, and alleys.

Amongst them, however, he discovered a wine
merchant's, and there the poor penitent tried to find
consolation in absinthe. He managed to do so.
But a fresh fit of repentance soon overtook him.
And it is this which supports his friends in the hope
that he will win salvation. He has faith—simple,
firm, childlike faith. It is works alone which he is
lacking in. Nevertheless there is no need to despair
of him, since he himself never despairs.

Without entering on the difficulties as to pre-destination—and they are not inconsiderable—nor weighing the opinions expressed on this subject by St. Augustine, Gottschalk, the Albigenses, the Wycliff-ites, the Hussites, Luther, Calvin, Jansenius, and the great Arnaud, one may venture to believe that Gestas is predestined to eternal felicity.

"Gestas," said the Lord, "enter into Paradise."